THE FRONTIER SERIES
Illustrated

The YOUNG PIONEERS

THE

CABIN IN THE

NORTHWOODS

BY

DR. C.H. PEARSON,

ILLUSTRATED

Published in 1870 Re-Published 1998
(Protected)

Mantle Ministries
228 Still Ridge
Bulverde, Texas 78163
Ph 1-830-438-3777 Web http//www.mantlemin.com

CONTENTS.

THE YOUNG PIONEERS.

CHAPTER I.

THE FAIRY OF THE FORT. — PLEASURE AND SORROW.

"WHY don't he come?" and Alice McElroy's fingers glided impatiently over the keys of the piano-forte.

She glanced again into the square below. There stood pony, saddled and bridled, pawing the paved court, restlessly awaiting the presence of his young mistress.

The morning was superb — a cloudless Minnesota sky of intensest blue; the air dry, balmy, bracing, delicious; the velvet green of the immense prairie prismatic with glistening dewdrops.

As the fair-browed maiden skipped to the other side of the fort building, and gazed from the window upon the scene, she drank in its wondrous beauty with a wild delight.

The frontier fortress was built on a swell of land remarkable for prairie land. One would think that nature designed it for just such a structure as crowned it with the murderous munitions of war. Strange that in the heart of that vast savanna there should rise a huge mound, or half hill, of height and circumference sufficient to command the entire wide-stretching landscape. Over this flower-enamelled plain, sloping from the fort on every side to the arching horizon, the kindling eye of the young girl wandered with worshipful enthusiasm.

"I shall wait no longer!" she exclaimed, decisively. "Charley has been set to some task, I warrant, and there's no guessing when he'll get through. What's the use of always having a *boy* escort. As if I cannot take care of myself! There are no Indians about now. I shall go alone for once. Pony is as good company as I wish."

And tripping down stairs, and out into the court, she mounted her miniature steed. There was a clattering of dainty hoofs, and she was flying across the plain.

These early morning rides were Alice McElroy's special pleasure. Horseback exercise on the open prairie had been prescribed by the fort physician on account of the delicacy of her constitution, and the cough, which, though slight and inconstant, gave him, of late, some concern.

But never before had she gone without an attendant. And as Mrs. Jones discharged the duties of governess to the McElroy children, Alice and Willie, and she knew her own son Charley to be brave, manly, and discreet beyond his years, he was often detailed to accompany Alice.

As we have seen, Alice expected Charley to attend her on this occasion. But as he did not promptly make his appearance, glad to assert her independence, she ventured without him.

The truth is, Alice, although affectionate and noble, was towards Charley petulant and innocently imperious at times. What queer creatures girls are, indeed! Mr. Jones, with his family, occupied a log cabin near Spirit Lake at the time of the fearful Indian uprising, and Charley distinguished himself there by his romantic adventures and heroic conduct — a mere lad that he was. He was, therefore, petted by the soldiers, and fairly doted on by Alice's mother and General McElroy, commander of the forces at the Fort.

Alice also liked him as a playmate, and admired his fine qualities; but to have a *boy* for guide and protector on her prairie expeditions, and she a young lady in her teens, "what an idea!"

With an exuberant sense of freedom from re-

straint, and of superiority to juvenile guardian-
ship, Alice dashed along, now putting pony to a
round trot, now to a full gallop, then resting the
reins on his glossy neck, permitting him to take
his own way — just as she was doing with so
much comfort to herself.

Between pony and rider there was perfect sympathy.   An intelligence and devotion almost human characterized the wee horse.   It was a rare
animal, — a thorough-bred specimen of a species
once famous but now nearly or quite extinct in
this country, — for which the general paid a fab-
ulous sum, presenting him as a birthday gift to
his only daughter for her sole use.

Never was beast better loved and treated.
Winding her white arms around his curved neck,
she would talk to him as if he understood each
word.   And are we certain he did not?   You
could not make Alice think him so stupid.   She fed
him with dainties from the table, and plucked for
his mouth the sweetest grass-tufts.   And her voice,
her step, her hand were "all the world" to him.

How pony drooped with failing appetite when
for three weary weeks his gentle little mistress
lay sick !   When, convalescing, she was supported to the window, it was affecting to watch him
as he waited beneath the sill for the feeble word
of recognition from her pallid lips.   And when
she first stepped out of doors, pony rushed fran-

tically to her side, and would not be pacified, despite the outcries and protestations of the frightened nurse, until she repeated his name and caressingly laid her soft hand on his forehead.

Pony took short steps, but nimble, and got over the ground much faster than some longer limbed coursers I have seen. He liked so to go — no working one's passage, whip or spur-wise, with him.

Doubtless high feeding and light work has much to do with the muscular thrill of speed experienced by the well-handled and mettlesome steed. But the loved form on pony's back, so graceful and unburdensome, full of glee, praised and patted him, and encouraged his best efforts; and away, away he sped, the fairy rider's eyes sparkling and cheeks abloom, and wavy silken tresses floating on the breeze, as they skimmed along, unmindful alike of distance and of time.

Alice McElroy gave a sudden start, when at length she descried just before her a piece of woods. Had she ridden so far? She saw no trees from the fort, only commingled grass and flowers extending like a sea of verdure to the bending sky. But pony was sweating. How nice, she thought, to rest a while in the leafy shade, before returning!

Riding in among the trees, she stopped the horse a moment, listened and gazed about, to be sure no danger was near. How silent the sheltering retreat! Not a sound broke the pervasive stillness, save a plaintive bird chirup in the dim solitude.

"O, isn't it perfectly lovely!" she ejaculated. "And yonder's a river. How clear and smooth the water is! And what splendid flowers, — there's the cardinal flower, if I live, — magnificent! Now, pony," she added, dismounting, and leaving the reins loose, "you just get cool, — don't wander off, — mind, now, while I gather a bouquet for darling mother and my dear good governess; then we'll start for home."

At which pony, with contented air, fell to nibbling the grass, displaying his nice taste by nipping, too, a bright blossom now and then, out of regard, perhaps, to Alice; and she, with an occasional glance at him, to be positive he staid near, strolled by the river brink culling flowers. They grew in tempting profusion, and she soon had a bountiful store. And reclining on the yielding moss, among the feathery ferns, she began to arrange the wild-springing beauties.

"Perfectly beautiful!" she murmured. "Won't mother and Mrs. Jones be surprised when they learn how far pony and I have been to-day all alone!"

"Pony, are you there? Yes, I see you now. You're a dear good pony! How much nicer

THE SURPRISE. Page 15.

it is to ride all alone! One can do just as one
pleases. Besides, Charley is so boyish! There's
Tom, now;" and a slight flush crept to her
temples; "how grand it was, his pushing off
the cliff that horrible savage that was creeping
up to murder him!"

At this point she stopped soliloquizing, and
hummed to herself a while.

"Yes, Tom's studying to be a minister. I suppose he wouldn't *dare* to play as Charley does.
Soldiers can play, but ministers must pray."
Then she laughed. "I shouldn't like to do nothing but preach, and pray, and think about another world, about preparing to die. Death is
frightful; though, if one is good enough to go to
heaven, and *old* — but I'm only — "

A slight rustling of the bushes snapped the
thread of her musing; a heavy hand was laid
on her shoulder; she glanced backward; a hideous savage bent over her. The blood seemed to
freeze in her veins at the sight. She attempted
to scream, but the sound died on her lips. Her
eyes became fixed and glassy. The Indian's
face wore a fiendish expression, as he held his
tomahawk above her head. She tried to fall on
her knees and beg for mercy. Then Indian,
trees, water, swam confusedly round. Her eyes
closed in darkness and insensibility.

The savage for a moment looked down upon

the rigid features of the white girl as if unde-cided whether to strike or not. That doubt arrested the descending weapon. Something connected with her dress caught his attention.

"Ugh," he grunted, and, stooping, detached from her belt a shining gold chain and locket, the latter containing the likeness of her mother.

This appeared to turn the current of his inten-tions; for, taking the girl in his arms, he bore her a short distance up the river side, dragged a canoe from out the thick shrubbery, placed her in it, gave it a quick running push, and dexter-ously jumping in after, paddled the light boat along.

When Alice recovered her consciousness, she found herself lying alone in the bottom of a canoe, and an ugly-featured Indian sitting in front of her.

At first she deemed it a dream. Then, bewil-dered, she rubbed her eyes with her hands to be certain she was awake. Soon, like lightning flash, the horror of her condition broke in upon her mind. In a frenzy of fear she roused her-self to attempt escape.

"Squaw, keep still!" spoke the Indian, an-grily. "Think swim, run, get 'way? No. Wa-ter deep. Injun killee you!"

"Dear, good Indian," pleaded the terrified girl, "don't kill me. Take me back; let me go home, and father'll give you —"

"Squaw speak no one word more!" grunted the savage, with an ominous look.

O, the agony of that moment to the captive! How she wrestled with her emotions, striving not to provoke her fierce captor by unavailing outcries!

Crouching in the swift-moving, fragile craft, as it shot through the dim woods, now hidden by the pendent branches, now lighted by ruddy sunbeams, hurried on to what fate she knew not, minutes were as ages.

By and by they came to shoal water. The Indian now laid his paddle in the bottom of the canoe, and employed a long pole to propel with. Soon he stranded the airy vessel, and ordered her to get out. Easily lifting the canoe on his shoulders, and driving her before him, they tramped a long way through the woods, away from the water.

At last they came to a spot not covered with trees. Back of it, and somewhat remote, was a line of smoke rising, indicative of an Indian village.

But the Indian did not take her there. Turning to the left, they struck into the forest again, continuing their journey till they reached an old tumble-down wigwam. Entering, he pointed Alice to a corner, took from a pouch at his side a thick piece of smoked venison, tore off a strip with his teeth, handed it to Alice, saying,—

"Squaw hungry; eat!"

Alice was faint from fear and fasting, but too wretched to partake of the untempting food. Dreading, however, to arouse his resentment, she tasted a morsel, and concealed the remainder.

When night fell, her captor stretched himself on the ground in his blanket, near the entrance to the wigwam, and was shortly asleep.

O, the long, long watch that night to Alice! She could not sleep. The heavy snoring of the savage in the gloomy wigwam, the hooting of the screech-owl and howling of the wolf without, the tumult of fright, grief, and foreboding within her throbbing breast, thoughts of her father's and mother's distress because of her prolonged and mysterious absence, — under these circumstances her eyes were as wide open as if they never could close again, and her brain active well nigh to insanity.

She was still awake when the pioneer streaks of morning penetrated the hut. After a while the savage bestirred himself, arose, lighted a filthy pipe, seated himself in front of her, cross-legged, and smoked in grim silence.

With sharpened intuitions, Alice studied his physiognomy, to discover, if possible, some human quality to which she might appeal. But the paint-streaked copper-face staring stolidly at her, though evidently that of a youngish war-

rior, was repulsive and malignant in the extreme.

"Where am I?" gasped the girl, at length,
with clasped hands.

"In wigwam," laconically replied her captor.

"Yes," answered Alice, startled at the sound
of her own voice, "but, I mean, how far from
the fort?"

"Twenty, fifty, hunderd mile; big way; no
git back, never!"

"O, do carry me there," cried she. "You
shall have money, anything. My father is General McElroy; he'll pay you all you ask, and
more too!"

But at mention of her father's name a terrible
scowl corrugated the brow of the savage, and,
emitting great puffs of smoke, he muttered, —

"Injun no do it. White chief kill Injuns,
many!"

Alice poured forth a flood of entreaties, sobbing heart-brokenly.

The savage drew his scalping-knife, bent a
threatening gaze on her, and said, —

"Squaw hold tongue; Injun cuttee out!"

And the girl was silent and hopeless, but
shook with an aguish terror, her sad eyes fixed
on her captor, full of anguish and supplication
more moving than speech.

The Indian puffed serenely at his pipe a while

longer, then, putting it by, drew from his dirty pouch more dried meat, and tossing her a portion, commanded her to eat. This time, half famished, she obeyed, which appeared to please her captor, who, after regarding her intently, as if deciding a matter of importance concerning her, said, peremptorily, —

"Squaw stay in wigwam!" and disappeared in the woods.

Alice, with beating heart, watched the fading figure of the savage till lost to view.

Where was he going? How soon would he come back? When he reappeared, what would be her destiny? If he did not return, what then? Alone in the wilderness, without food or fire, and no means of procuring either! It was frightful to expect his return, and starvation if he staid away.

The appalling novelty of her position brought into ascendency a new class of feelings. She had a bright intellect, and military blood coursed in her veins. Reason and courage reasserted themselves.

"If I perish, I will do so trying to escape," she resolved. And strong in this purpose, and buoyant with a sensation of freedom now that the Indian was away, in her eagerness she ran into the forest.

But suddenly stopping, she pressed her hand to her forehead in deep thought. Which way

should she go? Grave question that. Sinking
to her knees, and whispering an earnest prayer
for guidance and protection, she hurried into the
hut, picked up the venison she threw away the
night before, and set out on her perilous and uncertain undertaking.

CHAPTER II.

A RIDERLESS PONY. — THE BUFFALO WALLOW.

PONY appreciated the tender herbage, and the grateful shade of the wildwood, for he was "a dear lover of nature," after his manner, and perhaps would have voted, if admitted to the right of suffrage, to spend the remainder of the season there, could winsome Alice be near. He might cast his ballot thus, were it not for two objections — the grain he would miss and the titbits from the McElroy table, and the insects that abounded in the forest.

Flourish, and flirt, and lash his luxuriant tail, shake his comely mane, toss his shapely head, stamp his delicate feet, suddenly trot to a fresh place, no matter what violence or strategy he used, the hungry flies would persist in trying to suck the life-current through his sleek skin. In fact, his exertions, whether offensive or defensive, increased his troubles, attracting his foes from afar, till the air swarmed with whizzing, buzzing, trumpeting blood-suckers.

Strange, is it not, that so insignificant a trifle

as a tiny fly can so harass and baffle a quadruped heavy enough to outweigh millions on millions ot such enemies?

Pony endured the torture and fought the battle with as much patience and valor as, perchance, you or I would, were we subject to his annoyance. But even horseflesh will not bear everything; and pony, desirous of permanent relief, darted out from under the ravenous cloud of pitiless parasites, and trotted to where he left his gentle young mistress, attaining the flowery bank where she had sat, and uttering a questioning whinny simultaneously, as much as to say, —

"Please, Miss Alice, shall we not hasten out upon the breezy prairies?"

But the pretty wee animal saw no Alice there!

He snorted, pricked forward his tremulous ears, smelt of the earth, then of the bunches of flowers; neighed loud and shrill; waited, trembling with excitement, for the familiar reply, — furiously shaking his head and whisking his tail the while at the pursuing insects, — dashed down the river bank, scenting the ground as he went, like a hound on the track; turned, and smelt up along the border of the stream; paused suddenly, as if to deliberate, then wildly wheeled about, and, with mad swiftness, struck a straight course for the fort.

How wonderful is instinct! What so excited pony? Why did he hunt for a trail that should guide to the missing girl? Why his alarm and concern? What caused him precipitately to relinquish the search, and speed homeward as if on an errand of life or death? Ah, if the dumb, yet ofttimes singularly intelligent brutes could all speak, as did the prophet's wiser beast, what might we not learn from their now sealed lips! What an infinite gulf between their inarticulate muteness and human speech! O, what our condition, were we like them unable, as a race, to embody our thoughts in words! God be praised for the gift of speech, for who but He give it us and denied it to them?

"Miss Alice, whar' you be?" and black Nancy's ebony face peered into closets, clothes-presses, behind doors, and under beds. "Now you jist stop foolin'! Dinner's bin coolin' more'n half an hour, and yer father and mother are that worried. Can't yer make strouble 'nough widout hidin' away when eberyting is a spilin'! Come, honey, dat's a good girl; come eat yer dinner."

But remonstrate, scold, reason, and coax as the affectionate negress would, there was no answer.

Perseveringly the servant continued her search, hoping each instant that from some place of concealment her frolicsome charge would spring forth as she was wont, and, with ringing peals of laughter, fling her dimpled arms around her neck with a kiss, or scamper through the halls, challenging pursuit.

The colored waitress's brow became knitted with anxiety, and reëntering the dining-room, she said, —

"Please, marm, I can't find Miss Alice no whar!"

"O, well," pleasantly returned the lady, "she is probably in at Mrs. Colonel Thomas's. You just step across the square, and inquire."

The general and his wife were rising from the table when black Nancy returned, reporting that she had visited all the officers' rooms, and could get no tidings of Alice.

"It is certainly very strange," observed Mrs. McElroy, going to the window. "But what does this mean?" she quickly added, as the sound of a horse's feet smote upon the ear. "Pony has rushed into the yard, covered with sweat and foam, saddle and bridle on, but riderless!"

"Call Charley," gravely said the general.

The lad instantly made his appearance.

"Charley," asked the general, "have you been to ride with Alice to-day?"

"No, sir," he replied.

"Do you know if she went?"

" I do not."

Black Nancy now recalled with dismay, that Alice apprised her, the night before, that she intended to ride in the morning, requesting her to tell Charley to be ready to attend her, all of which had been forgotten till this moment.

" I fear she ventured alone, and something has happened to her," remarked the mother, turning pale. "When did you first miss her from the house, Nancy?"

" Dunno, missus, zactly. 'Parently 'twas 'bout eight, missus, when de hat was taken from de place whar — "

" Eight o'clock; who was on guard, husband, at the gate, then?"

" Call private O'Connor," said the general.

" O'Connor, did my daughter pass out on her pony when you were on duty this morning?" asked the general, as that worthy entered.

" An' indade did she, the blissed craythur," answered the Hibernian.

" Was any one with her?"

" Not a sowl, yer honor, save her own swate self, sure; an', says I, the Howly Vargin be praised, but if there's a saint in heaven, sure an' she's that same, her hair stramin' an' her eyes sparklin', a ridin' off so light an' aisy — "

" Rub down the pony, and put him up," sharply interrupted the general. Then addressing his weeping wife, he said, —

"Don't distress yourself, dear; I will go out at once with men enough to scour the prairies far and near. We shall certainly find her."

As if by electricity, the sad news of the loss of Alice went through the fortress, and, as if by magic, a force duly instructed, well mounted, and provisioned so as to be able, if necessary, to remain through the night, was departing for the search, each member of the expedition ambitious of being the one to restore the missing girl to her parents.

As the company left, O'Connor was leisurely grooming pony. A remarkable insubordination seized the little animal.

Jerking at the halter, and kicking with both hind heels to impart force to the jerks, and at the same time keep the Irishman at bay, the strap parted, and pony, at liberty, started after the soldiers.

"Howld, howld, ye baste!" shouted O'Connor, running to head pony off; and by a short cut getting in front of her, he furiously brandished the curry-comb. But pony had a will for once, and a temper, too.

Laying flat her ears, and drawing back her lips, disclosing double rows of formidable teeth, she made directly for the Celt, as if to eat him.

With a wild whoop Erin fled, pony following, her glistening ivories within an inch of his pate. The spectators in windows and court, overcome at the ludicrousness of the rare spectacle, laughed and applauded, forgetful, for the moment, of the loss of Alice, till Erin took refuge in a friendly doorway. Then pony galloped out upon the prairie, and joined the cavalcade.

That wise and experienced officer, General McElroy, had laid out the work of hunting up Alice with far-sighted and systematic skill. The men were divided into squads, each with its distinctive mission, and all to report often to him. Signals were appointed which would enable the most widely separated corps to communicate with each other, and with the commander-in-chief.

How like clockwork is military discipline! In this instance, however, there was one connected with the expedition irreducible to rules. That was pony, the volunteer. Defying orders, signals, and the ordained plan, the bantam steed would proceed in *one* direction, and that only. He even aspired to lead — the usurper. If the cavalry followed, how pleased he seemed! If they swerved from the route he preferred, he would curve and canter up to them, then back to *his* track, neighing for them to come also.

Pony's mute though eloquent appeals and manœuvres attracted the attention of Captain Manly. He was a close observer, was versed in natural history, and passionately fond of good horses. He was aware that not alone that useful animal, but the dog, the elephant, and others of the dumb kingdom, frequently exhibit a marvellous sagacity. Thrusting his spurs into his own beast, he was quickly at the side of his superior.

"General," said he, making the military salute, "the horse your daughter rode this morning having, it appears, broken loose from confinement, is hovering near my men. The little animal acts, I think, as if it would lead us to some particular locality. It may be a whim of mine, but I fancy it might not prove amiss to humor the creature, and see what comes of it."

"Singular, very," ejaculated the gray-bearded veteran, levelling his glass at pony. "Every movement of the animal is instinct with intelligence. Do as you please, captain, and if anything turns up, signalize promptly."

"I have great faith in horses," remarked the captain, on rejoining his command, to a brother officer. "They differ in intelligence just as men do. Some are stupid, others acute. Some love their owners, others care only for the stall — mere eye and trencher servants.

"Observe what a sensitive organization has that pony. His nostrils and ears, — the latter ever in motion, alert for the faintest whisper, — trim limbs, clear, bright eye, proud, self-conscious carriage, — there's a world of affection and good sense in that beast. I owe my life to a horse like that — except that mine was large and powerful.

"It was on the plains. A messenger arrived at our station, stating that a stage had been attacked by Indians, and imploring relief. Most of my command had been detailed as escort to an immigrant train ; but taking ten men with me, we hurried to the scene of action.

"The crack of rifles and yell of savages urged us forward, and, rounding a bluff, we were at once on the battle-field. The stage had been captured, and was filled with Indians, while a redskin sat on each of the four horses. The fellows, with gory scalps dangling, were enjoying a ride. Several bodies of dead and wounded whites lay around, while in the distance the fight was still raging, showing that some of the passengers had survived the onslaught.

"I comprehended at a glance how matters stood. The plains, you know, are all dotted with round hollows, say a dozen feet across, called ' wallows.' To these the huge buffalo resorts to roll, covering himself with a coating of moist earth, to rid himself of the lively little eaters infesting his shaggy hide.

"In one of these buffalo wallows four men had found refuge, their heads being just visible ; and riding dexterously and rapidly in a circle about them, shooting arrows or fire-arms, were not less than a hundred and fifty Indians. The cunning copperfaces would keep their bodies on the side of their ponies away from the white men, making a galloping breastwork of each horse.

" The danger was, that the whites would exhaust their ammunition; then the rascally savages would show no favor.

" The Indians were between us and the men in the wallow, and the intervening bluff had concealed our approach. Giving word to charge on the savages, in order to break through to the rescue of the whites, whose fire was slackening, we rushed, with a cheer, to the onset. The surprise was complete, and at first successful. But perceiving the handful I had with me, the scattering savages rallied, and assaulted us with great ferocity.

" An arrow-head struck my arm. The reins dropped. My horse reared; I lost my balance, and was hurled violently to the ground. Before recovering from the shock, a savage was upon me to take my scalp.

" Utterly at his mercy, he would soon have finished the job, when, with a defiant snort, my faithful beast swept up, and seizing my assailant in her capacious mouth, dragged him over, and trampled him with her fore feet. How she smote and bruised him! It was a terrific sight.

"I had by this time regained my feet, and re-mounting, being better armed, we succeeded in putting the Indians to flight."

"The instinct of the brute is a great puzzle to me," remarked his comrade, "it is so marvel-lously quick, subtle, and unerring. It seems, in certain respects, to surpass reason. There, for example, is the honey-bee. The honey-hunter repairs to the fields provided with a little box containing honey. Catching some bees, he shuts them within, and through the glass top watches till he sees that they have loaded themselves with the sweet liquid. The insect is then liberated. It rises in the air, flies round in several widening circles, till, having ascertained the direction of its home, it makes directly for it, the hunter fol-lowing, sure that if he retains the bee in sight, he shall find the honey-tree.

"Now, how does the insect — no matter how far or where the hunter bore it while imprisoned in the box — find out the right way home, and not only so, but reach it by a perfectly straight, or, as it is termed, 'a bee line'?"

"The horse will do the same thing," said the captain. "I had ridden one day forty miles across trackless prairies — an entirely new route to me. On returning, the sky became overcast, and not having a compass, I got lost. Giving the reins to my horse, the sagacious animal chose an opposite course from that I had been pursuing, carrying me across marshes and streams, and through almost impenetrable thickets, by, I subsequently learned, an almost mathematically direct line to my destination. And yet the country was as new to him as to me.

"But see, there are woods! Pony is entering them. Ah, yonder's a river; and what is this on the bank?" he earnestly exclaimed. For there lay Miss Alice's hat, containing a few withered flowers, and near by two partially arranged bouquets!

CHAPTER III.

THE FLIGHT FROM THE WIGWAM. — INDIAN
WATCH-DOGS.

WHEN Alice McElroy awoke to consciousness, and to find herself in the canoe with the
savage, two opposite states of mind and feeling
were induced. Overpowering terror and grief
swallowed her up in a tempest of horror, and yet
her faculties were preternaturally busy in noting
the course she was being transported, so as to be
able, if chance occurred, to retrace her way.

Little did her pitiless captor imagine that the
young girl who lay by turns moaning and pleading in her sorrow, or speechless from fright,
observed objects they passed with a vividness
that photographed their image indelibly on her
memory.

When, therefore, she took flight from the wigwam, her first endeavor was to discover the real
direction homeward.

The Indian had said that they had come a
"big way" from the fort. But, judging from
the slow progress they had made, on the whole,

she was convinced that he had purposely exaggerated the distance. Perhaps it was only a few miles to the river. Perchance her father might be there searching for her.

But what dangers and difficulties might be between her and rescue she dared not anticipate. A giant elm, lightning-blasted, she had seen in coming, and there, a mile or so away, she could discern its ghostly outline, stretching its bare branches heavenward. This welcome landmark decided her course, and the assurance she felt that the decision was correct gave her courage.

What did she not suffer in that dreadful journey! struggling through thorny bushes and interlacing shrubs, tearing hands, face, and neck till blood trickled from the smarting wounds, bewildered in bushy labyrinths where the confined air was so hot and suffocating as to cause her to pant and gasp for breath, sinking knee-deep in mud and ooze of slimy marshes, startled by sounds of she knew not what wild creatures. But the fearful apprehension that her captor, discovering her absence from the wigwam, would pursue and overtake her, stimulated her lagging energies.

About noon she came to the margin of a small lake. In the tops of the tall, overhanging trees were large birds, of black plumage and odd shape, with great, coarse, red throats. The water beneath was black, and thickly covered with broad, floating leaves. On the shores grew poisonous plants with brilliant blossoms and sickening scents. Here, weary and trembling, she sat down, and drawing from her dress-pocket the dried venison, ate a little. Then descending to the border of the pond, and scooping up some water in her hands, she eagerly drank.

Now, recollecting that she did not see this lake while carried off by the Indian, the conviction that she had wandered from the path startled her. Frantic at the thought, on she went, looking sharply to descry some waymark that would set her right again. Walking and resting in turn, afternoon wore off, and evening twilight fell.

The sun went down, and darkness brooded on the forest. Urging her weary limbs along in the awful gloom, slipping, stumbling, falling over moss-grown tree-trunks, scratched and clasped by remorseless branches, all at once she heard the howling of wolves, as if hundreds of them were assembled in grim concert. Then, in the direction of the howling, she saw a lurid light and dusky figures moving about.

She was too well acquainted with frontier characteristics not to recognize in the scenes before her an Indian encampment; for she had heard her father tell that the coyotes, or prairie-wolves, will surround a camp at nightfall, and at nine or ten o'clock commence their serenade chorus, and that the Indians will not kill the discordant voiced animal, regarding him as a watch-dog. For, let any one approach the camp, and the wolf-music instantly ceases, and the Indians know that somebody is about. Then they keep away from their fires, and watch for the intruder.

When the knowledge of her proximity to an Indian encampment burst upon her, Alice sank to the ground, overcome with conflicting emotions. If it was the same encampment that she passed with the Indian, then she had returned unconsciously on her own steps, and must still be near her captor's hut, and when morning dawned he would certainly retake her. The conclusion was appalling. How ought she to act under the circumstances? How would it do to enter the encampment and claim protection? Might not some in the barbarous community, for the hope of generous reward, extend it, and restore her to her father?

A faint hope sprang up in her heart. Softly gaining the summit of the mound she was on, she gazed earnestly at the encampment. Those swarthy forms, how hideous and terrifying! Turning, she fled into the covert of the woods like a bird chased by the cruel hunter, and toiled with the energy of a mortal fear to put as much space as was in her power between herself and those "habitations of cruelty."

Sitting down, at last, her strength all spent, she leaned for rest against a craggy oak. "I must not sit here but a moment," she said to herself. But a resistless drowsiness benumbing her sensibilities, with an ineffectual attempt to shake off the spell, she dropped into a deep sleep.

A sharp report aroused her. Starting to her feet, she saw, with wonder, that the sun was up: she had slept till morning. And a second wonder — a few rods in advance was the river. With a cry of joy at the familiar sight, — to see which she had dared and endured so much, — she sprang forward, purposing to descend the bank, and if the stream at that point was not too deep, wade over.

A warning buzz in her pathway brought her to a stand-still, for a few paces ahead, coiled ready to strike, was a large rattlesnake. She retreated backwards, the reptile darting out his forked, fiery tongue at her till assured of his own safety, then slowly uncoiled itself and glided away.

Making a circuit she began once more to go down the bank. A mat of dried rank sedges and osiers was before her. Stepping upon it, a score of snakes beneath the treacherous covering rattled and hissed, and with a shiver and a scream she fled back again.

A gun was now discharged in the distance

across the river. Then she dimly discerned a soldier's uniform. Her heart gave a bound — it was her father's men looking for her. She was about to call to them, when a great flat hand was placed sternly and silently over her mouth.

It was the Indian. Lightly throwing her over his shoulder, he bore her rapidly away. In vain she struggled and tried to cry out. The iron grip relaxed not, and in sight of final escape she was a captive once more.

Not long had the savage, with his victim, gone, when the fort soldiers appeared under the trees opposite.

"I am sure, captain, that it was a girl's voice. It was as genuine a scream as I ever heard," said one of the men.

"I heard it," added another, "and something like a dress went fluttering over the bank yonder!"

Instantly the eager soldiery forded the stream, and penetrated every part of the adjacent wood. But no trace of human existence was found, save a bit of dried venison under the tree where Alice had reposed.

Through the concealing bushes, the adventurous red man carried the girl, with the ease and swiftness of a panther, to a point low down on the stream. Here he pushed from its hiding-place a canoe, and tying his captive's mouth with tight folds of dirty cloth, he laid her in the boat, and paddled noiselessly along.

Long and diligent was the search for the lost maiden. Prairie, forest, and river were scoured, and large rewards offered for her recovery, but without avail. Weary weeks, melancholy months, rolled round, bringing no news of fairy Alice.

CHAPTER IV.

THE TRAGEDY ON THE RIVER.

"Husband, ar'n't you coming to get some rest? We've had a long journey, and we've a great ways to go yet. And you know we land before morning. You will be all tired out; and I can't sleep, I worry so about you."

It was a loving womanly voice that uttered this, and a pale, care-worn face it was that peered through the little aperture over the state-room door, the blue eyes glancing anxiously about for a glimpse of the person addressed.

"Coming soon!" was the hearty response, though the tones sounded strangely, borne on the night air along the dimly-lighted steamer. "Wait till this steamboat passes;" and Mr. Willard kept his solitary lookout, spell-bound by the magic of night, on the Mississippi. How varied and bewitching the scene! Ploughing the liquid element was the monster leviathan, rushing, thundering by, spouting fire, while star-like from the shore glimmered the lamps of village, and city, and farm-house. Is it strange that Mr. Willard lingered to gaze as if fascinated?

He was an affectionate, kind-hearted man, but impulsive, excitable, and, when aroused, headstrong. He had inherited a small property from his father, which, with his daily earnings, provided a snug home for himself, wife, and three children, in a growing town in Maine.

His "lot" joined the old homestead where his wife was born, and well contented was she to settle for life, as she supposed, by the side of her parents, and among the scenes of her childhood and youth. With reasonable frugality, her husband was able to maintain the family respectably, and a mile away was the school-house and the village church, so that the intellectual and religious training of the children need not be neglected.

But Mr. Willard contracted the "western fever," and announced to his wife his determination to sell their property, and start for the cheap, rich lands of Minnesota. The announcement was to her as the tolling of a funeral knell. And with gentle reasoning she sought to change his purpose.

"We are happy here," she tearfully said, "and have met with no reverses. It is not necessary for us to go west, as is the case with many. If we were suffering for the comforts of life, or likely thus to suffer, I would not shrink from any change that promised an improvement in our circumstances."

But the more he read, and thought, and argued, the stronger his wish to emigrate; and, with a foreboding heart, the wife prepared for the removal.

The pleasant cottage, with its productive vegetable garden and smiling flower-beds, and the household effects, were sold, and the morning for the departure of the Willards witnessed a sad sight.

The family had many friends, who called to utter a last word to those who that day were to leave them, never, perhaps, to return. Mr. Willard and wife were both members of the church, and the pastor was there also to add his blessing.

But when the aged father and mother came to say "good by" to the favorite daughter and the petted grandchildren, the old man bracing himself tremblingly on his cane, while the tears flowed down his furrowed cheeks, Walter Willard's conscience smote him for causing so much sorrow. It was, however, too late to retreat, and the train soon bore them from view.

The husband's ardent temperament quickly threw off depression. They were now really on the way to the Great West — the Eldorado of his day and night dreaming. Each hour the swift-

winged cars were bringing him nearer the goal
of his hopes.   The thought of this speedily swallowed up parting regrets.   How many acquaintances he made on the road!   What delightful
chats with those going, like himself, towards the
setting sun!   How companionable and confiding
he became with his new associates! — informing
them of his history, his plans, his expectations,
his means, his destination.

"Husband, is it safe to let those men know
how much money you carry with you?" the more
prudent wife ventured to inquire.   But the caution was soon forgotten.

And now he was floating on the great river he
had so longed to see; and as the late hours wore
on, with "his soul in his eyes," he continued
gazing at the ever-changing scenery.

It was a densely inhabited hive — that boat.
But Sleep had long since with velvet fingers
closed the eyes of the jaded travellers; not a
passenger was up save the enthusiastic Mr. Willard.

Not one?   Who is that, past midnight, creeping stealthily by the berths of the hard-breathing
sleepers?   Why moves he so noiselessly?   Sometimes he is motionless; then he skulks warily
along: his manner, movements, attitudes, show
him to be one whose deeds are more of the night
than of the day.

And see, another figure. The two meet; they whisper together with rapid and significant gestures; they part, and then reappear, approaching on either hand the lone emigrant looking unsuspectingly off over the water.

Suddenly they clutch him by the throat; his arms are pinioned and mouth gagged; greedy fingers take his watch and money; there is a struggle, — a heavy body goes overboard, — a splash, a gurgle — and all is still. The prowlers separate, glide away, disappear.

Mrs. Willard awoke as if struck by a blow.

" Walter! Walter! where are you?" she called. "Children, which of you will go and find father? Perhaps he has dropped asleep in another part of the boat."

"I'll go for him," answered thirteen-year-old Georgie; and, rubbing open his eyes, he threaded the forsaken passages, repeating, —

"Father! father!"

The lad approached the scene of the robbery just as the unhappy victim was precipitated into the stream. In the darkness he saw a confused conflict, and the thrusting over the boat side of a dark body, and heard the dull plunge; but, hastening to the spot, all was silence and vacancy.

Had he been dreaming? Was it illusion? All at once his heart stood still, for that form cast into the current, indistinctly outlined in the starlight, looked like his father!

Overcome of terror, he hurried back to the state-room with horror-blanched cheeks, unable to tell what he had seen.   Then the mother, hoping and fearing, clasping the son's hand, went forth to the search.

One o'clock. Two o'clock. The porter knocks at the Willards' state-room. The steamboat bell gives notice of a "Landing."

"Hurry!" says the porter to the lingering wife; "the boat stops only a minute!"

"But where's my husband?" she asks, weeping, and calls distractedly, "Husband! husband!"

"Mother," the boy whispers, with white lips, "I saw two men throw father into the river!"

The boat grazes the rude pier. The plank is out for the passengers. The baggage is thrown ashore.

"Hurry! ma'am, hurry!" reiterates the porter, seizing the arm of the bewildered woman, and pushing her over the narrow crossing, which is instantly withdrawn, and the steamer is off.

But what of the mother and children left in the damp twilight on that strange shore?   What of the husband and father?—for he comes not. What of the money he had with him? the avails of the neat New England home, with which he was to build up another home in the wilderness.

There stands the stricken group by their heaped-up boxes and trunks, in fright and agony.   How different it might have been had the ill-fated man considered his wife's happiness before adventuring west! or if, on the road, he had preserved the reticence of the discreet traveller!

And, O, what black deeds the darkness hides from every eye but One!

CHAPTER V.

THE LITTLE HUNCHBACK. — AUNT ESTHER, THE IMMIGRANT.

"MADAM, can I assist you in any way? You seem to be a stranger, and in trouble."

Mrs. Willard was naturally retiring, and withal distrustful of strangers. She glanced scrutinizingly at the speaker. His frank, open, manly face, instantly disarmed suspicion.

"Fearing, from your conversation on the boat with the porter," he continued, "that a serious calamity had befallen you, I succeeded in getting off at this landing to aid you, if you need assistance."

"O, sir," she wailed, "I know not what dreadful thing has happened. My husband disappeared in the night; and my little boy, here, says he saw two men throw him overboard. Can it be that my poor Walter is murdered, sir? It seems as if my heart would burst, I am so terrified and wretched!" And the ghastly face, and clasped hands, and piteous tones, might melt adamant. "Georgie, darling, tell the gentleman about it."

"It is not necessary, madam; it would only distress you," answered the young man. "I overheard the story. It may not be so bad as he thinks. Perhaps an accident happened to your husband, and he will yet make his appearance. It is always well to look on the bright side, madam."

"But what shall I do?" she inquired. "Mr. Willard was taking us to Minnesota. He had the money with him. What can be done to ascertain what has become of him, and if all is indeed well,"— and she spoke more cheerily, — "to let him know where we are. He'll be worried about us. And," she added, hesitatingly, "if he has been injured, I shall want to take care of him. Do — you — really — think — sir," and the words now faltered and dragged as if the horror-palsied tongue refused its office, "that — he — was — robbed — and *thrown into the river?*"

Her pleading eyes were fixed on his, as if she would read his inmost thoughts.

"Ah, yes, you think so!" she cried, wringing her hands.

Her listener turned away to hide his emotion.

"You believe my Walter was murdered. My dear *husband!* The *father of these boys!* Cast into the river! Children, we are now alone! Alone in the far west! Without friends! with-

out home! without money! And he murdered!"

The bitter agony concentrated in accent, look,
and attitude cannot be portrayed.

"Woman," abruptly interposed the young
man, "for your own sake, for your husband's
sake, should he still survive, for your children's
sake, be calm. This is no time to abandon yourself to grief and despair. God is alive. He will
not forsake you. Rouse yourself for action.
These boys look up to and depend in this hour
wholly on you. For their sake, I repeat, be
calm."

This timely exhortation, uttered with magnetic
force, was not without effect.

"You are right," she meditatively replied, "I
must not selfishly yield to sorrow. Counsel me.
What course ought I to pursue in these fearful
circumstances?"

A few rods up the shore stood a tavern. A
servant lingered near. Calling him, the young
man said,—

"Take this lady's baggage to the house."

And when he had seen it all safely conveyed
there, he led the stricken group after.

"Now," said he, as they seated themselves in
the "Ladies' Room," "you need, madam, to sum-
mon all your resolution to consider your position
and duty as composedly as possible. Because

of your family you must even be heroic. A true mother will hold up her offspring when affliction comes, teaching them by her own sublime example how to meet the storm."

"True, sir, true," remarked the lady, quietly weeping.

" It would be wrong to disguise the painful fact that circumstances appear to indicate that your husband has been foully dealt with, that your boy's conclusions concerning his father may be correct. Scoundrels of the deepest dye take passage in the immigrant trains and on the Mississippi steamers for the purpose of finding out who has money or jewelry, and, when opportunity favors, of plundering them. Your husband may have made dangerous acquaintances on his journey, and paid the sad penalty. But, even if he was thrown into the river, he may have been picked up by some boat, or gained the shore. It was farther down stream that the affair happened, — if it did occur, — and we must make inquiries at various places, and see if any intelligence can be gained concerning him. I will with pleasure attend to this. Remain here till I report results. There's a down steamer's bell, now ; keep up good courage, madam, till I return."

And running to the rude pier, he sprang into the boat.

And now that the young man has gone, let us

notice more in detail the little company he has felt so much interest to serve.

Besides Mrs. Willard, at a discreet remove from her, is her maiden sister, "aunt Esther." She is of light complexion and hair, — the latter very abundant, — natural; is somewhat stoutish; has a large, firmly-carried head, an ample forehead, and a fine face. Each article of her apparel, from neck-ribbon to gaiter-boot, fits nicely, showing her to be orderly and exact. She rarely speaks, but when she does it is to the point. She makes no demonstrations towards any one — not even towards a baby. If obliged to notice such a morsel of humanity, it is in a tenderly stately style, without lullaby or petting.

When Mr. Willard broached the subject of immigrating, she lifted her neatly-arched eyebrows in lofty surprise; and when at last she expressed her opinion, it was decidedly against the scheme.

"If Mr. Willard wishes to banish himself to the world's end, he may do so. *I* shall not stir an inch on such a wild-goose chase, and his wife is foolish if she does."

But when the Willards started, without previously hinting her intention of doing so, she descended from her room clad in a tidy travelling suit, rode to the depot, had her trunk checked, and seated herself in the cars. She did not even bid adieu.

to her acquaintances; perhaps her lips were too firmly closed to open for so slight a civility. Her face was, however, unusually pale.

"O, Esther," exclaimed Mrs. Willard, as the reticent maiden sank into the next seat, "are you to accompany us? How glad I am!"

"I did not say so," was the unbending rejoinder. The maiden lady's ear-drops grew pendulous from some smothered emotion. "I shall go a little way, to see that you and the children are properly cared for. Men are so inefficient!"

The boys, however, noticed that their single relative had *coupon* tickets in her reticule — though each was secretly torn off in succession for the conductor. "Little pitchers" have sharp eyes and wits as well as "big ears," and the lads drew a pleasing inference from what they saw. For, odd and uncommunicative as was aunt Esther, they loved and respected her. She had done them too many cross-good turns for it to be otherwise, and they very well knew that her judgment was golden.

"I bet aunt Esther is going all the way with us," gleefully said Georgie to his mother. "I peeped over her shoulder into her carpet-bag, and she had a string of tickets a mile long."

"Hush, chiid," answered the mother; "she will overhear you. But I must think you exaggerate a trifle."

"And then her trunk is big as all out doors."

"Not quite," quietly said the mother.

But the self-reliant, cool-headed, authoritative maiden lady, in the emergencies of the journey, was worth her weight in diamonds.

When the hackman at Boston demanded, with oaths and threats, an exorbitant fare of Mr. Willard, the latter, to avoid a quarrel, would have acceded to the unjust charge had not aunt Esther, majestically confronting the bully, bade Mr. Willard put up his purse, saying, —

"I'll settle this bill, sir," tendering the astonished Jehu the legal amount. Eying her an instant, he pocketed the money without a syllable of protest.

Farther on, a baggage-master would have collected three dollars and a half for his private benefit, had not aunt Esther come to the rescue.

At Buffalo, the hackman, who had engaged to take them directly to the waiting steamer, landed them instead at a hotel, saying the boat had gone. But while trunks and bandboxes were with remarkable rapidity being conveyed into the over-hospitable house, the urbane proprietor standing smiling on the steps, waiting to bow them in also, aunt Esther, leaning from the carriage, inquired by whose authority they were brought there.

"Too late for the boat, to-night," answered the driver; "step along, madam," taking hold of Mrs. Willard's arm.

"Sir," exclaimed aunt Esther, "you contracted to put us aboard the steamer in season. You shall do so, or pay the damage to us of our detention, or I'll report you to the police."

Hackmen are quick at reading character—and landlords no less so. The twain whispered together, the baggage was ill-naturedly restored, the vehicle whizzed for the wharf, and they were aboard the boat a full hour before it sailed.

You are now introduced to the "old maid."

If we slight the boys, we shall offend the mother. Georgie you are slightly acquainted with. He is a bright, active lad, his leading weaknesses being a disposition to fret for the sake of a scene, and an inordinate love of peppermint and sugar in hot water — indulged in for his "stomach's sake and often infirmities;" a very handy boy at almost anything.

Ferdinand, the eldest, in his seventeenth year, manly, smart, and muscular, somewhat vain of his extreme age, and also of his handsome face and figure and personal prowess; slightly too fond of dress also.

Between these is Frankie, "going on" to thirteen, nicknamed Little Hunchy, because of a spinal curvature with which he is deformed.

Frankie is a character. When about five, he was playing on the ice, when a drunkard came reeling by, pelted with snowballs by rude boys, and, I am sorry to add, girls. Too much intoxicated to discriminate between the innocent and the guilty, seeing little Frankie, he seized him in his blind rage, and dashed him to the frozen ground, and staggered on.

The child did not appear to be seriously hurt at the time, but a year afterwards it was observed that his back was bent, and in spite of medical skill, intelligent nursing, and carefully adjusted gymnastics, the vertebræ kept pushing outwards. As is the case in such affections, the *sternum* (breast-bone) also curved outwards. This double crooking sadly interfered with his bodily development otherwise.

Ten years after the cruel concussion, his legs and arms were singularly slender and feeble, his height much below that of youth at his age, while the disproportionate humped back and chest gave him the appearance of "old head" and shoulders "on young" legs.

Frankie's head was a study. Long from the frontal region to the lateral, and widening in its sweep; a prominent perceptive forehead; calm, reflective, dark-gray eyes; the upper lashes singularly long, and curling boldly upward; heavy eyebrows extending nearly to the ears; a picked snub-nose, the incomplete nostrils causing the end of that organ to set up the more decidedly;

hair abnormally coarse, erect, and bristling, in a line from neck to forehead, imparting a belligerent aspect; face serious, depressed, sagacious, defiant. Such is a rough portrait of the deformed child-man.

Child-man I say, for in stature and physical ability so almost infantile, but the surmounting so very, very old! Then his voice. Then his voice! You would expect from that massive, sage-like, impressive head, deep bass tones. On the contrary, from the perked-up, compressed chest issued marvellously thin, yet slightly harsh, piping sounds.

A sad life had Frankie's been since rum laid its bloated, blasting hand upon him. Strangers saw him only to cry out, "What a deformity!" Neighbors exclaimed, "If he had been my child, I had rather he had died than live to be so unshapely." Wherever he went, he attracted attention, and few guarded, even in his presence, their thoughtlessly expressed commiseration. He had heard thousands of lips declare him a monstrosity — a being only to be exclaimed at and shocked by. Yet he was possessed of an exquisite delicacy of feeling, and was too sensitive, even had he remained well formed.

Consider his condition. He was little; the large looked down on him. He was weak; the strong could assail him. He was distorted; the compliments paid to the comely were condemnation to himself.

At school he was unable to join in boyish sports, and could, therefore, contribute little to the general stock of amusement; and being so queerly made up, so different from his mates, like a speckled bird all the rest picked at him. Alas for the poor, the unfortunate, the deformed, in this superficial world!

So, poor, unfortunate Frankie, as the years wore on, came to look on mankind as so many social foes. When a new comer opened his lips, Frankie expected him to make some stinging criticism on his bodily infirmities. He had experienced small consideration for his feelings, and he did not anticipate much. And as "self-preservation is the first law of nature," it became a habit to be always mentally on the defensive, ready to return glance for glance, or, if need be, word for word, although, for the most part, he endured the criticisms of the rude with a sort of savage contempt.

As a result of all this, Frankie seldom smiled, talked little, and as his reliable means of protection lay in his looks and oral remonstrances, his precociously mature face assumed more and more an antagonistic, forbidding, consequential expression, which inarticulately said to the starer, " Mind your business ! " and to those tempted to undue familiarity, " Hands off, or take the consequences ! "

And when he rebuked impertinence, his countenance expressed terrible things — a method of defence harmless, it is true, yet often more effective than if, with less repelling power of physiognomy, he had possessed more executive ability.

I alluded to the peculiar appearance of Frankie's hair. The effect of the emotions on the human hair is well known. Excessive terror causes it to rise — to " stand on end," as the common phrase is. Grief or anxiety turns it white. Is it improbable, then, that the hair on Frankie's cranium grew stiffly perpendicular because of his life-long unhappiness? Disappointed, suspicious, resentful, incessantly irritable, — might not these feelings, so deep, perpetual, controlling, have changed the structural character of his hair? We propound the query for others to answer.

Yet, let us repeat, Frankie was exquisitely sensitive and tenderly affectionate. He loved those he did love deeply, strongly, undyingly. His mother knew this. His brothers intuitively had glimpses of the fact, gruff as his manner was towards them, and boyishly inconsiderate as they too frequently were of his happiness.

Ferdinand and Georgie were blessed with an exuberance of animal life. They inherited a good constitution, and were sound in health. To run

climb, leap, wrestle, swim, were much easier than
not to.   Praised for their fine figures, by acquaintances, in the same breath that Frankie was pitied,
it was natural that they appreciated their physical superiority to their unfortunate brother.

With infinite longing he would watch them at
their games and their light tasks. O, were he
only like them!   And how familiar became their
reiterated question, natural, yet triumphant, —

"Don't you wish you could do this, Frankie?"
as they displayed before him their strength and
agility!   How Mrs. Willard wept one day, when,
some lady callers having in his hearing compli-
mented Ferdie and Georgie, and pitied him for
being distorted and dependent, after they left,
the little hunchback, sad-eyed, pale, yet tearless,
his shrill, minute voice tremulous, said, —

"Mother, do you wish I was dead?"

"Why, no, child," she replied; "what makes
you ask such a question?"

"Everybody pities you on my account," he answered, adding, with a pain too poignant for
tears, "I don't see of what use I can ever be to
you."

But does a mother ever love a crippled or mal-
formed child less than the more favored?   Mrs.
Willard pressed the dwarf to her heart, the big
old-young head strained to her throbbing bosom,
and exclaimed, —

"Wish you dead, my darling Frankie? No; better they all die than you. You are the dearest child I have."

From that moment Frankie never doubted her, but increasingly distrusted the carping world.

CHAPTER VI.

THE IMMIGRANT WAGON.

"There he is!" cried Mrs. Willard; and she turned pale.

It was early morning. A heavy mist enveloped the river; but her eager eyes, piercing the fog-curtain, recognized, in the foremost passenger descending from the steamer, the young man who had so nobly volunteered to search for her husband. The three days the stranger had been absent were weary, anxious days to her. Not a boat touched at the landing, even in the darkness, but she heard the signal bell — hopingly, forebodingly watching for tidings of her lost companion.

But, impatient as she had been to hear from the young man, now that he had arrived she trembled at his approach. Ah, how much, at some solemn crisis, is crowded into a brief interval! Was she a widow, and her sons without a father? A word now, and that awful question would be settled.

The young man walked towards the hotel

slowly and gravely. With womanly quickness she saw that he came with an unwelcome message, else his step would be eager and light.

"Well?" she whispered, inquiringly, as he entered.

"Madam," said he, — and he paused, as if deliberating how to word what he had to communicate, — "I have learned nothing favorable or unfavorable. Nothing has been seen of Mr. Willard at either of the landings. Still he may have been rescued from the water, and carried to some obscure cabin among the bluffs ; or possibly a steamer may have taken him aboard. I have, however, sent back to Dunleith, to have posters printed describing Mr. Willard, and calling for information concerning him. A copy will be put up in every conspicuous place, circulated on the steamers, and among the settlers along shore. I see no alternative but to await the effect of the handbills."

Meanwhile the whole family, entering the room, had clustered about their new friend, breathlessly listening.

Slightly aside was aunt Esther, her face partially averted, her lips firmly knit together, and her countenance worried, yet resolute.

Ferdinand leaned against the door-casing, in a pensive, thoughtful attitude, weighing each sentence freighted with so much significance.

Georgie, his hand clasped in his mother's, gazed into her face, as if more troubled for her than aught else.

The Hunchback had drawn a chair to the plain centre-table occupying the middle of the apartment, his sharp elbows resting on the stand, his great head propped on his weak little hands.

"I am sure, sir," said aunt Esther, breaking the terrible silence that had settled on them all, struck dumb as they were by the blow that had smitten the husband and father from their side, — "I am sure, sir, that we are greatly obliged;" but she did not finish the acknowledgment; her words choked her, and simultaneously they all began to sob.

"Madam," said the young man, addressing Mrs. Willard, "may I ask if you will deem it best to return east immediately?"

"I could not," she faltered, "while my poor husband's fate is unsettled."

"But," he gently suggested, "to board long at this hotel would be very expensive. You mentioned that Mr. Willard had the money with him. Will you be offended if I inquire what your condition is financially?"

"Fortunately," was the reply, "I persuaded Mr. Willard, on reaching the boat, to let me take charge of a portion of the funds. Here is what he handed me;" and she counted from her purse fifty-five dollars.

"A sorry amount for a family," was the response. "Now, I have been revolving this subject, and have a plan to propose. You would scarcely wish to go back to New England at present; that is plain. And had you means, it would be imprudent to tarry here. There have been copious rains this season. The Mississippi, therefore, overflowed wide tracts of land. The freshet is now subsiding, leaving the submerged vegetation exposed to the sun. This will create sickness; and here, shut in among these bluffs, the air is, you have reason to know, intensely hot, so that the miasma is developed more rapidly, and acts with a deadlier influence on the system. Remain here two weeks, or perhaps even one, and some of you will be down with ague and fever, or some other bilious disease. Now, my idea is, that you had better go off upon the healthful prairies, away from the miasma of the river, among the large-hearted prairie farmers, take up land, and set to work improving it while waiting to hear from your husband. How does this strike *you?*" he inquired, turning to aunt Esther.

"This is my sister, Miss Esther Willard. She disapproved of our removal west, and only came out to accompany us on the road," explained Mrs. Willard.

"Then she does not fancy the frontier?"

"No."

" Her opinion will not, therefore, be biassed in favor of my plan. Miss Willard, have the kindness to express your views freely on the point."

" How far, sir, would the family have to go to find good, unoccupied land? "

" O, not a great ways, necessarily ; but I would advise from sixty to eighty miles."

" How would they get there? "

" I doubt not a conveyance can be obtained."

" Who would do the farming? "

" These boys," returned the young man. "Two of them are active and strong ; the other would be a safe companion and adviser. Farming on the fertile prairies, you must recollect, is vastly different from what it is in rocky, sterile New England."

" What would land cost? "

" There are," he replied, "two sorts subject to settlement. First, 'school lands,' so called because reserved to be sold for school purposes. These, at some appointed time, will be offered for sale at public auction. This may not take place for years. Until then the squatter or occupant has the use of it free ; and when it is disposed of, usually by courtesy of the neighboring settlers, he has the first chance at bidding. The other lands can be bought at one dollar and twenty-five cents per acre, a cabin and a few

other improvements being requisite as proof that
the preëmptor is an actual settler, and not a mere
speculator."

"What would the boys do for school and
church privileges?"

"O, their aunt could teach them for a while,"
he smilingly responded, "should she decide to
share their fortunes till they get fairly started.
But immigration is rapidly coming in. Educa-
tional and Christian advantages will soon be enjoyed, and railroads must shortly be built. Land,
if well chosen, — and on the route I would mark
out one could not select amiss, — can but rise in
value; so that, while waiting to hear from Mr.
Willard, instead of getting sick and consuming
what little means the family possesses, they will
gain in health and vigor, and perhaps attain a
nice property. Now, what say you to this scheme,
Miss Willard?"

The maiden lady's calculating nose seemed to
lengthen, the sympathetic ear-drops waxed tremulous, her features worked as if a tenacious
prejudice and strongly repressed emotions were
fighting against conviction. At length she
said, —

"I suppose you are correct, sir."

"And you will not forsake your sister in her
trouble?"

There was a painful struggle. Dear, orderly

New England, — where neatness, thrift, and plenty reigned, where she was born and nurtured, — and forms of friends she might not again behold! She was thinking of all this, and putting it in contrast to the loneliness, toil, and deprivation of the wild prairie. Could she, for others' sake, give up the old associations and comforts for the new scenes? Crushing the rebellious regrets, she answered, —

"I shall not leave the family."

"And," pursued her interrogator, "how do the boys vote on this question?"

"I'm for the prairies," cried impulsive Georgie.

"So am I," added Ferdinand.

"And Frankie?" inquired the young man.

But little Hunchback looked grave and depressed, and sadly shook his head.

"What are your objections?" asked the young man.

"I think the plan may be wise, but these boys never can carry it out. They haven't counted the cost," replied the dwarf. "A great deal of hard work will have to be done, and they don't like too much of it. They'll get discouraged in less than a week."

"O, little Hunchy's blue!" interrupted Georgie. "I guess we'll do as much as he will."

"True," replied the Hunchback, gloomily; "but I can do nothing."

"Well, all seem to regard the plan as a good one," said their adviser.   "Next comes the matter of ways and means.   Perhaps, however, it will give you more confidence in the project to learn that I am well acquainted with pioneer life.   My name is Thomas Jones.   My parents were originally from the east.   They emigrated in consequence of my father's losses in business, and the persecutions of creditors.   His difficulties unsettled his mind in a certain direction, and we led a roaming life in the wilderness, too often removing to get ahead pecuniarily.   He got to be a famous hunter and marksman, and was cool and brave in danger.   He removed at last to Spirit Lake, and was mortally wounded there while defending the settlers at the time of the Indian uprising.   My sister Sarah, too, was killed, and Charley and little Bub only escaped by concealing themselves in a hollow tree.   Soldiers from a frontier fort came to the relief of the cabin so bravely defended by my dear father, and subsequently returned for Charley and Bub, who had taken possession of the forsaken dwelling, and defended it against a second attack of the Indians.   After father's death, which occurred at the fort, my mother, having been well educated, became governess to the two children, Alice and Walter McElroy, of the commander of the fortress.   Through the generosity of a friend, and the kindness of the good missionary at L——, I was subsequently sent east to study for the ministry, and am now on my way to spend vacation with my relatives and acquaintances of the frontier. Good by, now, for a little while. This evening I will see you further concerning our plan."

"What a splendid fellow that is!" exclaimed Ferdinand, gazing gratefully and admiringly out of the window after young Jones. "Wasn't it fortunate that he happened along just as he did?"

"*Happened* along!" repeated his aunt, looking shocked. "Do you believe in *chance*? God sent him. Who of the thousands we saw on the journey paid us any generous attention? Did they not each 'take care of number one'? And how remarkable that he, of all that crowd on the steamer, should be just where he could hear us speaking of our dreadful trouble! Boys, this is a providence. God's hand is in it, and this assurance leads me to think we shall get along on the frontier."

"Does God order everything?" piped little Hunchie, crossly.

"I know what you mean, Frankie," kindly replied his aunt. "There are laws which, if we break, we must suffer the penalty. If we carelessly expose our money, we may be robbed. We are free agents, and can choose good or evil.

If a man chose to rob another, he can do it. We are not machines. But when we suffer for our own faults, or through the wickedness of others, God, in pity, often sends his servants to our assistance. And *I* do not doubt he sent Thomas Jones."

Ah, what a prop in adversity is faith in One who not only has a father's loving interest in his children, but who wisely and powerfully befriends them, causing "all things to work together for their good!" How much more rational and ennobling such trust than to suppose ourselves and the great universe to have *happened* into existence, an existence without forethought, intelligence, order, or end, to be whirled remorselessly about by blind and pitiless Fate!

Aunt Esther's words sent a thrill of hope to Mrs. Willard's heart, and, sadly smiling, she remarked, —

" O, if indeed the mighty God is watching over us, I must not despair."

" Ferdie, Frankie, Georgie, where are you? Come out here," shouted a cheerful voice in front of the tavern.

The lads seized their caps, and hastened to see what was wanted. In a huge Pennsylvania wagon — "long enough," as they say in that state, "to reach from one mud-hole to another "

— sat the speaker, reins in hand. It was
Thomas Jones. The boys started in surprise,
and dolefully exclaimed, —

"O, you are not going away — are you?"

"Not yet," was the smiling reply. "How
would you like to travel in a carriage of this
sort? Ask your mother and aunt to step this
way."

As the two ladies approached, the young man
dismounted, and said, —

"Mrs. Willard, how would you and your household fancy a trip into prairiedom in this establishment? Not very elegant, you perceive; but
please glance in, and see how much room there
is inside." And he gently constrained her to
mount to the driver's seat. "It will accommodate you all, and goods enough almost to furnish
a cabin. And there are the horses, not handsome, but serviceable. It will be delightful wan-
dering over the prairies in this way! Believe
me, you will enjoy it."

"Whose team is it?" asked Mrs. Willard.

"Yours, madam."

"*Mine!*" she ejaculated.

"Mother's!" echoed the boys.

"The horses will stand. Let us go into the
house, and I will explain. You see, madam, I
was very much perplexed how to get you on your
enterprise. Stage-coaching would eat up your

means, and leave you distant from unpreëmpted land. As I was walking up the street, turning this subject over in my mind, before a shop-shanty was this team, and the owner was engaged in bargaining to buy out the store. All that stood in the way of a trade were the wagon and horses. The immigrant, if he went into trading, would not longer need it, and the shopkeeper did not wish it. Here, perhaps, is a providence, thought I; and stepping up, I inquired how little money would pay for the wagon and span.

"'Wal, stranger,' answered the immigrant, 'bein' as I'm bound ter have this ere shop, I'll part with the hull concern dog cheap.'

"'I'll consider it,' said I.

"Returning, I entered the bar-room. I'm seldom in there, you are aware, madam. The room was filled with smoke and smokers. Walking straight to the bar, I said to the landlord, in a loud tone,—

"'That's a hard case.'

"'What?' he asked, still stirring toddy for a toper.

"'Why, about that woman up stairs, whose husband was lost in the river.'

"'I heard about that,' said he, indifferently.

"'But,' I persisted, speaking louder, 'it's a *very* hard case.'

"'What's the row, friend?' asked a lounger.

"'I'll tell you,' said I; and I rehearsed the whole account, having the fixed attention of all present.

"'Is she gwine back ter the east?' inquired a rough customer, knocking the ashes from his pipe.

"'No; she thinks too much of her husband. She's bound to stay till she hears what has become of him.'

"'That's the kind,' he replied.

"'She ain't gwine ter board here on *that* onsartinty — is she?' he further inquired.

"'No; she and her boys are too smart for that. They are going out on the prairies. But,' I added, 'the husband had most of the money with him; and how the women and boys can get there is what puzzles me. There's a good wagon and span for sale up here, and if I had the money —'

"'Stranger,' broke in a burly fellow, pulling out a greasy wallet, 'I'm 'most dead broke; but ef yer don't let me have a finger in that pie, I'll know the reason. Here, gentlemen,' he continued, passing round his jammed and ancient hat, 'put in yer shiners fer the women and the boys.'

"The result is, the team belongs to Mrs. Willard, and if she don't use it, I don't know what will become of it. But come, Ferdie," he instantly added, "let us go and put up the horses; then I'll make suggestions concerning the route."

It was late that night when the Willards and their young pioneer friend separated, for he had much advice to give, and numberless questions to answer. Besides, he was to leave by stage in the morning, and this was their parting inter-view. With pen and ink he sketched their course geographically, and also presented them with a pocket map of the country. These Fer-die took charge of.

"Good by, Mr. Jones," cried the lads in a breath, as he left.

"Boys," he replied, deeply moved, " my moth-er, brothers, and sisters always called me Tom. Don't *mister* me again."

"Tom, dear, dear Tom!" cried Georgie, throwing his arms around his neck; "I *do* love you so!"

CHAPTER VII.

" BURR-OAK CIDER."

IT was a bright morning when Tom took stage from —— Landing, on the Mississippi, for the frontier prairies.

There was a full load aboard, albeit every public conveyance can always accommodate " one more." A merry company they were, too. All men, journeying from various quarters for various purposes — health, pleasure, speculation, to " locate," or to visit immigrant friends in their wilderness homes.

Well may you imagine that the " unruly member " enjoyed a gala day in that crowded vehicle, for a stage-coach is a social institution anywhere, but especially so where the freedom of western manners bears sway.

A " light-weighted," wiry, ever-at-motion Hoosier, with twinkling black eyes, and a saucily upturned nose, started conversation by plying each in turn with personal questions, put with the familiarity of an intimate acquaintance, his interrogatories being always answered cordially, sometimes wittily. They could the less resent the liberties he took, since at the outset, in a few characteristic words, he sketched his own history, announcing himself as "a shoolmaster from Ingianny, going to Minnesoty to teach school, if he could get one; if not, to hire out farmin'."

"What is *your* name?" he began, directing his attention to a portly gentleman of forty-five, occupying the right hand corner of the front seat.

"Hammond, Dr. Hammond," was replied, with frank good humor.

"Where from?"

"The wooden nutmeg and pine wood pumpkin seed state, erroneously called Connecticut in the geographies."

"Got a family?"

"Too young to marry."

"Calc'late to settle in these parts?"

"If 'twill pay."

"Going to invest in land?"

"May *risk* a trifle where it's a *sure* thing."

Passing thus in regular order among the passengers, with an assurance, volubility, persistency, and ingenuity that kept the company in a roar, sometimes putting a new question before the response to the previous one was fairly out of the mouth, he reached the last person but one — a young man in hunter's garb, and carrying a rifle. He was of Scotch-American descent, hardy and opinionated; had been, he said, on the frontier five years; was recently from a hunting expedition on the Red River with friendly Indians. This experienced youth the "Ingianny" man bored with numberless inquiries concerning the climate, soil, productions, growth, and population of the country.

"The settlers are from most all parts, I reckons."

"Yes," answered the hunter, naming different nationalities represented, ending with "Norwegians."

"Norwegians! What sort of folks are they?"

"Don't fancy them, nor their heathenish jabber," was the narrow reply.

"Are they peaceable?"

"O, they never make any trouble, are generally hard-working and honest. But for one, I can't relish the idea of these *foreigners* coming over here and getting the best land. And of all the foreigners, I despise the Norwegians most. They are different from anybody else. I can tell one as far as I can see."

"And where are *you* from?" asked our questioner of the remaining passenger — a man of thirty, of fine physiognomy and gentlemanly bearing.

"From Norway," was the affable response.

"Then you are a Norwegian?" returned the astonished Hoosier.

"I am," he pleasantly replied.

An embarrassing silence fell on the party at this unexpected *dénouement*, from the effects of which even the versatile and irrepressible "school-master" could not rally, while the imprudent youth, whose eyes were so keen for Norwegians, looked chagrined and chopfallen enough at the sharp rebuke his prejudice and evil-speaking had received; for the comparison which the incident led us to make, between the young hunter and the well-bred stranger at his side, was not over-favorable for the former.

"Big spring! Wud ayther iv the gintlemen like a taste uv the warther?" shouted the wide-awake Irish driver, as he reined in the horses, and, seizing a pail, hurried to a ravine a few rods off, followed by the passengers.

The limpid water, cold and sweet, gushed from the earth in a powerful stream.

"Magnificent!" ejaculated the doctor, swallowing great draughts. "Wouldn't take a thousand dollars for this spring, if it was on my place at home! Will you try some?" he added, rinsing his flask, and passing it, refilled, to Tom.

Despite the slight flavor of whiskey that still clung to the drinking-vessel, Tom could but join in his enthusiasm; and, as they resumed their ride, a number of accounts of remarkable springs were given by several.

But Erin's dulcet tones again resounded, as he proclaimed, —

"Those gintlemin as wish can git something to ate here."

They were now in "the barrens." Stretching along a gentle ridge, in a singularly orderly way, presenting a striking resemblance to a New England orchard, were the "scrub" or "burr" oaks. Among the trees nearest the road stood a log house, over the door of which, on a rough oak board, was the inscription in red chalk, the letters staggering, as if formed by a drunken hand, —

"Burr-oak Cider."

"Cider!" repeated the Norwegian, as they dismounted. "I thought that was manufactured from apples."

"An' sure," interrupted the driver, slyly winking at the doctor, "they make it here without the fruit at all, at all, an' it's the *gin*-i-*wine*, an' no mistake."

The plain meal of corn-cake, fried pork, eggs, and coffee innocent of sugar or milk, was despatched, and Tom had quite forgotten about the "cider;" but on returning to the stage-coach, the smell of the doctor's breath, and the unnatural excitability that prevailed, led him to suspect that some "beverage" stronger than the poor coffee of the table had been patronized while he was walking beneath the oaks — a suspicion that became knowledge, when, an hour later, the doctor, in the glow of his feelings — perhaps I should say, stomach — drew his flask, filled with "burr-oak cider," *alias* whiskey, from his coat pocket, and sent it the rounds, all partaking except the Norwegian and Tom. When restored to its owner, he held it up to the light, shook it, and looking at its contents with a professional air, said, —

"That is what I call one of God's good creatures!"

"And yet," boldly replied Tom, "how many accidents, losses, quarrels, murders, deaths, what poverty, wretchedness, crime it causes! It is on this account that so many of the great and good stigmatize it as the *worst* of *man's* creatures."

"O, I mean rightly used," answered the physician, with a touch of condescension.

"Used as it has been here, for a common drink?" inquired the young critic.

"Boy," he replied, with doctorial dignity, "I contend that there is a principle in whiskey, which, as a tonic, is invaluable."

"May I ask," politely interposed the Norwegian, "in which of the drugs employed in manufacturing and flavoring the article you find that principle?"

"Sir," returned the whiskey advocate, getting nettled, "need I state that I refer to pure old Bourbon!"

"Pardon me, then, for reminding you," courteously responded the Norwegian, "that one seldom sees *old* Bourbon, much less old Bourbon *pure*. And surely the liquor called 'burr-oak cider,' sold at that wretched loggery, cannot be of the kind or quality you mention."

"Besides," broke in Tom, "when you prescribe a 'tonic,' — *cinchona*, for example, — you are careful about the size and frequency of the dose — are you not? Why, then, take the whiskey 'tonic' in such large quantities and so often? A tonic is to strengthen the body when weak; but those addicted to the 'Bourbon tonic' use it when weak or strong, and continue it till it beggars or destroys them. It would be mal-practice to administer a tonic to those already over-stimulated. But suppose, doctor, one should weigh two hundred, his face and eyes were red, the blood too much in his brain; would not an intelligent practitioner recognize such a person as apoplectic? and would not tonics be hurtful and dangerous to him, especially whiskey tonics? Hence, is not, after all, your defence of alcoholic drinks, on medical grounds, a pleasant little piece of professional strategy? Do you not really hold to them because they are agreeable to the taste?"

"You are a little personal," rejoined the physician, heartily laughing; "and I don't know but you are about right. But it is not best to be social bigots. An occasional glass cheers, enlivens, disperses the blues, leads a man to feel at peace with all the world, and forget care, fatigue, and sorrow. It promotes good fellowship, arouses the intellect, and enlarges the heart. How dry and insipid are public dinners without wine! And on a journey what introduces strangers so gracefully, and quickly makes them acquainted!"

"An eloquent eulogy!" observed the Norwegian. "But, doctor, I have read of a custom in France, before the revolution, that adhered more faithfully to fact.

"When a great personage, a marshal of France, a prince, duke, or peer, passed through a city of Burgundy or Champagne, the corporation of the city waited on him, delivered an address, and presented him with four silver goblets, in which were four different wines. On the first goblet he read this inscription, *monkey wine;* on the second, *lion wine;* on the third, *sheep wine;* on the fourth, *swine wine.* These inscriptions expressed the four descending degrees of drunkenness: the first, that which enlivens; the second, that which irritates; the third, that which stupefies; the last, that which brutalizes."

The physician, like one of Victor Hugo's characters, combined, with admirable art and in masterly proportions, the thirst of a guzzler with the discretion of a judge, and had preserved his mental equipoise notwithstanding the whiskey. But the nervous little Hoosier had by this time become unduly "elevated," and posturing as if about to fiddle, sawed away with one arm across the other, and struck into a dancing tune.

"*Monkey* wine," Tom murmured, nudging the doctor's elbow. "The 'tonic' is taking hold."

From imitating the violin, the "Ingianny schoolmaster" proceeded to describe incidents in his history which showed that he had seen more of life among rowdy Mississippi raftsmen than in the school-room.

"The 'tonic' is introducing to us the raftsman," whispered Tom. "What can so 'quickly make strangers acquainted.'"

The Hoosier ended his stories with a coarse song.

"*Swine* wine," exclaimed the Norwegian, in disgust.

Erin, on before, broke out also in rude strains, alternated with swearing at, and furiously lashing, his better-behaved horses.

"The 'tonic' has mounted to the driver's head," said Tom.

"*Monkey*, *lion*, and *swine* wines," chimed in his ally from Norway.

But the deepening ravines made their way uncomfortably rough, the wheels now sinking into heavy ruts, anon surmounting some jagged rise of ground, while the driving was reckless in the extreme. Tom shouted to the driver, —

"Be careful, or you'll turn us over!"

"O, be aisy, me by," he roared in return, whipping the horses anew. "Dennis O'Brien's been acrass the prairies before to-day. Get ape, ye bastes!"

A moment more, and the stage canted threateningly, righted, then came down, Tom's side, with a crash, his face resting on a sharp object protruding through the intervening leather. He was too closely pinioned by the passengers over him to move, and lay helpless, expecting each instant the horses to run and drag him thus. But the animals, becoming disengaged from the whipple-trees as the coach went over, although spurred on to the moment of the casualty by the drunken Jehu, waited quietly by for orders, like good temperance beasts, who had taken no 'tonic.'

When the door of their prison-house was opened, the passengers emerged, a sadly jolted and bruised set, happily, however, without serious injury, only to the stage, which was pretty well "smashed," obliging them to "foot it" to their destination, a distance of two miles. The

Norwegian and Tom, however, enlivened the walk by reminding the doctor that it was "one of God's good creatures" that, turning the driver's brain, upset the stage.

"Admirable 'tonic'! powerful 'good creature'!" ejaculated the Norwegian. "By all means, doctor, when again we travel together, bring some burr-oak cider aboard; it helps so on a journey!"

"How true the old proverb," suggested Tom, 'Wine is a mocker; strong drink is raging; whosoever is deceived thereby is not wise.'"

"Young man," said the doctor, as they entered the little frontier village, "to what part of the east do you belong, did you say?"

"No part," frankly answered Tom. "I was brought up in a log cabin on the prairies, but have been east studying."

"Medicine?"

"In part, but mainly for the ministry."

"So you were a boy-pioneer?"

"I was."

"And now you propose pioneering it in religion and reform? Let me tell you that you will find it a mighty sight harder battling vice and sin than fighting poverty and Indians. But you've the pluck for it. I wish you success. Good by."

As Tom left, the doctor muttered, —

"Well, if *he's* a sample of what pioneering it does

for body and mind, pity that there were not fewer
dwellings of luxury, and more cabins! But how
that youngster walked into my arguments! Fact
is, I had a sorry cause to defend. Drinking is
poor business."

"Mr. Jones," said the Hoosier, drawing him
mysteriously aside, "if I should light on your
neighborhood, and get a school there, perhaps
you'd help me out, if I got in a hard spot. Now,
'rithmetic isn't a mite nat'ral to me. You see I've
had no great chance for schoolin'. You'd give
an old acquaintance a lift on the diffikilt sums, I
s'pose?"

But the Hibernian driver saved Tom the trouble
of replying, by asking, in a business-like way,
"the gintlemin" to be sure and ride with him on
their return, or not in the opposition line.

"And get upset again?" suggested Tom.

"An' sure an' the accidint wud niver have occurred at all, at all, if it hadn't been fur the — "

"Whiskey," added Tom.

"Faix, an' yer honor's right there," answered
Erin.

Tom scanned the countenance of the young
Irishman. He had a clear blue eye, an interesting, intelligent face, and his brown hair curled in
beautiful, clustering ringlets over a fair, open
brow.

"What a pity," observed Tom, "that a young

man of your smartness should permit his head to be turned by the vile stuff! You'll marry one of these days, and be, perhaps, a drunken sot of a husband, and break your wife's heart, if you get the appetite fastened on you. Yet you might be a good and useful member of society."

"An', indade, sir," exclaimed the warm-hearted Celt, touched by the frankness and sincerity of Tom's manner, "it's married I am now;" and he dashed off a tear. "An' wut wud me angil uv a wife say had she seen me droonk to-day?"

"Where is she?" asked Tom, much interested.

"She's in the ould country, sir; an' I'm getting the dollars together to bring her over — her an' the babe."

"Steer clear of the whiskey, then," said Tom, "if you wish to get them here soon, and make them happy after they arrive."

"All the angils bless yez, sir! The reverend clargy couldn't spake bether nor yez. An' Dennis O'Brien is no fool to kape ter the drink that's harrmed many an' many a wiser an' a better than he. An' sure it's not to the credit of a docthor ter be a recommindin' it to the likes o' me."

CHAPTER VIII.

TOM'S RIDE CONTINUED. — THE CHIEF'S DAUGH-
TER. — SINGULAR ADVENTURE.

FORTY miles north-east of the landing, where
Tom parted from the Willards, was a wide belt
of woods, through which, down in its dim depths,
ran a foaming river. The irregular limestone
bluffs, forming its banks, were wild and pictu-
resque in the extreme. Few, save the Indian,
and the hunter, and trapper, ever entered these
labyrinths.

On the stream, farther down, where the woods
ended in rolling prairie, a young town had started,
and, using the water power, furnished lumber to
villages less favored; for the settlers deemed
themselves fortunate, if, by going a score of
miles, they could procure a load of boards, to be
used in building their cabins.

At this place the stage deposited Tom — the
route continuing no farther. The young Scotch-
American also stopped there, who, on learning
Tom's destination, stated that his father's cabin
was twelve miles distant on Tom's path, and, as

he would return next day with horse and wagon, offered to take Tom and his trunk along for company.

"I shall get here by two in the afternoon, to-morrow," he said.

Next morning, to "stretch his limbs," Tom started alone, on a short exploring walk up the river, amusing himself on the way gathering botanical and entomological specimens, and noting the varieties of birds that flitted on the wing, or floated on the water.

Absorbed in thoughts of the dear ones he was going to visit, and in what he saw, he had gone some distance into the woods, when, coming to a widening of the trail, he saw, quietly preceding him, an Indian girl, of from sixteen to eighteen years of age. She was walking slowly, apparently unaware that any one was near. Rumors of Indian hostilities were afloat, and this evidence that he was in the vicinity of an Indian encampment was anything but welcome.

His first impulse was to turn about, and noise-lessly retrace his steps. A second thought showed the folly of this, for he had been shouting to awaken the echoes, and singing, to express his enjoyment, and crashing the dry twigs, up to the very instant of the appearance of the tawny maiden ; so, despite her seeming ignorance of his presence, he felt assured she was aware of it.

Making, therefore, the best of his uncomfortable situation, he hurried to overtake the stranger. Approaching, he was struck with her exceeding beauty, while the ornaments upon her person proclaimed her a chief's daughter.

Her form was symmetry itself; her jet black hair, elaborately dressed and braided, was long, silken, and glossy; her carriage was graceful and dignified; while row after row of many-hued beads encircled her neck and shoulders, and embroidered her moccasons. And such face and eyes! the former, delicately tinged, perfectly regular, interesting; the latter, soft, lustrous, shaded by long, dark lashes.

In his boyhood, Tom had read, in some high-wrought romance he chanced to meet, an ideal sketch of an Indian maid; this prodigy of nature fully realized that glowing portraiture.

Scarcely, however, had he reached her side, when a short, dry cough, the insidious "coffin cough," so often heard in civilized dwellings, fell on his ear.

"Indian girl sick?" he inquired, awkwardly striving to make himself understood.

No answer was returned, nor did the movement of a muscle of the features, or a turn of the head, give token that she saw or heard him. Again she involuntarily coughed.

Taking out a well-stocked medicine case, he

drew forth a vial, and, displaying it to view, said, —

"Indian girl sick; medicine, perhaps, make well!"

Without a responsive glance or word, a little yellow hand was stretched out, the slender fingers glistening with rings. Pouring some medicated globules into the open palm, she gravely swallowed them, and continued her silent walk. Soon the cough softened a little, the irritation of the respiratory organs was soothed, and feeling that, possibly, on her favor his very life might depend, he sought, fruitlessly, to engage her in conversation.

Suddenly, however, she disappeared down the side of the bluff. A profound silence, broken only by the rush of the stream, and twitter of birds, succeeded, yet that ambushed eyes were watching every motion he could not doubt.

Retracing his way with assumed carelessness, he had not gone far, when from the thickets leaped a band of yelling savages, naked to the waist, their hair flowing in wild disorder over their brawny shoulders. It was a startling onset; but, understanding Indian character too well to manifest fear, he scrutinized his captors with a coolness that astonished himself.

"Money! money!" they shouted in rude English, thrusting their grimy paws from every side into his face.

"No money!" he replied, shaking his head.

Dancing, grinning, jeering, for a few exciting moments, they at length vanished in the woods.

Feeling uneasy, and uncertain as to what the discovery he had made might forebode, he thought he would see if he could find their encampment. So, pushing his way through the bushes, and down the declivity, he discovered, hidden under the overhanging ledge, several Indian tents.

Before one, tightly stretched from two stakes driven into the ground, was a deer's hide, the pelt of which an old hag was rubbing soft and smooth with a sharp-edged stone — a slow and laborious process.

Just shooting into view from the other side of the river, and propelled by a squaw, was a canoe, laden with the limbs of trees for the fire; while in a lodge squatted the lazy "lords of the soil," playing games of chance, the paint on their faces showing that, if not on the war-path, they perhaps intended mischief to somebody.

Feeling that in view of the Indians having recently left him unmolested, he might enter the camp without special danger, and as he wished, if possible, to ascertain their designs, he at once descended the ledge, and entered the tent. Seating himself, he watched their play. No notice was taken of him. One of the players, whose cruel leer, and the contortions of whose supple body, made him think of a human snake, struck into a savage song, swaying back and forth to keep time.

Tom found it difficult to conceal his apprehensions, and the better to do so, in a frank, "at home" manner, he had just taken his turn in drinking from the dubious-looking pail of water that stood near, when the chief appeared, accompanied by his daughter.

"Medicine for pappoose!" he said.

"Yes," Tom gladly replied, and, carefully taking out the powder, showed him what was a dose, making him comprehend that the remedy was to be taken three times daily, saying, —

"Make pappoose better!"

"Good, good," answered the Indian, adding, "white man, go home bimeby, quick! Indian no hurtee him."

Taking the hint, Tom departed, reaching the little settlement, thankful at his easy escape. Did the gratitude of the Indian maid, operating through the love of the old chief for his strangely beautiful child, give him a safe return? Long did he ponder his strange adventure.

It is an old adage, "All knowledge will come into use at some time." Tom's splendid constitution, thanks to the tug and toil of his varied experiences as a squatter's son, permitted him to study more and faster in a day than if he had been tenderly reared. Long deprivation of school privileges had also made him brain-hungry. As an inmate of an eminent physician's family, he had a taste awakened for anatomy, physiology, and the knowledge of diseases and their treatment.

"Christ was physician of both soul and body; why should not I be?" he argued. Little did he think, however, as he waded through Diagnosis and the Materia Medica, and rode and talked with the knowledge-imparting doctor, that the first use he would have for the medicine case the physician had presented him at parting, would be to relieve an Indian girl, and thereby, perhaps, save his own life.

He was aware that a frontier missionary must needs prescribe for the sick, or stand idly by and see them suffer; and from benevolent considerations he had informed himself in medicine. He had begun to receive the reward, sure to accrue, sooner or later, to those who seek the good of others.

CHAPTER IX.

" HOG'S BACK." — THE SOLITARY HORSEMAN.

THE capacious immigrant wagon was packed over night, Mrs. Willard's, aunt Esther's, and the boys' trunks put in first, side by side, back of the second seat; for there were two seats — the driver's, then one behind that. On the trunks mattresses were laid to recline on, if necessary, while riding, and to sleep on at night.

Against the side of the canvas-top, hung in straps, handy for service, was Ferdinand's gun, — a Christmas present, — his name engraved on a brass plate screwed into the breech. Then came two sharp axes, a hammer, hatchet, and a small handsaw, a knife in a leather sheath, and a leather bag containing an assortment of nails of different sizes. These articles last enumerated were part of the original outfit of the wagon.

Packed under the seats were cooking utensils, bags of grain for the horses, a sack of flour, and " bix box, little box, bandbox and bundle," belonging to the women. Suspended at the back of the vehicle were two water-pails.

The humble hamlet at which the Willards were tarrying, called a landing because steamers, on their trips up and down the river, touched there, was located in a gap in the limestone bluffs rising from the river's bank. Like a mighty wall these huge bluffs extended along the shore, with here and there an opening, as if a giant hand had cut through to facilitate communication between the commerce of the Mississippi and the inland region.

Rising on either hand, from the little port towered precipitous ledges, the opening narrowing as you left the water, — something as if you had started from the base of an irregularly acute angle, — and lessened in depth till, continuing to ascend, you emerge from the ravine, and stand on a level with the heights of the bluffs.

It was morning twilight when the Willards were going up the ravine. Ferdinand, by right of seniority, elected himself driver, and holding the reins in his left hand, — he said that was the way *experienced* horsemen did, — and a massive whip in his right, walked with an authoritative air beside the team, to favor the horses. Frankie and the feminines rode, and Georgie ran eagerly on before, turning every few minutes to tell Ferdinand which was the way, — wholly " a work of supererogation," as the theologians crack their jawing jaws to say.

The sun showed his round, red face — blushing to find himself so late — just as the white-topped wagon gained the summit.

"Hurrah!" cried Georgie, tossing his cap high up in the air; "why, mother, did you ever see anything so splendid!"

Ferdinand bellowed "whoa," in a gruff, commanding tone to the horses, and his mother and aunt, accepting his invitation, got out to survey the scene.

What a sight met their gaze! For miles and miles the great river wound along — a stream of molten gold, dotted with green islets, and spotted by steamers looking like monster water-birds.

"Wonderful! wonderful!" exclaimed Mrs. Willard. But soon she began to weep.

"Hurrah!" cheered Georgie again; "how cool and beautiful it is here!"

But Frankie, who had been viewing the river from the driver's seat, his large, old-young face peering solemnly around the wagon side, displeased at George's boisterousness, frowningly piped, —

"Stop your noise, George!" adding, authoritatively, "Ferdinand, it's time we were starting."

At which the latter, as if accustomed to obey the dwarf, politely assisting his mother and aunt into the wagon, he and Georgie got in too, and the steeds were once more in motion.

" I am sure I don't know which way to go," said Ferdinand, suddenly reining in the horses, and looking around in dismay. I expected it would be smooth prairie. I am afraid we shall tip over."

" The prospect is not very encouraging," replied Mrs. Willard, leaning on his shoulder the better to see. " We must have mistaken the path."

The ground was broken into sharp ridges, extending outwards in irregularly parallel lines, the ridge they were upon being much the highest, and apparently too narrow to pass along in safety.

" Why don't you examine the paper Mr. Jones gave you for a guide?" asked Frankie, impatiently.

Ferdinand fumbled first in one pocket, then in another, for the chart. It was not there !

" What *shall* we do?" exclaimed his mother. " We cannot get on without that chart."

Ferdinand took everything from his pockets, and turned the latter inside out. An amusing medley of articles of all colors, kinds, shape, and uses came to light, but not Tom's sketch for their route.

The little Hunchback's great sharp eyes were

fixed reprovingly on his older brother's face during the fruitless search.

"I knew you'd lose the paper!" he piped. "You'd lose your head if it wasn't fastened on!"

"I'll run back to the tavern, and see if it's there," said Georgie.

"You keep still!" commanded the Hunchback. "Drive on, Ferdinand."

"Drive where?" retorted the latter.

"I knew you'd forget," said the dwarf. "Didn't Mr. Jones say that the land would be in ridges up here, and that in leaving the ravine by the main — the travelled path — we would find ourselves on the highest ridge, called, from its shape and position, 'Hog's Back'? and that we must ride straight ahead two miles on it?" Go 'long now — not keep us waiting all day!"

Ferdinand had fallen into the habit of generally minding the dwarf, he had such a manner, and was so knowing; so he doubtingly chirruped to the horses.

"Steady! steady!" said the dwarf; "'twon't answer to be careless."

The caution was timely; for the ridge, rising somewhat like the spine of the animal for which it was named, was scarcely wider than the wagon, and steep and sloping.

But our immigrants soon mastered their apprehensions, and journeyed over the queer road, pleasantly chatting.

"Only think," said Georgie, "two women, three boys, two horses, and a big wagon, all on a hog's back. I should think he'd squeal!"

"And the hog two miles long from snout to stern," added Ferdinand.

"He hasn't a bristle, though!"

"The grass is his bristles."

"Steady, I tell you!" interrupted the dwarf.

Silence fell on the family, for the hog had his back pretty well up at this point — in resentment, perchance, to the lads' personalities. Shortly, however, the ridge slightly widened, — more pork, and less bone, — then they began to descend; and quickly there lay, outspread before their eyes, an immense expanse of land, as even to the sight as if art had made it so.

"Hurrah!" burst from Georgie's lips; and Ferdinand stopped the span, and the women bent forward to feast on the sight.

"Beautiful! charming!" ejaculated Mrs. Willard, enthusiastically.

"Sweet fields arrayed in living green," quoted entranced aunt Esther, with an accent that carried the listener to a landscape eye of mortal hath not seen.

"What course shall I take now?" asked Ferdinand — an inquiry that transferred our travellers from realms of reverie back to matters of a practical nature.

But who was to decide? Before them stretched an illimitable meadow, destitute of house, human resident, or road. Is it strange that, bewildered, there was no reply?

The dwarf, however, was cool.

"I thought you'd forget," he reiterated, in thin, querulous tones. "At the termination of Hog Back Ridge lies Looking Glass Prairie," he repeated, word for word from Tom's directions.

"Wonder why it's called so?" asked Georgie, looking relieved.

"Because," explained the dwarf, testily, "a looking-glass is smooth. Now hold your tongue!"

Then he continued, —

"Three wagon tracks; take the middle one. Here it is," pointing with his shrivelled fore finger. "Start on!"

"Isn't it jolly!" cried irrepressible Georgie, "from off a hog's back, two miles long, we go down smash— horses, wagon, and all — on a looking glass large enough to hang up on the sky. The hog didn't move nor grunt, and the mirror don't crack. I guess the glass must be thick."

And now that it was level, Ferdinand treated the travellers to a trot. This suited Georgie. He boiled over with mirth and fun. Ferdinand, the driver, behaved with the dignity befitting his responsible trust. At his side was the dwarfed Hunchback, grave, reflective, curt.

But Georgie was nowhere long at a time. Boy-like, he tried all attitudes, places, posts, and positions — racing by the horses, hanging on with the buckets, scrambling over aunt Esther to lie upon the beds, jerking the lines when Ferdinand was off his guard, starting up the steeds, abstracting goodies from his mother's reticule.

Indeed, the novelty of their situation wrought wonders in withdrawing the thoughts of the family — as Tom had foreseen — from their great sorrow.

Tom was a *practical* philanthropist. Doubtless he had read in a certain old Book these words : " Love not in word, neither in tongue, but in deed and in truth."

Many devout persons never saw that passage. Such impart excellent counsel to the starving, and recite Scripture to them, and then leave them to their fate — like a wealthy lady I knew, who seeing a barefooted child of poverty bitterly weeping over a pitcher she had broken, for which accident she expected a beating on reaching her miserable home, the lady, in the excess of her goodness, stopped, and using the child's misfortune for an illustration, addressed her on the uncertainties and disappointments of earth, and then presented the expectant girl with — a few pennies to buy a new pitcher? No; a tract.

When the saint in silks and diamonds glanced back at the recipient of her charity, what was her pious horror to see that printed page in the mud!

We commend to these cheap philanthropists the story of the kind-hearted old gentleman in Maine, who, riding along in his carriage one hot day in July, saw a toad lying in the road, gasping with the heat. In the kindness of his soul, the elderly man (who was very fleshy) climbed down, moved the poor melting toad *into the shade of his carriage*, then complacently climbed up again, and *drove on*.

"Mother," sputtered the Hunchback, "hadn't George better wait till the rest eat? He's helping himself to the doughnuts."

"When are we going to eat?" asked Georgie, the words working their way out with much difficulty, because of the cramming.

"We shall reach the halting-place pretty soon," answered the dwarf, "and then mother will get breakfast."

"There's the spring," said little Hunchback, breaking a marvellously long interval of silence. "We'll stop there."

It was in a gentle ravine; for, level as the prairie appeared at the outset, it had its depres-

sions, as is the case with many persons who seem
outwardly to be perfectly happy. This, however, was the first notable irregularity of the
ground with which they had met since bidding
adieu to the Hog's Back; and when Georgie saw
it, he clapped his hands, saying, —

"Mother, the 'looking-glass' *is* cracked, after
all!" a misfortune that did not seem to lessen its
value to the hungry immigrants, if we may judge
by the interest they took in its utility on the present occasion.

Ferdinand, with George's lively aid, unhitched
the horses, as Tom had advised, to rest them, and
permit them to graze. "They are accustomed to
it," said Tom, "and will not stray away." But
one of the steeds made preparations to roll in the
grass.

"He'll break his harness all in pieces," cried
aunt Esther; and Georgie, glad of an excuse for
"driving" the horse in some way, started him up,
and began to remove the harness. Both horses
were then relieved of the hard, heavy leather —
their working dress; and much did they seem to
appreciate their freedom. And they rolled and
kicked to their hearts' content.

Meanwhile, the immigrants had seated themselves on the soft turf, convenient to the spring.
Mrs. Willard, having spread a clean white cloth,
on which were deposited sandwiches, made of

two slices of bread with ham between, a paper of cakes, and another of doughnuts. Then on a piece of newspaper she put some slices of cheese.

"There are no plates, knives and forks, or spoons on our table," said she to the group; "but it is an old saying, and I dare say a true one, that fingers were made before forks."

"I declare," said Georgie, "I never ate anything so nice before. Did you fry these doughnuts, auntie?"

"They are from the same cooking that you disliked at the landing. It's the good air that makes the difference."

Yes, the pure, bracing, prairie air, how appetizing!

"I'm fairly ashamed of myself," remarked Ferdinand, who prided himself on gentility in eating. "I'm getting to be a regular glutton."

And if certain young ladies east, — don't be alarmed; we shall not mention names, — who went into ecstasies over his foppish airs, had seen him suck the grease from his finger-tips, using his "handsome lips" for a napkin, after finishing his fifth sandwich, they would have exclaimed, horror-struck, "How vulgar!" and straightway composed their shattered nerves by a delicate lunch of pickled limes, slate pencils, *terra alba* candy, mince pie, and ice-cream.

An hour fled swift-winged.

"Come," said little Hunchy, "it's time to be stirring."

Ferdinand and Georgie went to catch the horses. But the animals, having little wish to forsake the grass and freedom for fasting and toil, refused to be captured.

"Don't those boys know anything?" muttered the Hunchback. "Mother, call Georgie!"

"*G-e-o-r-g-i-e!* G-e-o-r-g-i-e!" screamed Mrs. Willard, in ear-piercing treble.

"You needn't call so loud," said Hunchback; "you could be heard for miles in this clear prairie air. Don't you see? That man heard you!"

A long distance off, distinctly outlined against the sky, was a horseman. At Mrs. Willard's call, he turned his horse about, and was now coming towards them.

"Make haste," said little Hunchback to Georgie; "take one of the pails from the back of the wagon, put a few oats in it, and tell Ferdinand to toll the horses here as fast as he can."

Ferdinand coaxingly approached the refractory steeds, shaking the pail so that they might hear the grain rattle. Often had they been fed from that vessel, and, with a neigh, they came trotting after Ferdinand, as he retreated towards the vehicle.

"Take off the other pail now," said little

Hunchy, "and put oats in that, and let both horses have some; for if you deceive them they won't come next time."

And while the horses were eating, and the boys were harnessing them, the horseman drew slowly near. The beast he rode was an unusually fine one, but the man rode as if unaccustomed to the saddle. He was a heavily-built man, with a dark, bad eye, but an insinuating manner.

"Anything to pay? Thought I heard a woman scream?" said he, reining up near the boys.

"Nothing," replied Ferdinand, frankly, "mother was calling Georgie."

"Ah," he ejaculated, coolly surveying the party; "yer ain't journeying alone with these youngsters, marm?" addressing Mrs. Willard. "Where's your man?"

"Father, and the other gentlemen, are just behind," interposed little Hunchback, his great, grave eyes fixed ominously on the comer. "We don't need your help."

The stranger looked the dwarf curiously over, the latter returning the scrutiny with a boldness and audacity oddly comporting with his diminutive stature. But the long, black eyebrows seemed to deepen in color, the forehead grew dark and threatening, his whole bearing hostile and defiant.

"What are you? a human porcupine?" asked the traveller, riding contemptuously round little Hunchy.

The dwarf made no reply, but kept his magnetic eyes fastened on the man.

"I can't make out what you are, man or boy," said the horseman, repeating his circuit; "but you don't fancy my company any more than I do yours. Well, good by to ye all!" and off he paced.

"O, how glad I am that he's gone!" gasped Mrs. Willard. "He's a monster, I know. I was frightened 'most to death."

"Lucky he didn't touch little Hunchy," said a boyish voice from the wagon.

They looked up. There was Georgie, on the driver's seat, with Ferdinand's gun.

"I would have shot him dead, had he laid a finger on one of you," added he, waxing heroic, as he perceived himself now "the observed of all observers."

"How would you have done it?" inquired Ferdinand.

"With your gun," replied Georgie.

"But you couldn't; there is no cap on it!"

"O, I didn't think of that," said Georgie, crestfallen.

At noon they camped again for dinner, and to bait the horses, reaching, at twilight, "Sun

Prairie " — a vast stretch of land, different from
" Looking Glass Prairie," the surface being more
undulating.   Just over the line separating the
two were a shallow stream and a clump of trees.
Here it was decided to spend the night.

CHAPTER X.

A NIGHT ON THE PRAIRIE. — DANGER.

THERE was no moon, but the blue vault above was brilliantly studded with stars. The little Hunchback lay on the mattress beside the wagon, his great thoughtful eyes turned skyward. At his back rested Ferdinand in deep sleep, while the regular breathing of his mother, aunt, and Georgie, who occupied the mattress in the wagon, assured him that he alone was awake.

His bodily littleness had been to him, through all his days, one of his greatest trials. Dwarf! how he hated the word! To be small was to be despised. He never hinted, even to his mother, the intensity of grief and chagrin arising from his incomplete stature. Those physically active and vigorous, and of large frame, he regarded as so many reflections on his own feebleness and insignificance.

And now, as his clear gaze, wonder-struck searched the overarching depths, he felt of less importance than ever, and seemed to shrink to an atom. Those orbs, world on world, systems of worlds, universes of universes, what was he compared with them?

Never had he witnessed such a spectacle; never swept with his aspiring gaze such star-gemmed spaces, undimmed, unobstructed, rolling, in infinite majesty, from horizon to horizon, the air-medium pure as crystal, not a veiling vapor, nor a disturbing zephyr's whisper. How very, very small he felt!

Yet, somehow, this shrinking into nothingness did not wound his self-respect. He was not measuring himself with his fellow-man, but with the mighty heavens. And suddenly there came sweeping down to him the words of the ancient singer, —

"When I consider the heavens, the work of Thy hands, the sun and the moon which Thou hast ordained, what is man, that Thou art mindful of him, and the son of man, that thou visitest him?"

The dwarf started up. Did a voice repeat that song? No, it was memory, he said to himself. As he pondered the words, they filled him with profound self-abasement — with deep, un-ruffled, unresentful humility.

"How great is God, the omnipotent, all-wise Creator and Upholder!" he said to himself. "Why should He deign to notice me — a mote in His limitless empire?"

INTRODUCTION OF SIMMONS.   Page 108.

Just then there came floating to his ear the remainder of the royal hymn.

"Thou madest him a little lower than the angels. Thou crownedst him with glory and honor, and didst set him over the works of Thy hands."

He raised himself again in increased surprise. Surely it was no illusion this time. Some tongue recited that passage. But solitude reigned from the bare prairie to the stars. "How my brain tricks me to-night!" he said. "What a strange spell is on me!"

Then his mind was led to meditate upon the singularly-suggested language.

"Thou crownedst him." "Then the mighty Maker of the universe has exalted man," he soliloquized. "Has *crowned* him; constituted him king, sovereign of creation."

"And *you*, dwarf," added the mysterious voice, "are therefore a king!"

"Who is speaking these comforting words to me," asked the dwarf, gazing around. "How weak I am! It is my own mind."

Yes, queer contradiction, they seemed foreign to himself, yet a part of himself.

"My head is hot," he ejaculated "I'll go to sleep;" and he closed his eyes.

"Set him over the works of Thy hands," whispered the voice. "The elephant is a towering mass of bone and muscle, yet man, king of nature, captures and governs the huge beast. Oxen are sturdy, but man yokes them. The horse is swift and strong, yet man puts bits in his mouth. The fish of the sea, the birds of the air, nay, earth and ocean, man subdues to his own use."

"Yes," assented the still wakeful dwarf, "man is king of all things."

"And how does he rule?" asked the viewless teacher; "by physical might?"

"Ah, I see," replied the dwarf, "it is through the mind — the soul."

"And you are weak in body, deformed, and small in size; but are you not, nevertheless, a king? Assert your sovereignty, then; rule by the intellect with which God has crowned you."

"That's it," said the dwarf, sitting up in bed, and resting his chin in his small, white hand. "It isn't the body that's monarch, but the brain. A dwarf may rule as well as a giant."

Did an angel or spirit comfort the deformed child? or were his rapt faculties elaborating ideas for his instruction? We do not pretend to decide. Can you?

The angels brought "tidings of great joy" to the shepherds watching their flocks by night on the plains of Bethlehem. Perhaps one of the ministering host may have whispered to little Hunchback as he watched beneath the immigrant wagon on the star-lit prairie. One said anciently, "I am little and despised, yet the Lord thinketh upon me."

A sound startled him from the light slumber into which he had sunken. A moment more, with a wild cry an Indian shot by on a pony.

"What's wanted?" drowsily muttered Ferdinand, trying to rouse himself.

"Ferdie," asked the mother, drawing aside the blanket that curtained the wagon-front, "what was that noise? It sounded like a yell. You are not in a nightmare — are you?"

"It's all right, mother," said little Hunchback. "I'll take care of Ferdinand; go to sleep."

And the vigilant little dwarf listened long and anxiously, fearing he knew not what. Then he stole cautiously out to where the savage passed. There he found a narrow, hard-trodden path. Creeping on hands and knees, he carefully examined it.

"It is an old Indian trail," said he. "Only one pony been over it recently. There is no danger. Probably the savage was as much astonished at seeing our team as I was at seeing him."

And his old-young face expressing entire confidence in this conclusion, he returned to the mattress, and dropped asleep.

But a confused noise in the direction of the

horses led him to rise again after softly tucking the blanket against Ferdie's back, and go and see what was the matter. He found that one of them, having been tied to a small oak, had walked round and round the sapling, till he had wound himself so closely as to endanger his neck in his frantic efforts to break away.

The dwarf, with considerable difficulty, disengaged the fractious animal, and leading it to the wagon, fastened the beast to a hind wheel. Then, after shortening the rope with which the other horse was tied, — for it was so long that the beast had its fore leg entangled in it, — he sat under an oak thinking.

"Next time we camp out," he muttered, "I shall see that the horses are properly hitched, and that we are not near an Indian trail."

A long while he remained meditating.

"All is quiet. I guess I'll get another nap," said he at length. He crept quietly under the clothes, so as not to disturb Ferdie. He was now thoroughly weary and drowsy. He dropped into a deep sleep, from which he was startled by something cold creeping across his bare ankles. With lightning quickness he knew that it was a snake. Perhaps it was harmless, perhaps it was deadly. By a strong effort at self-control, he lay motionless. Slowly the slimy reptile worked its way along, attracted by the warmth, towards

the middle of the bed. What an age it seemed
till the serpent glided from his limb, and nestled
between himself and Ferdie!

The dwarf was now in terror lest Ferdie should
awake. What could he do to rid them of their
unwelcome bed-mate? He dared not stir, and
he dreaded, most of all, that Ferdie would. After a while Ferdie threw an arm out of bed. Instantly an angry buzz from the reptile was heard.
It was a rattlesnake! Ferdie was quiet again,
and the snake ceased its deadly warning.

Working his big head cautiously round on his
pillow, so that he might look in the direction of
the rattling, the dwarf saw the snake. The
blanket had become disarranged, leaving Ferdie's leg bare, and the venomous creature was
lying near the limb, on the unturned covering.

Should Ferdinand move it was certain death;
and that he would remain quiet long, the dwarf
knew was not probable. With singular steadi-
ness and dexterity he began to withdraw his own
thin limbs, and at the same time gradually
to raise himself so as to sit up. The snake's
head was from him, which was in the Hunchback's favor.

Twice the serpent, irritated gently, shook its
rattles. But so wary and adroit was the dwarf,
that his snakeship settled again to repose, till the
Hunchback softly sat up, pillow in hand. The

snake saw the movement, and turned upon his **adversary**. One point, however, had been gained, namely, to attract the attention of the reptile from Ferdie.

"If I am bitten it will not matter so much," thought the dwarf. "Mother couldn't spare Ferdie, he's so well and strong."

The snake's head was erect, and the red, forked tongue played spitefully. He was preparing to spring upon the dwarf, when, with unerring celerity, the pillow descended on the snake, and Ferdie was thrust from the mattress.

"What did you do that for?" demanded the elder brother.

"There's a rattlesnake in the bed," shrilly piped the dwarf. "Here it is," he added, jumping aside, as the poison-fanged intruder wriggled out from beneath the pillow at the Hunchback. But Ferdie, seizing the whip-stock, despatched it at a blow.

"When we camp out again," observed the dwarf, "we must fix it so the snakes can't get into our bed."

But streaks of light in the east heralded the advent of day. Immediately after, the sun peeped across the prairie, then shot up fully to view. Georgie said he seemed in a hurry. But our immigrants were a second time ahead of him, and again he grew red in the face; and no won-

der, the lazy, lubberly fellow, to be lagging behind women and boys.

Mrs. Willard and her sister were performing
their toilet at the stream. Ferdie and Georgie
had set about graining the horses, pouring about
two quarts of meal into each pail, and stirring in
water to moisten it.

"I should think the oats would be better for
them than this raw, cold hasty-pudding, without
anything on it," said Georgie.

"No," replied Ferdie. "Tom said oats were
more stimulating, but they wouldn't stand by like
meal. Meal gives permanent strength."

The dwarf now appeared with an axe on his
shoulder.

"Here, Ferdie," he said, "I want you to cut
a few sticks. There, those are just the article,"
pointing to some forked limbs.

These were driven into the ground a short distance apart, the crotchet ends up. Across them
another stick was placed horizontally. Then an
iron pot was brought from the wagon, and hung
from the centre. This was partly filled with
water from the brook, and a fire started under the
kettle.

When the water began to boil, aunt Esther
dropped in potatoes; and Mrs. Willard sliced
pork, and commenced frying it in a spider.
Plates, knives and forks, and cups and saucers,

were produced. A cloth was laid on the grass, and the little family were soon, with appreciative appetite, discussing the simple repast.

" I believe I never got up so much refreshed," observed Mrs. Willard, " as I did this morning."

"That's because you didn't sleep in a close room," sagely remarked Georgie.

" I was afraid you'd catch cold," said aunt Esther.

"Folks that live in the open air are not subject to colds," replied the dwarf. But he did not allude to the Indian, and he had charged Ferdinand to say nothing about the rattlesnake.

" It would only frighten the women," said he.

CHAPTER XI.

A PIONEER BOY'S OPINION OF THE EAST. — DISAPPOINTMENT.

WHAT a familiar aspect nature wore to Tom as he journeyed frontierward! Stonewalls, ledges, boulders, rocks, gravel, stumps, stunted corn, swarming, suffocating cities, *east;* but here, broad rolling prairies, deep fertile soil, waving grasses, beckoning flowers. He hailed the contrast with a bounding pulse.

It seemed to him as if he had not drawn a full breath since he left Minnesota. He had suffered for want of air and room, and been cramped, confined, fettered, by social artificialities.

Now he was back to pure nature — to boyhood associations. He was happy. Expanding his chest, and thumping it with his friendly fist, he drank in the prairie air as if it were the elixir of life, and proudly swept the wide expanse with his admiring eye, as if to say, —

"There's nothing like my dear, magnificent prairies, after all."

With what vividness, too, did these scenes reproduce the early days of his eventful history!

the long journeys in the immigrant wagon; the too frequent removals; the homely, smoky squatter's cabin; the murderous scenes of the massacre at Spirit Lake; the cruel tomahawking of his sister Sarah; Charley's romantic exploits; his father's brave, heroic death; his widowed mother's establishment at the frontier fort with the noble wife of the noble commander of the fortress, as governess of their two lovely children, Willie and Alice.

Alice! With that name uprose before him a vision surpassingly good and fair, setting his feelings into a tumult altogether too *human* for a parson in embryo. He tried to rally his budding professional dignity, and banish the enchanting apparition. In vain. Adown the long stairs, through the echoing hall, warbling bird-like, bursting blithely into the apartment, stopping in confused surprise, he saw again the blonde-haired fairy, just as he did on his first visit at the fort.

That image had never wholly forsaken him, and ever, when it stood freshly before his mind's eye, there was a glow at his heart of mingled worship and gratitude, the former for the sweetness, excellence, and beauty of the winning original; the latter, that despite his plain garb and humble circumstances, she could listen to his story that day with such respect, and no apparent consciousness of the inequality of their condition.

But what worldly imaginations for a candidate for the gospel ministry! And what was Alice to Tom?

"No doubt," murmured Tom, endeavoring to shake off the spell, "she's forgotten me long since. Her father is a military man. Of course she has plenty of dashing young officers as admirers; she would not think of the squatter's son!"

Tom's first visit was to L——, the village where lived the kind clergyman and the storekeeper who had enabled him to go east to study. What a pleasure to take these good friends by the hand! There, too, an inmate of the missionary's family was curly-pated Bub, the youngest of his brothers. "I wonder," cogitated Tom, as he neared the town, "if Bub will know me; and if he is the same prankish little pet as ever; and if he still rehearses for the pulpit." For Bub's highest aspiration had been to preach. And that he had not altogether lost his taste for the sacred calling, Tom had received evidence of in the shape of a printed note that Bub had contrived clandestinely to slip within a letter to Tom from the missionary. It ran thus:—

DEER tom i AM, GOING 2 B a BIG MAN LIK U. i PREATH SUMTIMS. THE MISUARY SAYS I MAY PREATH FOR HIM, WHENN I DU. I, CEND AKIS. I STODY HARD. I AMM A SPLENN DAD SKOLLER.

The day was warm, and Tom was not surprised, as he drove up to the clergyman's cabin, to observe that the door was open. He thought it somewhat singular, however, that, notwithstanding the bustle attending their arrival, and that the wagon in which he was brought was fully in sight from the house for quite a ways as it drew near, that no one looked out at the team. They dismounted, the horse was hitched, they approached the cabin. Silence and solitude seemed to dwell within.

"I fear the family are away," said Tom.

Glancing in, Tom's eyes opened wide with astonishment. In a chair, his legs stretched out before him, a man's white cravat around his throat, its broad folds enveloping also the chin, a man's hat on his head, glasses astride his nose, eyes fixed on a ponderous volume, sat a fat-cheeked urchin.

"Bub, you scamp," cried Tom, rushing in, and, regardless of ministerial proprieties and vestments, hugging the clerical imp, the missionary's hat rolling one way, and the Commentary, to show how *heavy* it was, falling with a slam to the floor.

Never were a couple of "theologues" more antic. If a Committee of Supply on the hunt for a candidate "suited to the large, wealthy, and fashionable congregation" at Upper-crust-

ville, had stepped in just then, I doubt if either
of the rollicking, rough-and-tumble young divines
before them had been in demand. Why, only
consider, Bub's cravat was actually tumbled, and
so was Tom's hair.

After a happy visit with the missionary and the
grocer, the former took Tom in the storekeeper's
carriage next morning, and they set out together
for the fort.

A cordial, affectionate, tender greeting awaited
Tom from General and Mrs. McElroy, his brothers, and his mother. She, Tom noticed, had
grown older; but her face was rounder and fairer,
bespeaking good fare and contentment.

"I conclude," said Mrs. McElroy, "that, charmed
with eastern people and privileges, frontier life
looks quite different to you from what it once did."

"Madam," heartily replied Tom, "there is much
that is admirable and grand in the older settled
portions of our country. But if they have many
things better than we, we are not without our
compensations. Here society is natural, and
neighbors are sympathizing and friendly; there
caste distinctions prevail, you know not who lives
next door, and fashion tyrannizes. There everything practicable is done for the culture of the
mind; but the young are not developed physically, and taught to be self-reliant, as among the
pioneers.

"In religion, I prefer our simplicity. It seems to me little short of sacrilege for Christians to display so much pride of dress in the house of God as they do east. And worship is maintained at such extravagant expense, that the poor are frequently debarred from the gospel, or are thrust into back seats, or banished to the galleries. Better our log-cabin equality than such a condition of things.

"I shall never lose the painful impression made on my mind by an incident that happened to me in one of these aristocratic churches.

"The fame of the Rev. Dr.—— led me one Sabbath to go and hear him. I arrived at his place of worship a little late. Entering the vestibule, I saw hanging before me two signs, on which were lettered, FREE SEATS ABOVE, an index finger pointing up stairs. Of course I inferred that there were no free seats below, and as I did not design hiring or buying a seat in God's house that day, I went *above*.

"In high, straight-backed, comfortless pews, a few of which were furnished with tattered and soiled cushions, was a collection of plainly-dressed people, with faces marked by care, poverty, and toil. An elderly woman, of feeble appearance and large frame, but saintly look, passed me her mutilated hymn book.

"I glanced below. Every pew was constructed

for comfort, if not luxury, and not more than one third of the sitting accommodations were occupied — whole slips in succession being entirely empty.

"The Scripture Lesson was from St. James's Epistle, second chapter — 'My brethren, have not the faith of our Lord Jesus Christ with respect of persons. For if there come into your assembly a man with a gold ring, in goodly apparel, and there come in also a poor man in vile raiment, and ye have respect to him that weareth the gay clothing, and say unto him, Sit thou here in a good place, and say to the poor, Stand thou there, or sit here under my footstool, are ye not then partial in yourselves?'

"This withering rebuke was impressively read by the pastor, and I scanned the countenances of the audience to see what their effect would be. But neither minister nor hearer showed the least consciousness that the language applied to modern assemblages. Fresh from our uninvidious gatherings, where, though a person may be in rags,

'A man is a man for a' that and a' that,'

the spectacle was — well, I cannot command terms to do justice to my feelings. They were destined to be intensified, too, by an occurrence at the close of the service.

"As I was descending the long, wide stone stairs

leading from the gallery, an exclamation caused me to look back. The scream was uttered by the aged woman who passed me her book. Being old and weakly, she had tripped and pitched head foremost. Springing to break her fall, I caught her on my shoulder. Why the weight and the momentum did not send me headlong, I do not comprehend; but I sustained her sufficiently long for others to come to our assistance, and we helped her to the sidewalk. Her ghastly face and trembling limbs showed how great the fright and shock to her.

"Was it not singular, that I, a stranger from the far-distant prairies, chanced to be there to save the life of that aged saint?"

"There are, however, devoted souls in those very churches—are there not?" asked his mother.

"Yes, many, dear mother. There are as earnest, unselfish, large-hearted Christians in the eastern cities as ever blessed any age. But while great numbers of professed disciples of the meek and lowly One attend church befrizzled and betrinketed as if at a theatre, thousands perish in the very shadow of Christian temples, as ignorant of Christ as the pagans; and multitudes lack the necessaries of life. These inconsistencies make infidels, on the one hand, who reject all that is sacred, and fanatics, on the other, who fly into all sorts of absurdities."

"Yes," said the missionary, "man, like the pendulum, goes to extremes. When I was east, disorderly classes of religionists arose, who plunged into the wildest excesses. A very singular form of fanaticism obtained at one time, called the Shaking Power. It had a queer history. Shall I tell you about it? It will, I think, be quite entertaining."

"O, yes; do let us hear about it," said the ladies.

The Shaking Power.

"Some forty miles from my home," said the missionary, "in a populous town, a 'meeting' was sustained with fanatical furor, composed of a motley assemblage from various sects and orders, and holding sentiments the most discordant, if we except the, with them, essential point—railing at 'the churches.' Here, members excluded for grave faults from the fellowship of Christians, restless, self-exscinded spirits inflamed by fickle isms peculiar to themselves, and those who never belonged, or expected to belong, to an orderly organization of any kind, met to sympathize and act in wild religious freedom, where everybody could be teachers, and anything be taught. Of members of Christian churches they were accustomed to speak as those who have the '*form* of godliness, but deny the *power* thereof;' meaning that these had system and decorum, and lacked those noisy and eccentric manifestations of zeal in worship which they themselves exhibited.

"Religion with these zealots was almost wholly a 'meeting' affair, and to exhort or pray in public was preëminently 'taking up the cross;' and to know, on such occasions, what to do, and how to do it, they sought to 'move as they were moved upon by the Spirit;' in other words, act out such impulse as chanced to seize them, whether it were to perambulate the sanctuary in sight of the congregation, and then kneel in the aisle and pray, or make remarks from the pulpit stairs. It mattered not how fantastic and foolish the impulse; it was to be unhesitatingly obeyed: indeed, the more senseless and erratic, the greater proof to their minds of the Spirit's power and control. As to preaching, it could not be known beforehand if there would be any, or who would be the preacher — this being left for the decision of the Spirit after the people had assembled, and one was as liable to be called to fill that office for the time being as another. A heavy 'cross,' indiscriminately imposed, was to go into the pulpit and speak and pray, so that in the course of an evening a dozen or more, old and young, male and female, would attain that conspicuous post; and if any one, after *ascending*, had to *de*scend without uttering a word, the boisterous shouts of

'Praise the Lord,' 'Glory to God,' showed that it was regarded as evidence of peculiar sanctity — the grace of humility had been tested, and had triumphed.

"A feature of this fanaticism, which took the lead in exciting wonder and inspiring the credulous with awe, ultimately operated as a cure of the evil it was designed to foster. It was called 'the shaking' or 'trembling power,' and originated with a farmer, who, though not without natural cunning, was below his class in intelligence, and whose life up to that time had borne meagrely, if at all, the fruits of goodness. He would meekly say he was 'slow of speech,' and 'as he could not speak like the rest, they must let him bear the cross the Lord had put upon him,' which was to shake. This was the utility of his gift: he watched the countenances of those present, and, if any one 'neglected duty,' he professed to detect it by the involuntary tremblings that shook his frame — their violence being in proportion to the importance of the duty, and the length of disobedience. Sometimes he called on the delinquent to 'do his duty,' — a call which was considered divinely prompted, and was at once obeyed.

"One evening our enthusiasts had met in a school-house. It was dark and drizzly without, and marvellously dull within — perchance the

effects of the weather, or a stupid reaction, the
sure sequence of spurious zeal. Silence reigned
for a long time. At length a man advanced to
the teacher's desk, and, in husky, monotonous
tones, helped on the general lethargy. A pro-
tracted pause ensued, which was broken by a
maiden lady suddenly springing to her feet and
commencing an exhortation. Her faded and
dirty linsey-woolsey dress, which she ' wore from
principle,' fell straight and close about her form ;
her coarse black hair was unevenly cut short in
the neck 'to shame pride,' while her wrinkled
skin, nut-brown complexion, stumpy gums, and
eyes wildly flashing as she paced the floor gesticulating violently, and with shrill voice denounced
'hypocrites and formal professors,' gave her a
weird and haggish expression. When her message was delivered, a dumpy man in semi-Quaker
garb, who sat in a semi-recumbent posture gazing
at the floor, remarked, without looking up, that
he was no singer *naturally ;* that he did not know
one tune from another ; but when the Spirit told
him to sing, he must sing ; and he gruffly chanted
to extemporaneous music, composed as he went
along, keeping time meanwhile with one foot, —

> 'The pure testimony put forth in the *Sperit*
>   Cuts like a sharp two-edged sword,
> And hypocrites now are sorely tormented,
>   Because they're condemned by the Word ;

The pure testimony discovers the dross,
While wicked professors make light of the cross,
And Babylon trembles for fear of her loss.'

An embarrassing silence again occurring, some one prayed the Lord to 'show them what it was that clogged the wheels of the meeting, and kept them from moving'— a prayer which seemed to them about to be answered, as a peculiar jarring of the floor and seats gave notice of the advent of the shaking power.

"This curious phenomenon was of an intermittent type, affecting first the lower extremities, imparting a tremulousness just perceptible, extending slowly to the whole body, meanwhile increasing in strength. Then passing off, a few moments would elapse before a recurrence in the same manner, each fit being augmented in length and intensity.

"The 'power' brother suffered one attack without speaking. While agitated by the second, he said oracularly, but retaining his seat, —

"'If anybody here has a duty to do, he had better do it!'

"'Amen! Amen!' fervently responded the brother-and-sisterhood, nodding approval, and exchanging relieved glances as they looked in the direction indicated. The candles burned dimly; but remote by himself, among some unoccupied seats, could be discerned the figure of a

man wrapped in a cloak, his hat drawn over his
eyes, his face resting on the desk before him.
The conclusion was, that it was some one bending under the weight of a too heavy cross; and
the shaking-power brother, after ineffectually
rising and saying, 'If the brother yonder
has a duty to do, I say he had better do it,'
with apparent difficulty dragg his trembling
frame across the room, and laid his hand authoritatively on the shoulder of the delinquent, when,
lo! the cloak slipped to the floor — there was no
one under it! It had chanc d to be left in such a
position as to look, in the uncertain light, as if
filling its wonted office to the human form —
hence the mistake. Fanaticism is proverbial'
ingenious in turning its most palpable blunders
into favoring arguments, but I never heard that
this one was so used. The effect of the scene
was irresistible. It dealt the shaking power a
blow from which it did not recover, and the meeting dwindled in interest and numbers, many of
the misguided attendants returning to their former
religious indifference, and others, who had been
honestly led astray, to happier spiritual associations."

"Mother," hesitatingly asked Tom, when
alone with her, "where are the rest of the fort
people?"

"That is a very sweeping question," she replied; "I do not understand it."

"I have seen the general, and his wife, and Willie," explained he, coloring, "but where is Alice?"

"Why, Tom, have you forgotten that she was lost?"

"*Lost!*" repeated the son, with strong emphasis. "Why was I not informed of it? Lost! how? when?"

"I wrote you the distressing intelligence; the letter must have miscarried." She then related the circumstances connected with her disappearance. When she had finished, Tom sat with drooping head, buried in thought.

At last, starting as if awakened from sleep, he exclaimed, "Mother, I know what happened to Alice. She was carried off by the Indians, and I have seen her!"

He then recited his adventure with the chief's daughter, ending by affirming that she and Alice were the same.

"You are excited, my son," replied the mother, soothingly. "There are no points of resemblance. Alice had light hair, the Indian girl black; then consider how fair Alice was — too white to be mistaken for a savage. Besides, why did she not, by word or glance, make herself known?"

These objections to his conjecture were unanswerable; yet Tom was not convinced that he was wrong, and replied, —

"Well, I shall hunt up Long Hair, and my visit shall be spent in seeking to unravel this mystery;" and he left the room, pale, bowed, and resolute, as if a weight of sorrow and of duty had suddenly fallen upon him.

CHAPTER XII.

THE DWARF'S DISCOVERY. — BRAIN OR BONE.

"I THINK we had better settle down somewhere," said the dwarf, "and not wander over
the prairies forever. This is not just where I
meant to stop; but Tom's chart was lost, and we
must make the best of it."

"But how do we know that the land here is
not preëmpted?" inquired Mrs. Willard.

"I'll venture that," replied the Hunchback;
"we are in the region Tom said was not taken
up. Besides, there are no signs of settlers."

The two women put their heads out of the
wagon, and looked around.

"We certainly should not be troubled with
neighbors in this solitude," observed Mrs. Wil
lard, dubiously.

"Nor sigh 'for a lodge in some vast wilder
ness,'" suggested her sister.

"But what *should* we do in case of sickness?"
forebodingly asked the former.

"Take care of each other," replied the dwarf.

"Suppose we were all sick at once?"

"Suppose the Man in the Moon should shoot us," gruffly grunted the dwarf. "We came out to get a farm, and we can't do it by remaining in the wagon all our lives, and conjuring difficulties. If we mean to do anything, let us begin, I say."

"Well, boys, what do you think?" inquired the mother, of Ferdie and Georgie.

But their courage was at low tide; and dispirited, they turned their faces aside without answering.

Arriving west and *going* west they had found to be very different.

Prospective pioneering and the reality were so unlike! They had not counted the cost in encouraging their father to immigrate, nor in accepting Tom's plan for them. Very romantic ideas had they entertained of life on the prairies. But now they were reduced to plain matters of fact.

"I am sorry we ever left the east!" fretted Georgie.

"We can't help that now," replied his mother.

"But how are we to get along in this miserable place?" asked Ferdinand. "No neighbors, no house to live in; nothing but land, land! How are we to live?"

"By thought, contrivance, and work," said the dwarf.

"O, yes, *you'd* do lots of work!" retorted

Georgie. "If you peel your own potatoes, you'll do well."

"I'll do my part, if you will yours," piped the dwarf.

"Yes, you'll *think*. Well, I prefer that part myself."

"I tell you," reiterated the dwarf, frowning, "I'll do my part if you'll do yours."

"My sons," sadly interposed the mother, "you'll kill your mother if you quarrel. We have met with great trouble. We must love and help each other. And remember, children, it is through no fault of Frankie's that he is not as strong as the rest of us. But how beautifully he remembered the route! I am not sure, with his strong memory and time for thought, but that he will be as useful in making our new home as either of us."

"Mother," said little Hunchie, softened by her soothing speech, "you know that I was the last to give in my assent to Tom's plan. I knew Ferdinand and Georgie were too excited about the prairies to weigh the matter. But we are here, and I believe we shall succeed nicely after a while. It is in our favor that there are no settlers, for we can choose the best of the land. Tom says this whole region is destined to be thickly populated. And don't you recollect how crowded the cars and steamers were with people bound to Minnesota? We shall have neighbors soon enough. We must select our claim as wisely as we can while there is so fine a chance, and hasten to improve it, so that new comers may not get it from us."

"Frankie is right," decided the mother. "Let us make a beginning. All is, if we can't get on farming, we shall have the claim to sell; and we can go back to the Mississippi, dispose of our team, and, if we wish, return to Maine."

"So we can," chimed in Georgie, brightening. "But what's to be done first? I'm sure I don't know."

"Select a site for a cabin," answered the dwarf, curtly. "Mother, you and aunt Esther get dinner, while we boys attend to this business. Unhitch the horses from the wagon, Ferdinand. You take one, and Georgie the other, and ride in opposite directions, and see what sort of a spot for a house you can choose. We ought to find a spring, if possible, as we shall not be able to dig a well, and river water isn't wholesome to drink. Tom said there is too much decaying vegetable matter in it."

"We shan't ride, and we are going together," said Ferdinand. "Come, Georgie;" and snatching aunt Esther's red shawl, and adjusting half to Georgie's shoulders and the remainder over his own, with arms around each other's waists, they sauntered off.

"They'll learn that it isn't all play," said Frankie, gazing after the scarlet-robed boys.

They had gone, perhaps, a half mile, when Ferdie suddenly slinging the shawl across his arm, the brothers ran, excitedly, different ways, describing a large circle. Then, waving their caps, they shouted, —

"Drive over here! This is the place. Splendid for dinner, too!"

So, the women and Frankie getting into the wagon, the latter guided the span there.

"It's perfectly charming!" cried aunt Esther, with unwonted enthusiasm.

They had reached a gentle swell of ground, at the foot of which was an oval-shaped lakelet, its turfy borders being as evenly curved as if done with the landscape gardener's tools, and the water was so translucent that the smallest object could be seen at the bottom. It was fed by boiling springs, several of which, at either end, were sending up fine white sand, while farther from the shore was still another, of great size and force. A mile and a half west was a fine grove.

"Well done!" exclaimed Mrs. Willard, with maternal pride. "You have won credit to yourselves. We can erect our cabin on the top of the eminence, and it will command a splendid view. The lake will furnish an unfailing supply of sweet and healthful water. And when we open our farm, every inch of it will be in sight."

"Now," cried Ferdie and Georgie in a breath, "we'll feed the horses, while mother cooks dinner."

"You may leave the headstall on the off horse, Ferdie," said the dwarf.

"What for? He can't eat with the bits in his mouth."

"Guess I'll have a short ride," answered the Hunchback. "Lead him alongside the forward wheel, Ferdie. Now, fold this blanket, and strap it on his back;" and springing from the wagon, the dwarf mounted the animal.

Ferdie and Georgie clapped their hands and shouted, the odd-shaped rider cut so queer a figure.

The slim, short legs and arms, and big head, the latter "beating time,' nodding and jerking with the motion of the horse, did indeed constitute a ludicrous picture.

"How his head bobs!" said Georgie, laughing uncontrollably. "It'll snap off, I'm afraid."

"Hush, boys," interposed the mother, in an undertone. "You will hurt Frankie's feelings. It is a noble head, if it is large. 'Tisn't all bone, like many big-headed folks, and it's properly put together. Then, raising her voice, "Don't be gone long, Frankie, or I shall worry about you."

The stout horse and small rider plodded slowly on, for the dwarf had never ridden a beast before, and his weighty top-piece toppled painfully when the animal trotted.

He was away some time.   The family became anxious concerning him, and Ferdie was on the point of taking the other horse, and riding to see if any accident had befallen him, when he emerged from the grove.   On his arrival, he silently seated himself on the grass, and ate the bountiful portion his mother had reserved, while his brothers and aunt Esther discussed which way the projected cabin should set.

"Tom said the door ought to be towards the south," remarked Ferdinand, "because it's the sunny and warm side."

"Then we will have it so," answered aunt Esther.

"Come, Ferdinand, harness up," interrupted the dwarf, wiping his mouth.

"Harness up?   Not by a jugful!   We are going to build the cabin here," cried Ferdie and Georgie at the top of their lungs.   "Aren't we. mother?"

"My son," said Mrs. Willard, laying her hand lovingly on the Hunchback's shoulder, "all of us deem this a delightful spot.   Don't you think we had better build our new abode here?"

"What shall we build it of?" asked he.

"Of logs," tartly replied Ferdinand.   "You didn't dream that we designed erecting a marble palace — did you?"

"Where will you get the logs?" persisted Hunchback.

"There are a pair of sharp axes in the wagon, and a grove yonder," returned Ferdinand, loftily.

"How will you get the logs here?"

"We suppose the span can draw them."

"And after the logs are brought, are you and Georgie strong enough to lift the great green tree-trunks upon each other, till the walls of the cabin are constructed? It would require a company of men."

As there was no reply to this, the Hunchback added, —

"Hurry, and tackle in the horses, and drive to the grove."

They were soon there.

"Now," said the dwarf, jumping out of the vehicle, "hitch the span; then all follow me."

Striking a narrow path, which he pronounced a deer's trail, leading through the wood, there, on the other side of the grove, sheltered from the north winds, stood a snug cabin. It was un-shingled, and without door or windows. There was, indeed, no aperture for the latter. A few loose boards composed the floor. Wide cracks yawned in the walls. Some rods farther on flowed the creek. Between it and the cabin was a copious spring of ice-cold water. Facing the dwelling was smooth prairie, and at a convenient distance was a small, unroofed shed, built of logs.

"I had been considering the case," remarked the dwarf, "and saw that we could not, unassisted, build a cabin, and that we must, therefore, locate near some town where help could be procured. But, you know, land is high in such places. We can fix this up, and manage to live for the present."

"What if the owners return and claim it?" asked prudent aunt Esther.

"No danger of that," affirmed the Hunchback. "See how dry the logs of the walls are, and there are no traces of footsteps. The cabin is very old, and has long been abandoned. Years ago, before immigration had penetrated so far, it was erected, no doubt, by the hunter and trapper. It is on Uncle Sam's land, and we may occupy it if we will."

Mrs. Willard drew the young-old head to her, and pressing a kiss on the dwarf's lips, presently said, —

"What should we do without our wise Frankie?"

CHAPTER XIII.

A STRANGE VISITOR. — THE MAN IN THE CHIM
NEY CORNER.

THE cabin which the Willards had appropri
ated was built of massive logs, through which
was an occasional loophole. For, when the
first pioneers took possession of the soil, the log
houses were constructed so as to be fortresses
upon occasion. Later comers, being less suspicious of their copper-colored neighbors, did not
provide against hostilities which they expected
not.

But the walls of the cabin, beaten upon by sun
and storm, had shrunken till wide seams let the
prairie winds — accustomed to their own way, un-
checked by obstacles — through and through the
dilapidated structure, whistling as they went, to
express their contempt for the architectural ex-
crescence. The zephyr, just from touching with a
respectful kiss the beautiful prairie flowers, would
pucker up its lips and dart through the unsightly
building with a *w-h-e-w!* as if ashamed of being
seen in so poor an abode. And it must be con-

fessed that a log house does not compare well with
the blossoming verdure amid which it squats.
Still, human beings, unlike wild flowers, must
have a house over their heads, and the homely
loggery has been the home of many a soul worth
more than worlds.

"I really believe," observed Mrs. Willard,
next morning after their arrival at the cabin,
"that I suffered more from the cold last night
than I did sleeping in the wagon," and she shiv-
ered as she spoke. "I guess, boys, you will have
to stop up the cracks in the walls, if you do not
wish mother to get sick."

"We'll set about it to-day," manfully answered
Ferdinand, entering.

"That's right," replied she, turning towards
him with a pleased smile. "Why, what have
you there, my son?"

"Partridges," responded he, proudly swinging
them into view. "Last night, after all were
asleep, and everything was still, I heard a rum-
bling sound in the grove. So, going noiselessly
out of doors, I listened. Soon it was repeated,
and I knew that it was a partridge drumming on
a log to call its mate. At daybreak I was out
hunting. Guess we will have a nice dinner to-
day," he added, triumphantly.

"And we shall be indebted to your smartness
for it," said aunt Esther.

"And now, Ferdinand, if you and Georgie will get me some wood, and make a fire, we will have breakfast."

"And I," remarked aunt Esther," will pick and dress the partridges."

"Those fowl are worth much more than their value to us as food," observed Mrs. Willard, with emotion, as the boys left. "Notice Ferdinand; how cheerfully he steps off with shouldered axe! His dear father bore the burden in the care of the family, and it is a new thing for the boys to do much for themselves or us.

"But even the shooting of those birds has given Ferdinand a taste of the happiness of self-reliance. Perhaps this pioneering is destined to develop him into a useful man. Hear their axes! How enlivening the sound! I must run out and see how they manage."

The grove in which was the cabin was principally of oak. Among the leafy trees stood here and there one killed by prairie fires. Two of these — they were not large — the boys were falling. The wood of the dead trees was sound, dry, and exceedingly hard, and the task of cutting them down, and chopping them into suitable lengths, was none too easy.

"How bravely you get along!" exclaimed Mrs. Willard, quietly loading her arms with some of the smaller sticks; and, notwithstanding Ferdinand cried out, "Don't do that, mother!" she carried them into the cabin.

But the boys quickly followed with lusty loads. Then they lugged in a huge backlog, and deposited it in the clay-stick-and-stone fireplace; more wood was added, and if the smoke did puff out into the room, ere long a merry fire was crackling, and tea-kettle and pot steaming.

"Chinking," or stopping up the cracks in the sides of the loggery, was a slower and more laborious job than the lads anticipated. The manner of accomplishing this, is to hew pieces of wood sufficiently narrow on one edge to enter the crevices; then, striking on the broad or outer part, they are driven closely in and nailed.

Oak being too hard to work, or even to secure, the nails often bending and breaking, the wood was so impervious, the boys chose poplar instead. This was soft and light, and proved just the thing. Several days elapsed, however, before the chinking had far advanced.

Next came "mortaring" the chinking. This, in a new country, is usually done with clay. The moist, tenacious earth is thrown violently, by the hand, between the logs.

"Jolly! I can do that," cried Georgie. "It will be like snowballing."

But he was glad to cease from the attempt. Nor did Ferdinand succeed much better. For, strange as it may appear to the uninitiated, this style of mortaring requires a powerful arm and no little physical endurance.

One afternoon, as the brothers, with lamed arms, were ineffectually laboring at clay-balls, they heard behind them the snort of a horse. Turning, there sat a rider coolly watching, with an amused air, their endeavors.

"You are not exactly used to that business," he remarked, dismounting. " Here, I'll show you how."

And stripping off his coat, and rolling up his shirt-sleeves, displaying a massive arm, he scooped up the clay, and threw it with great precision and force.

"Now, boys," he went on in a complimentary manner, "you are bright enough for 'most anything, but you haven't the muscle for this. Besides, it wants practice."

And while they looked on he continued mortaring and chatting, till quite a space was finished. Meanwhile the sun was declining. Suddenly it slipped off the edge of the prairie, and dropped from view.

For some time the boys had been feeling uneasy. They saw the afternoon waning, and tea approaching, and then night. And the stranger — who was he? How he lingered — so keen and self-confident! Was he a fit person to invite into the cabin?

The mother and aunt were not unaware of this presence, and the former delayed supper, hoping he would leave. The boys, too, though thankful, at the outset, for his efficient assistance, grew more and more uneasy at his tarrying. On their part, therefore, conversation was confined to monosyllables.

But the volunteer worker in clay paid no heed to their reserve. Nor did he take any hints, however plain, about the lateness of the hour, or resent it when the dwarf, making his appearance, told him bluntly, and in a suspicious, domineering manner, that if he had far to travel, he had better start, as *they* couldn't keep him over night.

"Ah, 'tis a trifle late, youngster, as you remark," he mildly responded. "What a bright star that is low down there in the sky! I don't much wonder *ef* you cud give the real name on't."

" I don't care about the star," retorted the Hunchback, wrathfully.

" When did you state you immigrated from the east?" asked the strange caller, seating himself on an oak stick.

"Mother," whispered the Hunchback, reëntering the house, "that man is determined to stay here. I tried to send him away, but he will not budge an inch. It's the very fellow who came to us on the prairie, when you called Georgie."

"So I suspected," she replied, anxiously.

"We shall bar the door against him," said aunt Esther, firmly. "Frankie, you manage to sly the boys in, and we'll fasten the chap out."

"But he'll steal the horses," suggested the dwarf.

"I didn't think of that," she replied. "Mercy! he's heard every word!" she instantly exclaimed; for near the entrance was the subject of remark listening to their conversation.

The demonstration he had thus received that "listeners never hear any good of themselves," did not, however, disturb his equanimity.

Passing, uninvited, the forbidden threshold, he said, with unruffled audacity, holding up his begrimed hands, —

"*Ef* you will have the kindness, madam, to obleege me with a dish of water to rense off this sile! I jist thought I'd give yer boys a lift mortarin.' Heavy work that fer youngsters like them!"

The spinster, with stately dignity, poured water in a basin, and giving it to Georgie, he set it on a bench without the cabin.

"A cloth, ma'am, *ef* yer please, ter dry me on," he said, putting his face within the door.

With freezing coldness a towel was held towards him.

"Thank ye, ma'am," said he, rubbing his

head dry. Then producing a pocket comb, he removed his hat, and turning his back on the women, proceeded to comb his hair, remarking, —

"Don't mind me, ma'am; I see yer tea is waitin'. An' the youngsters, no doubt, are hungry as pigs."

The Willards were, at this stage of affairs, convinced that they had met their match. On two trunks, arranged side by side, and covered with a cloth, waited the meal. What could they do?

"Perhaps you will eat with us," said Mrs. Willard, faintly, in an accent intended to elicit a refusal.

"Don't care ef I take a bite," brightly replied the repulsed guest. "I ain't a mite bashful among friends. Haven't tasted sich corn-dodgers for a month of Sundays. And that butter *is* a little the sweetest. May I ask, ma'am, ef it's yer own churnin'?" addressing the indignant spinster.

"No!" she emphatically replied.

"*Of* course not! Excuse me, ma'am. I might hev known from yer hands — so white an' delicate, that they'd never seen much tile."

Aunt Esther haughtily folded her hands in her apron, and lifted her eyebrows scornfully.

"Hands, ma'am," he calmly continued, "have a marster sight of meanin' to 'em. Here's one, for instance," laying his own on the table, "that was constructed for 'most anything — shootin', choppin', diggin', and, in circumstances of danger, say, fightin'. You see," said he, closing his fingers, "it's considerable of a fist, *ef* I do say it."

And a latent threat seemed to his excited auditors to pervade his tone.

"A man that's got to *knock* about the world has ter own a paw that can thread a needle or floor an elephant. But a *lady*," — and here his voice was low and soft, — " who stays ter home, or goes to dances, or keeps school, don't need a power of bone an' sinew, no more'n she needs a man's thunderin' lungs. Show me a person's paw, male or female, an' ten ter one I ken tell jist what natur intended him fer.

"An' now, ladies," he observed, rising, "*ef* it will be no offence, I'll jist take a whif, ter keep off the *dis*pepsy."

Then seating himself in a corner of the wide-mouthed fireplace, he drew some tobacco, and a huge knife, with a poniard-shaped blade, from one pocket, then an oddly-carved pipe from another, and carefully cut up the weed, and filling the bowl, inserted the slender stem between his lips, and puffed in quiet.

What a still group was that, that evening! By the flickering fire-light the Willards could see that the dark eye of their unknown, self-invited visitor followed all their movements, while the uncertain glow that fell on his features reflected no satisfactory insight into his true character. Contradictory elements predominated in the strongly-marked countenance, the expression of which was remarkably under the control of its proprietor.

At one moment Mrs. Willard would judge him to be a rough but honest specimen of the uncultured frontiersman; at the next, a shrewd villain, who had assumed the pioneer manner and dialect for a bad purpose.

Whatever the surmises of the cabinites, the mysterious stranger smoked silently on, pouring, in irregular alternation, the smoke out first in a dense volume direct, then from the right corner of his mouth; next, from the left, and lastly in two simultaneous jets from his nostrils; and all this in the easiest, at-home style conceivable, as if he of the pipe was owner of the premises, and smoking in that particular place and method a household institution.

Nine o'clock. Ten o'clock. He was still there. The boys stole out of doors, and engaged in earnest consultation, Georgie standing sentinel where he could report if the man left his seat.

"I shall order him off," said Frankie.

And with knit brow and threatening eye, approaching the intruder, he laid his puny hand upon the man's muscular knee, and said, —

"Come, mister, be starting; we can't accommodate you here!"

"Can't?" inquired the smoker, deliberately knocking the ashes from his pipe; "let's see. Two rooms. One at the foot of the ladder, and one above. I'll jist peep inter the loft."

And calmly crossing the apartment, and supporting himself upon the strips of wood nailed, in lieu of a real ladder, against the logs, he peered into the attic.

"Good enough for a king," said he. "There are just six of us, countin' myself. I've known forty ter occupy one floor in a smaller cabin than this. No, youngster, you're not agwine ter set me afloat on the naked prairie at this *on*reasonable hour. These ladies wouldn't permit sich barbarous proceedin', pervided *I* was willin', which I am not. 'Twon't answer at the west to turn the cold shoulder on the benighted traveller that way. *Ef* you're willin', ma'am," addressing Mrs. Willard, "I'll jist bring in my blanket, and roll myself up in it under the ruff!"

"We are not prepared — " began she.

"Never mind apologies, ma'am. I kin sleep *beautiful* so. All I wants is a board — ef it isn't the softest that ever was!"

And fetching in a roll of blanketing, he tossed it upon the boards overhead, saying, —

"I'll jist take a peep inter the shed, an' see if there's a corner for my beast."

And loosening his splendid steed from the sapling to which it had been haltered, the stranger led him to the little stable, followed by Ferdinand and Georgie.

"Why, youngsters," said he, glancing in, "you don't turn yer critters in *permiscuous* — do ye? It's a born mericle that they hadn't got ter kickin', and spilte one t'other afore now. We must fix some stalls ter keep them separate. Got an axe?"

Georgie brought one.

With singular handiness and celerity he hewed some thick poles flatted at both ends, and with the strong nails from the wagon pouch, also carried to him by Georgie, he constructed three rude stalls for the horses, and tying his in the one farthest from the door, the brothers secured theirs in the remaining places.

It had been aunt Esther's custom, before retiring, to read aloud a portion of Scripture, and then the family repeated in unison the Lord's Prayer. When the trio returned, after stating their habit, she opened her gilt-edged pocket Bible, and read the fourth Psalm. As she concluded the last verse, "I will both lay me down in peace, and sleep; for thou, Lord, only makest me dwell in safety," "There's no book like that," remarked their guest; and falling to his knees, he listened devoutly as the divinely-given petitions ascended.

"I shall sleep beautiful after that prayer," said he, as they arose; "it sounds natral."

Whether he was sincere or not in what he said, it is certain that the afflicted and lonely household was soothed and uplifted by their simple, unaffected service. On the solitary prairie, far from human succor, their hearts instinctively turned for protection to the ever-present Being who neither slumbers nor sleeps. And the two women retired, serenely committing themselves to the loving care of the infinite Helper and Preserver.

How much, however, their returning composure was due to the reverential deportment at prayers of their strange guest, I cannot decide. But Mrs. Willard whispered to her sister, —

"I am afraid we have been too suspicious of that man. Did you notice that he knelt with us?"

But aunt Esther doubtingly shook her head.

As for the boys, they did not ascend to their mattresses in the cabin garret, but camped beside their mother's bed, Ferdinand with an axe, and Georgie with the hatchet, while the dwarf sat in a dim corner, screened by trunks, with Ferdinand's gun ready loaded and capped. The three had resolved to watch till day. But soon the *boarder* fell a snoring in so masterly and systematic a style, that Georgie drowsily whispered to Ferdie, —

"Guess you won't hear the partridges drum to-night!"

"Yes, I hear one now," replied Ferdie; "he's on that man's nose!"

And after a convulsive giggle, they both dropped asleep.

But the Hunchback kept guard.

CHAPTER XIV.

SECOND IMPRESSIONS. — AUNT ESTHER AND THE PLOUGHMEN.

THE Willards rested undisturbed, save that, semi-occasionally, a climax snore from the attic lodger caused momentary disquiet. But thunder does not kill, neither does snoring; and there is a frank outspokenness about the latter quite reassuring under certain circumstances. Certainly, so long as a man suspected of fell design so loudly proclaims his somnolence, so long you feel secure from harm at his hands. And Mr. Lodger blew bugle-blasts of peace till the glowing east announced the empire of darkness overthrown — for a few hours.

With composed and serious mien, the wayfarer descended from the low-roofed chamber, and kind Mrs. Willard, as he bade her "good morning," marvelled that they had been such cowards.

"Madam," said he, "I owe you an apology for my rudeness last evening. Here on the frontier the latch-string always hangs out, and the traveller is made welcome. You are not used to such unquestioning hospitality. I forgot to make allowance for the fact, and was irritated at your cold, New England ways.

"My name is Simmons. I hail from New York, where I own a snug property. Am what is termed an old bachelor; not from choice, but never chanced to meet just the person I fancied. Took a notion to the frontier. Have spent a year or two riding round. Think I shall open a large farm, stock it, build a comfortable house, if I can find a woman of the right stamp to look after me and the establishment, — none of your flyaway butterflies, but a sensible, pious lady, in whom a man can depend for comfort and happiness.

"There you have my story. And now I've been thinking, as your boys are young, and green in pioneering, and my horse is overdriven, that if they'll let the creature stand where he is in the shed, and cut a handful of grass for him, and give him water, just as if 'twas their own, I'll return the compliment with interest."

The two women critically regarded their guest while he spoke. To how much better advantage he appeared by morning than by firelight! They began to feel annoyed at the offensive distrust of him. His *language*, too, how greatly improved! How much there is in one's manner!

Mrs. Willard did not at once reply.

" Believe me, I will not obtrude on your quiet. I shall not be here much myself, but when on the ground will gladly aid the lads in getting settled. My experience ought to be of service to them, and as for remuneration for the care of self and beast, I'll see that you don't lose by the operation."

The arrangement was entered into. Mr. Simmons, leaving his handsome horse, and crossing the prairie afoot, was lost to view.

" I hate his looks," said the dwarf, " and hope he'll die or the Indians will capture him, so that he'll never show his face in our house again."

" Why, Frankie," exclaimed Mrs. Willard, reprovingly, " what a wicked wish ! I am sure the more I see of Mr. Simmons, the better he appears. Doesn't he, Esther? "

" He's hard to understand," replied the spinster.

At twilight of the third day ensuing, Mr. Simmons returned.

" Ferdie," said he, familiarly, " I have a capital idea for you boys. It is too late in the season, you know, to plant, but it is magnificent weather for haying. I'd like a little exercise at it myself. Suppose we spend several days working up the grass — untold acres wait for the scythe. It's easy making it in this dry Minnesota air, and these **ceaseless breezes — cut and stack it the same** hour almost. Why, your sons, Mrs. Willard, might put up tons of it; and in the fall and winter, the immigrants, flocking in too late to hay, would buy of you, and pay all you asked. They must have it for their cattle; don't you see? And I'd rather give the lads a lift at it than not."

"A most excellent idea," said Mrs. Willard.

"I've lugged a scythe ten miles on purpose," he continued. "Here it is;" and he took it in from the side of the cabin, against which it leaned. "What say for a raid on the prairie grass to-morrow, boys? — if your mother will let me lunch on her nice corn-cake, and stretch my legs on a board in the attic."

"Certainly," replied that lady, with warmth. "Ferdie, some haying-tools came with the wagon — did they not?"

"Yes, mother," he answered; "two rakes, a large and small hayfork, and one scythe."

"How much will hay probably command next fall?" inquired the mother.

"It will be low, of course, compared with eastern prices; but the grass here grows wild, and it makes into hay vastly easier and faster. Your boys will dispose of it readily at from five to ten dollars per ton, and they can stack two tons a day, easily."

"That's the ticket," said Georgie, turning a summersault from the doorstep, where he sat listening. "We can pay for our claim that way. I'm in for it, for one. Hurrah for prairie hay!"

Mr. Simmons's suggestion was a good one, and commended itself even to calculating aunt Esther.

And next morning betimes, the pleasant and familiar sound of the mower sharpening his scythe resounded on the proximate prairie.

Mr. Simmons, with amazing ease, yet with hurry, cut great smooth swaths. Ferdie improved as he practised, abiding by Mr. Simmons's example and instructions. Willie and Frankie handled the rakes. Soon gigantic hay-mounds dotted the shorn plain, the man day by day stimulating the energies of the boys by his own disinterested efforts, and by assuring them that all the profits were to be theirs.

One noon, as they reclined eating their dinner, Mr. Simmons observed, —

"Boys, I move we vary our work this afternoon. I'm getting tired of that dark attic. Besides, the roof is so low that I can't get into bed without thumping my head against the rafters. Let us cut some light logs, and build a little hut between here and the cabin for me to occupy nights, and to store the tools in, and save carrying them so far."

So Ferdie and Georgie fetched axes, and a miniature cabin arose, which, from that time forward, Mr. Simmons slept in.

The haying went on prosperously, Mr. Simmons working with the boys, or omitting it, as he chose, but when in the field directing all that was done. He proved an efficient overseer.

He now frequently called in at the Willard cabin for conversation with the ladies, his many thoughtful suggestions and apt offices causing them to depend somewhat on his aid. Towards Miss Esther he became specially, but unostentatiously, attentive. And when, at times, he dwelt on the loneliness of his bleak bachelorhood, and pictured his idea of wifely qualifications, occasionally the blood would mount to her cheeks, as she fancied he had her in mind for the original.

"I declare, I believe the old bach is dead in love with you, sis," Mrs. Willard would assert, after he had left.

At which insinuation aunt Esther's ear-drops would indignantly vibrate, as she tossed her head, ejaculating, —

"What presumption!"

There was, however, one kindness that Mr. Simmons did aunt Esther that extorted her appreciative notice. She had — as who has not? — one infirmity: she was vain of her clear complexion — a charm she feared she should lose in the gloomy, begrimed loggery.

"I shall be black as Egypt," she sighed one

day, as the gallant "bach" entered. "It's as dark and smoky here as Tartarus!"

Shortly after Mr. Simmons remarked, —

"Ladies, I've been on a voyage of discovery, and have hit on a chance to buy a cooking-stove and some glass windows, cheap. Now, you could have an aperture cut for a window, and one fitted in very easily — Ferdie and I could do it, as to that. A temporary addition might also be built against the cabin, near the door, to put the stove in till cool weather."

"What would they cost?" eagerly asked Mrs. Willard.

"Not over eighteen dollars. The stove is second-hand."

She did not answer, for she felt too poor to spare the money. But when her eyes were turned, aunt Esther followed the bachelor out of the cabin, and inquired, dignifiedly, —

"When could the stove and windows be procured?"

"To-morrow," was the reply.

"The money is ready when they arrive," she said. "Come to me for it; but let it remain a secret between you and me."

Immediately, to the astonishment of Mrs. Willard, the boys and the bachelor attacked the dwelling. They were chiselling, pounding, thumping, sawing, in a most unaccountable manner, the entire afternoon, till at length daylight streamed into the log house through a civilized glass window, and the tea-kettle sang a song of steam in a veritable stove.

Nevertheless, the dwarf was still sullen towards the benevolent Mr. Simmons. And aunt Esther, despite his clever compliments and kindnesses to the household, shook distrustingly, though less confidently, her well-poised head. But with Mrs. Willard, Ferdie, and Georgie, the bachelor was immensely popular.

"What is that?" exclaimed Mrs. Willard, a week later, as stentorian shouting smote her ear from the direction of the haystacks.

Georgie hurried round the grove, and more quickly hurried back, his blue eyes wide with wonder, reporting that two men were there with a "*tremenjous*" big team, ploughing.

"On our claim?"

"Yes," said Georgie.

Mrs. Willard and aunt Esther, with the three boys, went to see for themselves. Sure enough, in front of the hut in which considerate Mr. Simmons performed nocturnal music, was yoke on yoke of oxen, drawing a mammoth plough through the virgin sod. It was an animating spectacle; but why were they ploughing there? and by whose order?

The lads hastened to ascertain.

"It's another of Mr. Simmons's generous surprises," said confiding Mrs. Willard. "He's having that land broken up for the boys. He *is* a good soul, there!"

"Mister," addressing the man of the whip, "who sent you to plough on our piece?"

"Hey?" blurted the driver, beginning a new furrow.

When he reached the end of it, Ferdie repeated the question.

"Git out of the way," he roared, flourishing the cruel lash, "or you'll git this round yer legs!"

Ferdinand retreated in consternation, and repairing to his mother, stated the brutal reception he had met.

"I'll inquire," said aunt Esther, her eyes flashing; "they'll not be impudent to me!"

The correctness of this conclusion, however, appeared doubtful as she neared the ploughmen. Their vociferous "gee-haw"-ing and terrible oaths discovered a determination, like Jeff Davis, to be "let alone." But Miss Esther advanced, with undaunted intrepidity, directly in the path of the team, and there she stood immovable as a granite boulder. The cattle stopped, the men ceased swearing, at the unexpected interference.

"Sir," said she to the teamster, "I wish to be informed by whose authority you are here."

"Wall, I ruther suspects," returned the man, "it's by the authority of him as owns this strip o' land."

"Who is he?"

"Wall, miss, it's the person what occurpies that ere shanty, and forked up those ere stacks o' hay!"

"O, you've made a mistake," she observed. "*We* built that hut, and made that hay."

"Didn't no one else have a hand in it?"

"A man who boarded with us helped — a Mr. Simmons."

"I don't know no Mr. Simmons; nor you nuther, as to that. But the individual what occurpies that shanty employed us to turn over this soil, and we're just a going to do it. Gee! git up!"

"Sir," interposed the lady, stepping to his side and laying her white hand on his bare, brown wrist, "*you* are a *man*, and *I* am a *woman*, and of course you are *gentleman* enough to hear what I've got to say. Come this way a moment," she added, authoritatively; and, ashamed to refuse, he followed her to the Willard cabin.

"Here's where we live," said she. "Which has been the longest built, this house or that hut, in which the one who sent you here slept a few nights?"

"This, in course," he answered.

"Then what right had that fellow — our *guest* — to call this land his, and send you to break it up?"

"Have you preëmpted, miss?"

"Not yet."

"Well, miss, I'm hired to do this small job, an' I shell do it. Can't afford to lose the pay. All is, ye'll have ter be spry, or you'll have yer claim jumped — that's all!"

"Jumped! I don't understand you."

"Well, you're mighty green, then. It's done over and often. You see, the one what gits fust into the Land Office, and swears he's got a cabin, and some breaking on land what's unpaid for, gits it. Now, that's what this ere Mr. Shimmey — or whatsomdever's his name — is arter, *you* bet!" and her blunt informant turned to go.

"One more question," said she. "You asserted that he owned that hay. What do you know about it?"

"Nothing much," was the answer; "only that I heard this ere man engage it to Edmonds at three dollars a ton. Edmonds is buying up all he can lay paws on, to hold agin it gits higher!"

CHAPTER XV.

ONE SWALLOW DOES NOT MAKE A SUMMER. — TRIBULATIONS OF A FAT MAN.

"I SHALL ask him, as sure as he sets foot inside this cabin again;" and aunt Esther's cheeks glowed.

"Do you suppose," said the dwarf, "that if he intends to jump our claim, he'd be fool enough to tell you beforehand?"

"I shall never believe that Mr. Simmons is tricky and dishonest," affirmed the charitable Mrs. Willard. "Why, I have been much instructed, and benefited, — I hope I have a right to say, — by his excellent sentiments. If I am not deceived, he's a truly godly person. And I still think that he sent that breaking team here as a generous kindness to us. It was a surprise — he's so delicate about intruding himself. You are unreasonable towards him, Esther, while he worships the ground you tread on; and he is doing these kindnesses in order to overcome your prejudice, and get you to look with more favor on his suit."

Aunt Esther grew pale with anger, but kept her firmly-set mouth closed.

"And *you*, Frankie, are much to blame for your aunt's coolness. You'd be suspicious of an angel; and you talked so hard against Mr. Simmons, that she has drank into your spirit. It is ungrateful, after all he's done to help us. I'm sure we *need* help out here on the prairie."

"Well, you'll find out," hotly piped the Hunchback, "after he's got our splendid claim! But, mother," he added, after a moment's pause, "it isn't best for me, or aunt Esther, or any of us, to let him know we suspect him, for that would put him on his guard. And if he *does* wish for the land, he would hurry and preëmpt it. We must treat him well, but *watch — watch* — keeping our eyes open when he supposes they are shut."

"That's it, Frankie," joined in aunt Esther; "we must conceal our suspicions, and unravel his schemes, if we can. But there he is, now!" And flustered Mrs. Willard became over-busy in her housework, and self-poised aunt Esther returned to her sewing.

"How do you all do?" he inquired, in an accent of sincere interest, and not in the careless tone of a commonplace.

"Quite well, I thank you," responded Mrs. Willard, intent on her baking.

"Pleased to hear it. By the way, did some men call here to do a little breaking?"

"Yes," she answered, ceasing to mould the dough, and, regarding him with transparent anxiety, instantly added, "they said *you* sent them."

"Happy to learn that they were so prompt. You see, by turning over the sod that it may lay exposed to the weather and the frost, it will be nicely rotted by spring. Fortunately I ran across that team while I was away; and as it is almost impossible to hire one for love or money,—especially for a small job, — there is so much prairie to be broken up, I persuaded the fellows to put in their plough for a little strip — only three acres. The boys will want a garden next season."

Good Mrs. Willard's expressive countenance displayed the pleasure she felt at his vindication of himself; and to help him out, she said, notwithstanding the dwarf's admonitory frown, —

"The boys thought it strange you told those men that this claim is yours."

"So I did," he explained, lightly laughing. "You'll set that down as a fib, I'm afraid, and mark me out of your books. But they were full of work, and I was obliged to make out a strong plea to get them here at all, and of course I had to become personally responsible for the contract. Men don't care to do business with women, and these chaps knew nothing about Mrs. Willard and sister, — estimable ladies as they are, and abundantly able to pay."

"How much is their bill?" tartly inquired aunt Esther, taking out her purse.

"A mere trifle," replied Mr. Simmons — "only twelve dollars. Another time will answer just as well. Ferdie and Willie, I wish to show you about the breaking."

"There," said he, as they reached the three acres, "this spot lies low, and I chose it partly because, being moist, it will stand a drought, should there be one next summer. It's no harm to be sure of *one* crop, at least. This will be your garden. You will have to fence it, to shut out stray cattle. And, by the by, I might spend a day or two helping in this, better than not, just now. Suppose we go at it this afternoon."

"Agreed!" cried the lads, as enthusiastic now as condemnatory before.

"If, now, Frankie was as smart and bright as his brothers," continued the bachelor, "it wouldn't take us long to get out the rails and lay them up. Pity he's so helpless and odd."

"I guess dinner is about ready," said Ferdie; "Georgie, you run and see."

The lad quickly reappeared to call them. And as the little family surrounded the rude table, Mrs. Willard hesitatingly said, —

"Mr. Simmons, perhaps you would say grace before we eat."

"If you desire, ma'am," he replied, and repeated a brief form of petition and thanksgiving, which so mellowed Mrs. Willard's sensitive heart, that she fairly loaded her guest's plate with the choicest of the food, and was concerned that his vigorous "appetite was so poor."

Their guest ate rapidly, and precipitately rising, excused himself, saying, —

"Boys, I'll get things ready, and when you are through eating, we'll go to work."

Mrs. Willard looked from the window after him till assured he was out of hearing, then gesticulating impressively with a fork, she said, —

"Now, Frankie and Esther, I trust you are satisfied. You have doubted and slandered a pious and true man."

"Frankie," she interrupted herself to scream, "come back and finish your dinner!"

But the dwarf disappeared behind a corner of the log stable.

"MR. SWALLER!"

That fat worthy was venturing very carefully to "work his passage" from the immigrant wagon to *terra firma*, and, at the inopportune instant when the shrew's shrill and imperative summons pierced his ear, was mentally and physically contriving how to descend safely, with a strapping girl of five under one arm, and elsewise, a nurse bottle, a basket of eggs, a flask of wine, a bandbox containing his wife's bonnet, and last, but not least, himself.

"*Mr. Swaller!*"

The rotund and encumbered gentleman alluded to was peculiarly situated. The horses were uneasy, the flies pertinacious, the ponderous wagon starting, just as he essayed, with one foot on the wheel, to make land. There was an awful and untimely lurch of the vehicle. The eggs slid in succession "to smash," and, stooping to catch them, his unwieldy legs became entangled, and, by a remarkable feat, considering his weight, he found himself on the ground, bandbox beneath him, child sitting on his nose, and milk running into his eyes.

The spectators to this extremely unique and striking *tableau* were the Willard household, and — *Mrs*. Swallow.

The flustered and perspiring *Mr*. Swallow gathered together his lower extremities, sat up, and gazed around, as well as cherub and milk would permit. The former, its unusually large mouth stretched miraculously, yelled "particular murder."

"Mr. *Swaller!* when *are* you going to bring that poor lamb into the cabin? There! you've stuck your thumb in its eye — put it out, of course, and no doctor to run for. On my Paris **hat,** too. I shall be a fright now. After all the pains I've taken to bring it all the way from the east, that's what I get for it. Don't put your foot into the rest of the eggs. You know I can't *exist* without egg and wine. Broke the bottle, eh! Here, darling," — to the child, — "come to me. What *would* you do if your poor sick mother was to die? Who'd care for you then, darling? To think that the *last* born of my *first* husband should be *pitched* out of a wagon at the risk of its innocent life! There, *h-u-s-h*, sweet. Here's some more candy for you."

And the stout, elderly lady tightly clasped the sugar-sucking angel, alternately lavishing kisses on its bedaubed mouth, and darting sharp sentences at her unfortunate "lord."

"Mr. Swaller, I *can't* go immigrating any more, and I *won't*. Came to save my life? So you did. But I'd rather *die* east than *live* west. *Creeping* along, like a sick snail, in a nasty emigrant wagon! Jolt, jolt; rumble, rumble; drag, drag. You're welcome to cure my lungs, but you *shan't* do it on the prairies! Nothing but grass, grass, *everlasting* grass, as if we were hosses, and not folks. I'm no better, and you can see it if you're a mind to."

Mr. Swallow listened to this sententious but rapidly-delivered harangue with a meekness and long-suffering worthy of commendation. It was evident he realized his position and responsibili-

ties as a "*family* man;" and though it was plain
he was not indifferent to the speeches of his
"better half," he bore the inflictions as if he comprehended that such was his duty.   He was used,
but not wholly hardened, to it.

Mrs. Swallow, as she has already informed us,
was an invalid — a martyr to real, or fancied,
pulmonary difficulties.   And the doctors, having
long been harassed with her *complaints*, and exhausted the Materia Medica in endeavoring to
effect a cure, had rid themselves of their patient
by recommending a change of climate.   And
Mr. Swallow, in accordance with medical suggestions and his wife's appeals, was journeying with
her in Prairie-land.

Recovering from his mishap, the dutiful husband hurried at once to load his arms with domestic goods, and to soothe the partner of his joys,
when, as overburdened and panting he approached
the cabin door where sat his afflicted spouse,
"darling" suddenly sprang from her mother's
embrace, and laying hold of his coat-tail, violently
jerked upon it, spitefully kicking his shins the
while with her patent copper toes.

"Mr. Swaller, see how you've hurt that poor
lamb's feelings — that's why she acts so.   And
no wonder—*pitching* her out of the wagon at the
risk of breaking her innocent neck.   Darling,
come to your mother."

But darling pulled the more desperately at the coat, Mr. Swallow straining to press ahead, when, lo, the garment parted, and "darling" was precipitated backward upon the ground, and Mr. Swallow forward into the cabin, a storm of toilet utensils, wearing apparel, food, a dish of molasses, and an umbrella and parasol, showering upon his loving helpmeet.

"You've done it now, Mr. Swaller! Do you think my head is made of iron, that a stone pot won't crack it? I do believe you'll be the death of me, and *that child*, yet. What would my *first* husband say, if he knew how his *last* born was treated! But I shan't and I won't go emigrating an inch further, lungs or no lungs. I'll die in a *galloping* consumption before I'll *creep* all over the earth in a frightful emigrant wagon. There are snakes here, too. You need'nt tell me there ain't. *You* saw one; and *I* saw one. A nasty big *rattlesnake.* What if he'd stung that child with his horrid-sounding rattles. Ma'am," addressing Mrs. Willard, "*can't* we stay here tonight? Yes, we can," answering her own question; "and to-morrer them hosses will turn tail about, and we'll jolt, jolt, creep, creep, drag, drag, back to the east—lungs or no lungs. They said 'twas a *climate* here. Climate! It's blowed like a harricane for more'n a week. And it's thundered for a whole hour; and it'll keep on thundering for a month without stopping to breathe, for what I know. *Climate !* "

Mr. Swallow, assisted by Ferdie and Willie, unharnessed and put up his span in the little stable, Ferdie hitching one of his outside, Mr. Simmons being, for a wonder, away.

" O, you've put up the horses — have you, Mr. Swaller? Well, I hope you've *locked* them up, too. To think, such a valuable horse as you lost, all through your own carelessness, Mr. Swaller. Nothing else — don't tell me. That beast was stole *right under* your *nose*, and likely's not these will be. Then where shall we be? Have to trot around on foot. Pretty figure you'd cut — wouldn't you? setting out to walk east, heavy as you are."

The Willards welcomed the arrival of bed-time, in the hope that sleep would fetter the tongue of the *twit*tering Swallow. She retired early, occupying Mrs. Willard's bed in the room below, while the Willards disposed themselves as best they could in the attic.

But Mrs. Willard was startled from a refreshing nap by a distressed cry from the apartment beneath.

" Mr. Swaller ! " faintly.

" *Mr. Swaller !* " louder.

" Mr. Swaller ! " angrily. Then desperately,

" Mrs. Log-cabin-woman ! *Mrs. Log-cabin-woman !* "

Mrs. Willard thrust her head through the opening in the attic floor, at the ladder-way, and asked, —

" What's wanted?"

" Mrs. Log-cabin-woman, won't you *wake* up Mr. Swaller. I'm sick!"

Mrs. Willard was amused and vexed. Comfortably in her hostess's bed lay the vixen visitress and offspring, while stretched on the trunk-table was the obese husband in shirt and pants, his head topped off with a yellow handkerchief, his abortive endeavors at snoring — consisting of a snort and a puff — attesting how happily oblivious he was to the agonies of his Eve.

" Madam," said Mrs. Willard, " your husband must be very much fatigued; hadn't you better let him rest?"

" Rest, when my head aches as if 'twould split? Wake him up, I say. I shall die if I don't have some *ice*-cold water to bathe it in."

" If you would be quiet, perhaps the ache would cease," mildly suggested Mrs. Willard.

" My poor lungs are so pressed — and he a trying to snore! And I so weak! — Mr. Swaller?" tenderly and inquiringly. " You *won't* wake up, *hey*? We'll see, then," she vociferated, bounding to his side and smartly shaking him.

" Wh-what's to pay?" he stuttered.

" Pay? Its *spring water* to pay, Mr. Swaller.

There's the pail. Quick! I'm most gone!" and she retreated, gasping, to her couch.

The model husband repaired to the spring, and, returning, bathed her forehead, till, tired of that service, she bade him stop, saying, —

"But you're not going to lie down again, Mr. Swaller; not a bit of it, after neglecting me so brutally. You shall *watch* by me, and if I survive this horrible night, you shall take me east in the morning. Live among these western savages? That woman wouldn't lift her littlest finger to rouse you, though I was most dead — and you a snoring there! No; you *can't* snore like a man; you're too fat. It's puff, snort; puff, snort; and that horrid *western* female standing, sniggering, viewing the scene!"

"Mr. Swaller," patiently preserved the perpendicular till daybreak, his wife in timely interpositions saluting his drooping lids with, —

"Not going to sleep — are you? You won't puff, snort, when I'm sick."

As the swallows were migrating next day, Frankie, addressing the man, said, —

"Didn't your wife say you had a horse stolen from you?"

"She did."

"What sort of a looking beast was it?"

"A splendid large black horse, with a white

spot in the forehead, and the scar of a flesh wound inside of the left hind leg, on the ham. I shall get posters printed describing the beast, and offering a liberal reward for its recovery."

CHAPTER XVI.

FRANKIE'S SECRET. — THE INVISIBLE PURSUER.

"AUNT ESTHER," whispered Frankie, "come out near the breaking pretty soon; I want to see you alone."

The prudent spinster repaired thither without attracting notice.

"Well, what do you want, Frankie?" she inquired.

"About this Mr. Simmons," he replied, coming directly to the point. "I believe he's a bad fellow, and will do us some mischief yet, if we don't get rid of him."

"Have you found out anything?" she asked, anxiously.

"Enough to make me determined to find out more," said he. "Did you notice how suddenly he left off eating that day the Swallows called?"

"Yes; and I thought it strange."

"So did I; but I know the reason. He's mighty quick to hear the least sound. He's like a cat watching for a mouse — only he acts sometimes as if he was the mouse, and was expecting the cat to catch him. He heard that woman's voice, and hurried to the stable. I followed without his seeing me. I'm on his track most of the time. He seems to know it, too; and how he glares at me when none of the family see! But he can't shake me off. Well, he hurried to saddle and bridle his horse, and ride away. You know he keeps his in the farther stall from the door. One of our horses happened to be in the way, and this Simmons kicked him terribly in the stomach, and swore like a pirate."

"Right after asking a blessing at the table!" murmured aunt Esther.

"Yes, the old hypocrite! I knew he did that to comb the wool over mother's eyes. Then hastening to mount, he drove to the other side of the grove, and waiting there till the Swallows had gone to bed, — the woman, saying she was sick, had us all retire early, — he drove like blazes across the prairie, the rain pouring down all the while like a deluge.

"But after the Swallows had left, he came back, tied up his horse, and went to work fencing as peacefully, as if he had staid by, and wasn't drenched to the skin in the shower."

"How queer!" ejaculated the lady.

"Isn't it queer, too," continued the dwarf, fixing his large eyes suggestively on hers, "that he's kept that splendid horse here so long?

When he agreed for the boys to take charge of the animal, it was for only two or three days, and because, he stated, that the horse had been overdriven, and needed to recruit.   But the creature is so ambitious and high, that Simmons will not allow him to be grained.   He's in tip-top order.   Yet his master never uses him to go out of sight of our cabin, but *walks* to and from the places where he so often goes.   What's all that for?"

"I'm sure I can't tell," she answered, perplexed.

"Well, *I* can," asserted her diminutive informant; "that's a stolen horse!"

"*Stolen?*"

"Yes!"

"What makes you suspect that?"

"Come with me, and I'll convince you," was the reply.   And the Hunchback, cautiously peering about to be certain no curious eyes observed their movements, led the way to the stable.   Then, pointing between the logs to the animal's head, he asked, —

"Do you see that white spot?"

"Certainly."

Then turning a corner of the stable, —

"And that scar on the inner side of the left hind leg?   Look sharp."

"I do."

"Mr. Swallow told me that the horse that was

stolen from him had those marks, and this animal in all other respects perfectly answers his description."

"That accounts for his hurrying off in the shower," mused the lady. "What do you propose doing about it, Frankie?"

"In the first place, mother and those boys mustn't know what we think about it, for they'd ask him if 'twas so, and thus put him on his guard, and perhaps he'd murder us all. He has a savage disposition, and a man that will lie as he has, and pretend to be pious, and steal a horse, would kill you if you were in his path."

Aunt Esther shuddered and turned pale.

"We are completely at the mercy of this cold-blooded schemer," she exclaimed. "He'll get the land and everything from us; and even our lives are not secure."

"We mustn't let him," interposed the dwarf, fiercely. "It's put upon me to foil this villain, and I will do it;" and the piping voice rang out shrill as a fife.

"Be careful!" remarked aunt Esther. "Some one may overhear you. Tell me what your plan is, and if I can assist in it," she added, resolutely.

"He'll be here to-night — it's his time — I've studied his habits. To-morrow he'll leave again, for he only comes now to see if his horse is safe.

Then I shall *follow* him; yes," added the dwarf, his tones dropping to a hiss, and his eyes gleaming, "I'll track him to his haunts, as a hound would a panther, and the instant I get the proof I want, he'll be in the hands of an officer."

"O, what if he should see you following?" she said, in terror.

"He won't.   Look, auntie!" and sinking into the grass, he piped, "I can hide at his very heels — almost."

"But you are weakly, Frankie; he can travel faster and farther than you.   You would not be able to keep him in sight."

"Wouldn't?" exclaimed the Hunchback, rising, and looking her confidently in the face.

"How do you know you could?"

"Because I've tried," chuckled the dwarf.   "I've tracked him mile after mile — been behind him — before him — at his right — at his left — sat down when he sat down — heard him talk to himself when he supposed only the prairie hens and the snakes heard him.   O, how lazy he is!" and his face expressed intense disgust.   "He walks lazy, and he works lazy.   He *can* be swifter and stronger than the swiftest and strongest man I ever saw?   But he won't — only for a little while, to deceive folks.   He managed to give those boys the heavy lifting and the quick moving; but he talked so glib, and bossed them so

well, that they thought he was doing his part.
He don't expect to get his living by hurry or labor, but by trickery and fraud. I've hovered
around the sneaking scamp till every crook and
turn of his body is as plain to me beforehand
as that the sun will rise and set. Ah, I'll fix
him!"

"I dread to have you follow this man," ex-
postulated his aunt, "for if he *should* discover
you —"

"Aunt Esther," interrupted the dwarf, "look
at me once more. Am I not ugly, mishapen?
Can I run, leap, wrestle, or swing the axe and
scythe? Doesn't every one wonder that I endure
to live? If he throttles me, better me than the
beautiful and the able-bodied. He cannot, however. But if I were too cowardly and selfish to
risk it, who would? And who can imagine what
mischief might fall on the family! It's *put upon
me* to do this, and I must."

"How far would you be obliged to follow
him?" she asked.

"Somewhere from twelve to eighteen miles —
can't judge exactly."

"Frankie, dear, I suppose I must trust you on
this strange and perilous mission. It's hard,
though," and the tears fell; "and you are so
noble about it! I shall pray for you. Here's a
little money," handing him a bill. "You may

need it to get out a warrant, or secure the services of an officer, — I don't understand these matters, — or for your own expenses ; " and struggling to appear cheerful, she re-entered the cabin.

Mr. Simmons, as Frankie predicted, tenanted his shanty that night, and on the succeeding forenoon, after patting Georgie and praising Ferdie for their smartness and ability at fencing, hinting at the reward in store for them for acting as hostlers, and lamenting that little Frankie was such a burden to them, took his departure, swinging along at a masterly gate, till an ample space was between himself and the Willards; then, with indolent saunter, he moved at the other extreme of pedestrian locomotion.

Behind him, in the distance, had he looked critically back with a magnifying glass, perhaps he would have detected a black speck moving after in the distance. It was the dwarf's cap in the prairie grass.

Mr. Simmons's well-developed figure stood distinctly outlined against the sky, but the pursuing pygmy was too near the earth to be easily discerned. The Hunchback's eyes were clear, determined, alert, though more than ever deep and thoughtful. His face expressed mingled satisfaction, wariness, and resentment. The unconsciously pursued instinctively hated his pursuer, and had he been aware of the latter's propinquity, how quickly he would have crushed him, with no hand to interpose!

But the Hunchback, though bodily contemptible, compared with Mr. Simmons, had a *head*, — you need not be certified of that, were you to meet him, — and his physical minuteness was, under the circumstances, to his advantage. Blessed are short legs when one on the prairies must not be seen! With his singularly precocious intellect, sharpened by sorrow, and roused by the emergencies of his present undertaking, Mr. Simmons had in the despised dwarf no mean antagonist.

What a scene! In front loomed Mr. Simmons's towering form; in the rear was the squat proportions of the pertinacious young Hunchback. And thus they proceeded for miles — the leader, in his careless indolence, barely putting one foot before the other, often stopping to gaze skyward, or at the various points of the compass, or to cast himself at length on the plain; the follower, steadily gaining on him, yet maintaining a discreet distance.

Across Mr. Simmons's route there flowed a shallow creek. Here he was accustomed to solace himself with a smoke. Of this circumstance the little Hunchback seemed aware, for striking into the luxuriant growths lining the banks of the stream, he curled himself up triumphantly within a few rods of his enemy. Evidently this was a feat he had before accomplished, and of which he was particularly proud.

Mr. Simmons rested, and the dwarf waited. An hour glided by, then another. Hunchback became impatient, he was so anxious to reach the end of his pursuit and face the villain, as he felt confident he was to do with the fist of justice — not his own fist; that lacked knuckle. Why did the man *laze* so? The dwarf obtained information on this point by a method on which he did not reckon.

"I see you, old boy!" said Simmons, suddenly resuming an upright position, and looking in the direction of the lad.

The dwarf trembled. Had the cunning horse-stealer been cognizant of his pursuit, and permitted him to approach, that he might deal out summary vengeance? His impulse was to rise and defend himself to the last extremity — a forlorn extremity indeed, for him. Flee he could not with the least chance of escape. But something held him quiet. How fortunate! For Mr. Simmons, forming a tube of his hands, shouted as if to some one remote.

"Ahoy, there!"

"Ay, ay!" was the response.

And the Hunchback, assured that he had not been seen, noiselessly turned to ascertain who the

AUNT ESTHER AND FRANKIE.   Page 188.

last speaker was. The long strides of the new comer soon brought him to view — a rough, ill-visaged customer, with bushy whiskers, and carrying a gun. Approaching obliquely, his course lay directly across the Hunchback's hiding-place. Nor did the dwarf dare move, for Mr. Simmons stood overlooking his concealment, and the least motion or rustling might betray him. He had, however, escaped one danger by keeping still; this encouraged him not to precipitate his fate by useless action. The friendly sedges put their blossoming tops together to screen him; but already he lay exposed to the advancing foot of the stranger, when the latter, springing aside, exclaimed, —

"A rattlesnake, old hoss, sure's you're alive!" And making a circuit to avoid the reptile, he avoided the Hunchback too.

"Even a rattlesnake can do some good," thought the dwarf, breathing freer.

"How *are* yer, Grimes?" said the stranger. "Give us yer paw!"

"Ah, *Grimes!*" soliloquized the dwarf; "then Simmons isn't his true name!"

"And you, Scroggs? They haven't nabbed you yet, hey?"

"No, nor you nuther. But jist you see here! Isn't that a purty toy?"

The Hunchback, peering from his nest, saw that it was a gold watch and chain.

"Took the critter from a cabin not more'n two hours ago. Door was open — walked in. Nobody there. This thing hanging agin the logs. Says I, 'It's no place for jewelry, in a log cabin,' and having an affection for sich trash, jist tuck it 'long. Scare up any *game* out here, old fellow?"

"Slim picking, compared with better. 'Tain't like the Mississip," replied Simmons. "Got a horse to sell, and some geese to pluck. Tell yer what, that animal is wuth five hundred dollars, if it's wuth a cent. Belonged to a rhinoceros in hat and boots — travelling for his lady's health. Isn't she a screamer? Took the horse off while she was trotting her man round doing family chores. Stabled him way off on the prairie, where he'll be safe from his *former* owner till the excitement's over; then he's on the market. Don't fancy waitin' 'fore realizin'; but I gets free gratis; the boys take care of the animal because they love me like a father; they've put me up some hay, — that's already engaged — and have fenced *my* breaking to help me jump *their* claim — ha, ha, ha!"

"*Ha, ha, ha!*" mocked the dwarf, in the grass, too angry to contain himself.

"What's that?" exclaimed Scroggs, turning around. "Did you hear that laugh?"

"Yes," replied his companion, "plain enough!"
Rising, they gazed silently about them.

"Wal, one thing's sartin," observed Scroggs, as they seated themselves again; "there's not a *human* on *this* prairie."

"But, Grimes, you spoke on the boys; whar's the old uns?"

"Wal, fust comes their dear mamma — the piousest shemale afloat — 'twould do your gizzard good, old hoss, to hear me pray over her cooking!"

"You didn't try *that* on!"

"I did, though; but it didn't come a mite natural. I expected an invitation to say grace, as they call it, and having a minister in tow, I jist noticed how he went on, and repeated it word for word — shut eyes — clasped hands — went the whole figger."

"Ha, ha, ha!" they roared, slapping their sides.

"Ha, ha, ha!" shrilly echoed the irascible dwarf.

"There's that sound agin — it fairly chills me," said Scroggs. "What you s'pose it is, hoss?"

"It must either be an echo or a bird, I judge," replied the other, deliberating.

"Next is an old maid, aunt Esther, my *sweetheart*, you understand — don't swaller soft soap as easy as the other. Then a miserable imita-

tion of a human with a hunch back. Blast him
— his eyes follow me everywhere. I'd *strangle
him* if I had a chance!"

"Eny money there?"

"Not much show. Don't know, though, 'bout
the old maid. She's close-mouthed as an oyster.
That's what I'm courting her for — to find out."

"You ain't mentioned the old man."

"Haven't any. That weasel of a Hunchback
told me, when I fust introduced myself to the interesting household, that they left *him* behind.
So they had, with a vengeance. The mother
opened her innocent heart to me pretty free. He
was robbed on the steamer, and thrown overboard."

His comrade rose, and laying his freckled red
hand on Grimes's shoulder, said, —

"Who do you s'pose did that job?"

"'Twasn't you?"

"Me and Brooks. That's why I'm here. I'm
doubtful if 'twas done thorough. His wife was
a callin' to him, an' his brat was comin' to see
whar he was, an' me an' Brooks clutched him in
a hurry, and I relieved him of his valuables, and
touched him up with the steel, and histed him out
of the boat all at onst, as you may say. An'
Brooks stands to it he saw him arterwards hugging a snag. Now, hoss, *ef* that's so, and he
was helped off by some one, I wouldn't jist like

to light upon him among folks. So I've taken
to travelling on the prairies till it blows one way
or t'other.

"But ain't you going to jine our company?
You're skittish, come to the scratch; a reg'lar born
coward; but you're cute. There's 'leven of us.
Has our headquarters on the river. Have a woman to cook, an' wash, an' spy for us; she's a
buster — fight like a tiger — cry like a baby."

"Where's your hiding-place?" asked Simmons.

"'Bout three miles an' a half, 'bove Cole's whiskey shop. Cave under the bluff. Nobody can
scent it. Small island just opposite — big tree
on't — dead — struck by lightning."

"What's the pass-word?"

"Whistle three times — so!" and he made the
sounds. "Our fellars'll be mighty glad to see
yer. Shall go back soon myself— dry pickin'
on the prairies."

"Well, I must start on," said Simmons.

"So must I," answered Scroggs; "good by,
hoss;" and the latter went his way, and the former his — accompanied by the vigilant and viewless dwarf.

CHAPTER XVII.

" GRUBBING." — HONEST MR. GREY.

PICTURE to yourself a man of fifty, of medium height, stoutly built, square shoulders, black hair and eyes, long, hooked, knowledgeable nose, solemn physiognomy, grave step — Mr. Grey, of Minnesota, reader !

No more honest-looking face than his would you see among a thousand. And as for his eyes, a neighbor, who had a theory on the subject, said she knew he was truthful from their shape ; while his worn suit of black, of which its ancient swallow-tail was noticeable, had a sort of classical air, tending to check any sense of the grotesque which might arise in the mind of the spectator.

He has of late been " hired man " to Mr. Parsons, the missionary at L——. He first introduced himself to the clergyman in a way that touched his sympathies. He hailed from Pennsylvania, where, he stated, his wife and children still lived, and whom he was anxious to bring to his present location, because the fever and ague prevailed in that part of the state. He said he had made "a claim" on the adjacent prairie, and "put up" a shanty on it, designing to make such "improvements" as the law required, and then from his earnings — for he was poor — meet the expense of preëmption and removal. He gave a glowing account of his family, whom he seemed greatly to miss, and was anxious that his companion should be informed as to his situation, and the character and prospects of the locality he had chosen.

"I am not used to writing," said he, "and I have called to ask if you will be so good as to write a line to my wife for me."

After some further conversation, the letter was written, met his approval, and, in accordance with his direction, addressed to the absent partner of his fortunes, Mrs. Angelina P. Grey, Readfield, Pa.

A few weeks passed, and he again made his appearance, full of trouble. No answer had been received to his affectionate epistle, and he was making little headway in his worldly affairs.

"Young men get all the jobs," he complained. "People don't like to hire old men like me. They think I can't do much now; but I can keep up my end with the best of them." He then offered to engage himself to the missionary at a reasonable price, to do anything desired.

There was one department of "new country

enterprise which those who lived in the "oak openings" found difficult enough.   It was "grubbing," — I do not mean "getting one's grub," although this was not any too easy.   The fires, which from time immemorial had swept the prairies, burned off, each year, the embryo trees.   But the roots, being comparatively uninjured, continued to grow, forming, near the surface of the ground, woody accumulations, round, gnarled, and tough, called grubs.   These must be removed by the grubbing-hoe — an implement having a pick on one side to remove the soil, and an axe on the other to assault the roots.   Mr. Grey's application was well timed, for Mr. Parsons had set his heart on a garden near his cabin, had spoken for a "breaking team," and was trying to do impossibilities in the grubbing line, when the sedate Pennsylvanian came up the path.

Taking up the hoe, which the minister had laid down, he said, pityingly, —

"Now this is too hard for such as you."

The fact was evident.

"It's what you don't know how to do," he continued, "provided you had strength for it.   Grubbing is as much of a trade as blacksmithing, and a mighty sight harder.   Just see here," added he, removing the earth from a beheaded grub; "the plough can never get through *that*.   'Tisn't cut off deep enough; for the twigs on top of

them, if not cut off, show just where the grubs
are, and the ploughman can keep clear of some
of them."

Which was all true.

"Let me show you how to do it," he exclaimed,
heartily.   And suiting the action to the word, he
extirpated, with surprising dexterity, grub after
grub.   Then leaning on the hoe-handle, and
talking in a confidential tone, he said, —

"Why, I've cleared acres and acres of these
'ere.   I was brought up to it, as I might say.
When's the team comin' to tear up this bit of
land?"

"A week to-day," replied the missionary.

"Well, you can't get these grubs out by that
time yourself.   Suppose, then, you let me do it
for you.   I'll have the piece all ready, smooth as
a picter, if I have to dig to the centre of the
earth.   Only I shall have to board with you
meanwhile.   I ain't a mite particular what I eat."

Deferring the ploughing till a later day to give
him ample time, — for the clergyman had heard
that Mr. Grey was very slow; some called him
lazy, — an unpardonable sin in the eyes of the
energetic frontiersmen, — the good missionary
set him at the task with the complacent feeling
which one has when he helps himself and his
neighbor at the same time.

At night, on inspecting Mr. Grey's work, it

proved satisfactory; and as urgent engagements
called Mr. Parsons from home each day until after nightfall, the grubbing was left wholly to the
workman.   But always, when he hurriedly returned at noon, the missionary could see him lus-
tily toiling.   Once, however, entering the house
at an unusual hour, his wife said, with a laugh, —

"Do see Mr. Grey perform.   I have watched
him till I have cried, laughing."

Stepping to the window, the preacher saw that
Mr. Grey was indulging "the resistance which
inactive matter makes to a change of state," to
his heart's content.   A prolonged look at the sky
northward, then a rest; then moderately spitting
on the ground *once*; next an examination of the
horizon eastward, followed by an inspection of
the hoe from top to edge; another gaze into
space; spitting again; at length the hoe is
raised, but only to repose a while on the capacious
shoulder.   At last, more by gravitation than muscular force, an ineffectual blow is struck.

With a ringing laugh, the wife declared that,
with certain characteristic variations, the same
movements had been enacted and reënacted
throughout the entire morning.

"Poor man," she kindly ejaculated, "let him
favor his old frame.   He has time enough to get
the land ready.   And," she added, "he seems to
make good progress, after all.   How clear the

ground is behind him! not a grub-sprout to be
seen."

One feature in the character of the hired man,
which covered a multitude of infirmities, was his
godly inclinations. He did not profess to be a
Christian, but described Mrs. Grey as a model
disciple, sighing because he was unlike her in
this respect. When his day's work was done, he
would take the large Bible, seat himself by the
light, spread open the book reverently on his
knees, and read, quite absorbed. No other reading could tempt him from that. At family devotions he knelt devoutly; and carefully washed,
shaved, and " dickied," he greeted the Sabbath
and its services. His conversation was mostly on
religious topics.

" I do not know," he contemplatively observed
one day, " as I did right in not having my babies
baptized, it would have been such a comfort to
their mother;" and a tear glistened in his honest
eye.

Listening to his domestic portraitures, the clergyman and wife soon felt quite acquainted with
Mr. Grey's estimable spouse, and his well-
trained Sophronia, — a successful school-teacher,
— and certainly sympathized with him in the
miscarriage of his first letter; and a second was
despatched to Mrs. Angelina P. Grey, county as
well as town being specified.

At dinner, at tea, Mr. Grey would groan over grubbing. "It was the most *straining*est business that ever a man did," he declared. How his back ached his listeners could only imagine by his woful grimaces, and the expressive habit he had of pressing his hand upon that part of the body whenever he straightened up from a stooping posture. Even the famous liniment which a pitying hand furnished him gave only temporary relief.

"It is because he gets so tired through the day," his gentle-minded critic would suggest, as his stentorian snoring set the baby crying in the room below, and spread panic among the rest of the youngsters. And the clergyman, with stately humor, said, "I must say that I have listened to many competitors in these unwelcome serenades, but never till now heard the leader of the world's nasal orchestra."

"I would like my pay for the grubbing," said Mr. Grey, as the missionary came in one evening.

"Are the grubs all taken out?" he asked.

"Not one left," was the reply.

"But I stumbled against some in crossing the lot."

"Yes," answered the workman, "there were a few small ones left in that corner, because they were of no account. The plough will go through

them without trouble. When I work for a man,
I wish to do by him just as I would do for myself. I could have spent time in cutting out every
little stub, but it would be a needless expense to
you."

"Well," said his employer, "I will slip down
and see how things look;" and holding the lantern close to the ground as he went, he found
that not a grub had been disturbed in that part
of the enclosure.

"What does this mean?" he inquired; for the
workman had followed.

He replied, unabashed, —

"I thought I would just knock off the twigs
on this side, my back was so lame; but I
shan't charge you anything for that, if you'll
pay me for the rest of the field."

"I'll examine the remainder first," rejoined
the minister; and, to his amazement, it was re-
vealed that after the first day's labor, the whole
had been gone over in the same deceptive manner!

"Pay me for *that*," demanded Mr. Grey.

"Pay me for your board," exclaimed the indignant clergyman, "and the damage you have
caused by breaking off the twigs and leaving
the roots in the soil out of sight."

The dishonest workman raised the ponderous
hoe threateningly — for he had it with him.

A sardonic smile played over his face, a murderous light gleamed from his eyes. He kept the weapon poised a moment, as if weighing the pros and cons, then put it down, and silently departed. The missionary felt that the man would have killed him, had he thought he could have done so safely to himself.

Not long after, an acquaintance accosted Mr. Parsons, saying, —

"Mr. Grey worked for you a few weeks since, I believe. How did he do while in your employ?"

Unsuspectingly stating what his conduct had been, the missionary was subpœnaed the next day, as witness in a case in law, in which, I think, Mr. Grey was plaintiff. The defendant had caused the minister to be summoned, he said, to "impeach" Mr. Grey. The county seat was some fifteen miles distant, and Mr. Parsons found that quite a number were going over on the same errand as himself, having also been defrauded by the crafty Pennsylvanian.

A brisk ride behind the village storekeeper's fine span, across solitary stretches of rolling prairie, brought them to their destination, an unfinished story-and-a-half house, hidden by an irregular growth of native trees. It stood on a slight swell in the outskirts of the town, and had a pleasant, well-to-do air, with its thrifty surroundings of ploughed fields, grazing cattle, and domestic fowl. It was also the village tavern, — as one might judge by the loungers.

The court sat in the bar-room. As the company from L—— entered, they were received with hostile demonstrations by the residents assembled, for Mr. Grey had taken up his abode in the place, — boarding at the tavern, — and having ingratiated himself in the esteem of the people, they supposed him a worthy and injured man. He did look prepossessing, Mr. Parsons thought, as, entering, he saw him parading the apartment, calm and neat. He was, however, a little disconcerted as one after another of his victims filed in. Such a meeting he had not anticipated. He had engaged shrewd counsel, who seemed at the outset to have confidence in him.

" I move," said a rowdy, full of fight, " that the services be opened with prayer," glancing defiantly at the missionary.

Mr. Grey's opponent, a swearing, loud-voiced boaster from New England, chose to conduct his own case. He soon got the justice enraged beyond self-control by his blunders, interruptions, and insults, as he raved around the room, lawbook in hand, goading the court with his insolence. The lawyer evidently enjoyed this aspect of the case hugely. Confusion reigned.

Meanwhile there was much private discussion

in which Mr. Grey's history was being rapidly
unsealed. Seizing a good chance, the missionary got Mr. Grey's ear, told him that his character was well known, and advised him to settle the matter with his adversary as soon as
possible. He grew frightened. Popular feeling
began to turn against him. The case suddenly
closed, I can scarcely tell how — in some summary frontier way, however. Mr. Grey's counsel, disgusted with him, and finding that he
could get no fee, called for his horse, and, as
the crowd stood watching his management of
the high-spirited animal, he started for his distant home. Off dashed the advocate; but before
he had got fairly under way, Mr. Grey, the picture of terror, ran frantically after, shouting,
while the spectators cheered him on, —

"Hold on! hold on! Don't leave me! Take
me in!" and catching hold of the back of the
vehicle with a desperate grasp, as the astonished
lawyer slackened his pace, he clambered in,
and was soon out of sight. And that was the
last they saw of Mr. Grey.

I scarcely need say that there was no evidence
that Mr. Grey was from Pennsylvania; that
Mrs. Angelina P. Grey was other than a myth.
He was, it was thought, an escaped jail-bird,
his vices being, perhaps, the natural fruit of
that parent sin — laziness.

"And," said Mr. Parsons's right hand man, good Deacon Palmer, "St. Paul's rule that 'if any would not work, neither should he eat,' is wise and just in more senses than one. The sluggard is ever a covetous man; as Solomon says, 'He coveteth greedily all the day long;' and as 'his hands refuse to labor,' and he is thereby brought to want, who so tempted to crime as he? The indolent man is by logical necessity a dangerous man, and I always give him a wide berth. You preachers, however, have so little practical knowledge of human nature, that though you preached 'total depravity' Sunday, next day a knave would make you think him an angel. You need to be taken in occasionally to reform this professional weakness." He added, after a moment's pause, "Many persons fling at the church because there are hypocrites in it, but Mr. Grey's case shows that there is now and then one *out* of it."

But when next the storekeeper and missionary met, the former, his coal-black eyes streaming lightning, and both arms in vigorous motion, — as was his manner when excited, — took the latter to task for advising Mr. Grey to close the case at the justice's.

"He's a double-dyed rascal, parson; and we ought to have nabbed him when we had the chance. Why, sir, a squab-up morsel of humanity, with voice like an asthmatic chicken, and pipe-stem legs, tracked that chap more than fifteen miles afoot, to expose his wickedness and save his folks from the villain's claws."

" Who did you say it was? "

" A young hunchback. It appears that this deceiver gave his name in that settlement as Simmons, and representing himself as a well-to-do bachelor in search of a wife, tried to inveigle a respectable maiden lady into matrimony. He was designing also to jump a claim belonging to two lone women, and had secreted a stolen — but no matter about that now. It looks mightily as if this Grey, *alias* Simmons, *alias* Grimes, — another of his names, — was in league with a horde of Mississippi River cutthroats. He won't trouble people this way again very soon, I'm thinking — more's the pity. I'd like to help string him up ! "

" Did you learn the Hunchback's name? " asked the clergyman.

" Willard," replied Mr. Cowles.

" Where is the Willard claim? "

" Customers came in, and I forgot to find out. In fact, as the Hunchback promised to be on hand with his mother and aunt, in season for Grey's case, I expected then to be better informed about them. Why he didn't come I can't decipher —'fraid something has happened to the brave

little squatty. I meant to have helped him on his
way back a piece, but he went away before I was
aware."

"I have wondered that I heard nothing from
that family," said Mr. Parsons. "Tom Jones
made their acquaintance at the Landing, and
directed them near us. He particularly commended them to the sympathy and kind offices
of the settlers here. I must look them up."

CHAPTER XVIII.

JOHN TOWER'S TOWN. — A WEDDING TOUR.

"SIR," said the waiter at the Winneshick Hotel, in Dacotah, putting his head in at the door of Mr. Parsons's, (the missionary) room, "a gentleman below wants to see you. Shall I show him up?" And in due time a man about fifty, of fresh, florid face and stout figure, entered the room.

Slowly unrolling a showily-drawn chart, on the margin of which was emblazoned *Prairie City*, he remarked, —

"Let me show you the new town, sir, which I am starting. We have got *the* location, sir," he continued, emphatically, swinging his chart into the light, "and we expect to make a wide-awake thorough-going thing of it, that will pay for the trouble ; and where, if a man invests in a lot, he can be sure of realizing something worth while from the investment. Here, you see, is Main Street," running his finger down the centre. "This is our principal business avenue. Here are our largest stores, storehouses, warehouses, and the like, you understand, as have all great commercial centres. Just here, sir, our steam-mills are going up. Not yet erected, you understand; but the companies are formed, and I have letters in my pocket stating that they will be on in the course of a week or two. Plenty of capital, you see; some of the stockholders old friends of mine, schoolmates, stirring men, who know just how to put things through. Two railroads have been surveyed and staked out, which take our place on the way. One we are sure of, both are probable. You can see at a glance, sir, what the rise of land will be when these improvements are completed. Our town lies on the direct line from Dubuque to St. Paul. Nature intended a railroad should go there — the only possible route, indeed. Any one can see that who will take the trouble to examine the make of the land. I lay this matter before you to give you a chance in the town. We want a minister, sir. I learn that you are one. I believe in the institutions of the gospel for a new place; calls in, you see, the best class of settlers, and makes them contented. Our well-to-do, reliable emigrants are generally brought up to be religious, and cannot do without schools and churches. I've watched this thing, and know that the coming of a clergyman into a young town is often the making of it; real estate always rises. And now, sir, what say you to casting your lot in with us? I'll give you an extra chance. Just say that you'll agree to put up a house, and I'll pledge myself to give you two of the best lots on the plat."

There are few things more interesting than the springing up of a young town on the frontier. Like the embryo plant, it is very small at first — a few cabin homes — while all around are broad prairies and thick woods, where may be seen the fresh trail of the Indian. Persons whose days have been spent in some long-settled locality, where generations come and go, and things remain much the same, if told that yonder cabin, with its blacksmith shop near by, and log tavern, constitute the germ of a town, and lots were offered them for sale in that rough solitude, would laugh in your face. But a year passes, and, perhaps, how changed the scene! As if by enchantment, the cabins are gone, and framed houses, stores, mills, churches, occupy their places.

Such a place was E——. When Mr. Parsons first happened there, he put up at the little, uncouth, log tavern, the only building in the place. The table was of picnic style, made of unplaned boards. In place of chairs was a bench of slabs and stakes. After dinner he started out for a walk, to view the town, thinking he was in its suburbs. The proprietor joined him.

"Where is the town?" asked the guest.

"This is it," was the reply.

"But," said the missionary, "where are the people, and the buildings?"

"Well," replied the landlord, "it's true, when you see my cabin, you see all there is now; but let me tell you, it won't be a great while before the people are here, and the buildings too. You are going farther on the frontier; let me advise you to stop here, and put you up a house."

The clergyman, at that period in his personal history, was unwesternized, and the forcibly uttered advocacy of this advice which followed he listened to very much as he would to the exaggerations of the auctioneer; and, turning on his heel, he left him to his day-dreams.

In one year and a half from that time, however, having business that way, he returned; and there stood a conspicuous, well-grown town, in appearance, at least, ten years of age. Two handsome hotels, a stone school-house, stores, tasteful dwellings, streets well laid out, and alive with teams and the din of the business mart, filled him with pleased surprise; and as his Yankee friend — the proprietor — introduced him to the realization of his expectations, and told him he left Massachusetts overwhelmed with debt, when he saw the competency he had acquired since he put up his cabin tavern, the guest's views of him and his schemes underwent a sudden revolution.

There was D——, also. A stage-load, one of whom was our clergyman, fresh from the Mississippi, stopped there one night. After tea they walked out to see the "lay of the land," and in their stroll many a sharp joke was cracked at the young town's expense. Along the margin of a small, shallow stream stood a few cottages and cabins, among which was one shanty-tavern ; and these constituted the place. Speckled trout peeped out at them from shady nooks with a boldness unknown in waters where the angler's bait is often thrown. Flocks of quails piped in the long grass, and prairie hens ran fluttering in their path, guiding their helpless broods. A friend of his, a shrewd Vermont farmer, who had two hundred dollars spare money, which he wished to invest to the best advantage, was besought, almost with tears, by one of the settlers, to take his cottage, eight acres of land, and improvements, for that sum, assuring him that he would realize something handsome for it ; that he had confidence in the growth of the town, but was too homesick to remain. The Vermonter knowingly shook his head at the urgent offer, and passed on. He lived, however, to regret it, for in less than two years from that time four acres of that land sold for eight thousand dollars.

With these and similar instances in mind, the missionary was disposed to listen candidly to the representations of his caller, although he had heard of " paper towns."

One day, some two years later, Mr. J——, a gray-haired man of sixty years, called on the missionary at L——, and taking him mysteriously aside, asked if he would come to N——, some five miles distant, and perform the marriage rite for him, the next day?

He requested the affair to be kept a profound secret, I suppose from fear of a celebration of the event by certain young men, who claimed the privilege of making night hideous with blowing tin horns, firing guns, and other discordances, whenever a bachelor or widower entered into matrimony.

Keeping the secret, however, was no light task, for the devoted bridegroom had already advertised the condition of his affairs by his attentive courtship; and as he was seen to call at " the minister's," — an unwonted thing for him, — he had, quite innocently, " let grimalkin out of the reticule." To save him from annoyance, it became necessary for the divine, if possible, to put the cat back again.

He discovered this when he went to get a horse for the occasion. The young man who had the care of the stable filled also the office of village gossip, and, as he curried the horse, asked, with an air oddly compounded of the deferential and impudent, —

"Who's going to be married *now*, Mr. Parsons?"

The clergyman's silence did not disconcert him, and he added, —

"*I* think old J——'s a little too old to marry again; but they *do* say he'll git a fust-rate wife, though. What do you think?"

"Is Mr. J—— going to be married?" asked the minister, parrying the attack.

"I don't know who knows if you don't!" he returned, laughing loudly; and then, leaving his horse tied at the halter ring, he entered the tavern, — it was the dinner hour, — and announced to the people at table that "the minister had come for a horse to go down and marry old J——."

The news flew over the village like wildfire, and having a presentiment that, to make assurance doubly sure, the curious would watch to see if he went towards Mr. J——'s, the minister mounted and rode slowly through the town in the opposite direction. Skirting some heavy woods by a generous circuit, he had struck a road leading to Mr. J——'s, when, just in the fork, his attention was taken by two men engaged in putting up a guide-post, on which was neatly lettered, "*Prairie City*, 15 *Miles*" — the index

hand pointing in the direction of his ride.   One
of the men turned to look at him.   It was the
proprietor of Prairie City, who at once came forward, and was soon arguing again the claims of
his town.

"We are going ahead nicely," said he; "prospects never better.   But we want a minister.
Haven't found one yet.   Just agree to put up a
house among us, and you shall have two handsome lots, as I said before."

Having little time for conversation, the clergyman left him, his parting words being eloquent
in advocacy of his "city."

The wedding was to be at the dwelling of the
bride, a widow of fifty.

Her snug cabin showed marks of the thorough
housekeeper.   Order was supreme, and she was
its living embodiment.   Each article of dress,
from the starched dress-cap to the shoes she
wore, fitted with exactness; and whether she sat,
walked, talked, or was silent, she was prim and
precise.   A most estimable woman she was, too,
and I scarcely wondered at the devotion of the
bridegroom.

Many years had passed since death took from
him his loved companion, leading him at last,
sad and lonely, to leave his desolate New England home, where every object reminded him of
the departed, and seek to forget his bereavement

amid the exciting scenes and vicissitudes of the frontier.

He preëmpted a "one-hundred-and-sixty-acre" farm, well balanced in prairie and timber; fenced and ploughed, and planted largely; fitted him up a cabin; read the eastern papers; smoked, chewed tobacco; lounged in the village store for society; grew careless in his personal habits, and very irritable. What was the matter? He missed the gentle presence of woman, and the solitude of his western home became more and more irksome.

He was a mere man of the world, quick-tempered, and, of late, when angered, shockingly profane. He had not, by his presence in the place of prayer, manifested the least interest in the higher wants of the soul, and Mr. Parsons was glad to find the bride elect to be a lady of piety, and much weight of character — a circumstance in which the bridegroom took great pride, showing that, hard and irreligious as he seemed, her upright christianly qualities had much to do in influencing his choice. Indeed, he evinced, on his part, a sincere sense of unworthiness for such an alliance, seeming to realize that morally there was a great gulf between them; and there was a nervous anxiety with him, lest, somehow, he should lose the prize. Ah, woman without goodness the wicked man shudders at as a monstrosity; woman with piety the profligate adores.

The ceremony was to be in the early afternoon, and to be followed by the usual wedding repast. The missionary, however, had been in the room but a short time, when he saw that something was going wrong. The bridegroom looked anxious, and the family friends embarrassed. Mr. J—— himself stated the cause. He had omitted to procure from the justice the legal right to be married. That officer lived miles away, and could not then be found. Mr. J—— was unreconciled to a delay of the ceremony.

"Well, then, let us step over the state line!" he exclaimed! "it's only three quarters of a mile; the law'll let us be married there without any preliminaries. Many a couple has done that!"

But the lady would consent to no irregularity. She would wait a week to be sure that every step was taken with due deliberation. So the bridegroom must needs make the best of the matter, and, with a disconsolate face, helped dispose of the nice edibles that had been prepared for the wedding.

"How shall I find my way to Prairie City?" said Mr. Parsons to one of the sons, who had followed him to the gate, as he was leaving. "As I haven't had the pleasure of marrying anybody, I guess I'll ride over there and see the place. And there's a family named Willard somewhere in this region. Very likely they are over there — so much has been said about the town ! "

" Prairie City," slowly repeated the young man. " I don't know of any such place about here."

" But I passed a guide-board to-day which said, ' Prairie City, fifteen miles,' and the hand pointed in this direction."

" O," said he, " you mean Mr. Tower's town. Well, I've never been over there. It's off the main road. Follow that track round the woods yonder, and keep straight across the prairie, and it's about ten miles, I reckon ; but you'll have to inquire."

The road was a lonely one, leading away from the settlements, which were mostly contiguous to the timber land. Mr. Parsons's imagination enlivened the loneliness with pictures of the flourishing place to which he was going. He could almost see its magic growth, and hear the din of its busy population ; and on, on he rode, until he began to wonder that the " city " did not come in sight, thinking he must have gone more than the distance specified. He was relieved at seeing a cabin near by, and rode up to inquire. It stood alone in the vast solitude, with no living creature about, save a lame old skeleton horse, spiritlessly nibbling at the grass as he hobbled around. The building had recent-

ly been occupied; for what purpose, and by
whom, in such a doleful place, it was hard to
guess; but the inmates were away. So, driving
on, again a cabin appeared.

"Where is Prairie City?" he shouted to a man
lounging in the doorway.

"No sich place about here, as I knows on,"
was the reply.

"Is there a man by the name of Tower living
anwhere in this region?"

"Tower, John Tower? Why, sir, you came
by his cabin more'n three miles back."

"You don't mean to say that the log house that
stands all alone, out on the prairie there, is Mr.
Tower's place! He told me he'd started a town
there!"

"Anything but *startcd*, I reckon, stranger; but
you ken see for yourself."

"Mr. Parsons," cried a young man, hurrying
through the hazel bushes to head off the missionary's horse, as he was returning to town, "so
old J——'s married, after all — isn't he?"

"Ah!" said the clergyman; "I am not aware
that he is married.   When did the event occur?"

"Why, didn't you marry him?"

"No."

"That's what I call sharp, for a minister," said

the man of the stable, as he took the clergyman's horse — " going way round them woods jest to throw folks off the track ! But you married old J——, after all ; I know that ! "

" How do you know it? "

" Why, you see, says I to myself, says I, Mr. Parsons has gone that way jest for a blind. So I jest took a ride down to old J——'s to make observations ; and sure enough, there you was, over to widow K——'s, the family dressed up in their Sunday best, ready for the wedding. Folks has got to get up afore day to git ahead of this child. I told 'em all that you've married the old widower."

" But I have not married him ! "

" You haven't ! " he replied, quite crestfallen ; then, rallying, added, " well, I'm really glad on't. Why, there's his daughter, Mrs. L——, has worried herself sick about it. She don't approve of the old man's marrying ; and I guess there's no love lost between 'em, they differ so on this matter. She's up to the town now, and I shouldn't wonder if she hails you, to know jest how the thing stands."

He was right. As the missionary was passing a shop, Mrs. L—— came out, and said, —

" Mr. Parsons, some say you've been down to marry my father, and some say you have not. I tell them, if it is so, I know nothing about it, for father hasn't said a word to me. But I wish you would tell me, that I may know what to believe. Did you marry him?"

"No, madam, I did not."

"There!" triumphantly cried Mrs. Cowles, the shopkeeper's wife, from the door. "I told you so! Didn't I sit by that window and watch to see which way the minister went? He didn't go towards old J——'s at all, but right towards Sallie Nason's, and he was seen on the road to her house. I don't object to folks marrying, but I don't see the use of being so sly about it."

"Can you tell me," said Mr. Parsons to a friend, "anything about this Mr. Tower, who says he is starting a town some fifteen miles from here? I see he has been putting up guide-boards of late. Has he capital for such an enterprise?"

"You can judge," was the reply. "He called on me yesterday with an old silver watch, worth not more than five dollars, which he wished to sell or pawn, in order to get food for his family. I suppose he wanted you to say you would come to 'Prairie City?' Well, it would have sold *lots* to his eastern correspondents!"

"Father," exclaimed Mr. Parsons's little boy, one delicious Sunday morning, two weeks after the incidents just narrated, "there's a large double wagon driving towards the house, filled with folks. I guess somebody's coming to get married!"

True enough. On board seats placed across the huge open vehicle were Mr. J—— and bride, with a goodly company in their best attire and very smiling faces. It was only an hour to service, and they had ridden through the main street of the village to the clergyman's house — sufficient evidence that Mr. J—— had lost his fear of publicity, and now preferred an open to a clandestine marriage — a change due, no doubt, to the good sense of his excellent and dignified lady. Mr. Parsons took this as a happy omen, and after uniting them in the holy bonds, said, —

"Mr. J——, it is nearly time for meeting. Let me invite you and your friends to go with me to the house of prayer. It would be a fitting beginning to your married life — one I am sure that your estimable wife would approve. Is it not so, madam?"

"O, yes," she replied, with a grateful look.

"Besides," he added, "I am to preach on marriage this morning, and it will be a pleasant coincidence to have you as hearers, after having just made you one."

He cheerfully assented, and the missionary spoke from the text, "Blessed are they which are called to the marriage supper of the Lamb." Mr. J—— listened tearfully, and his wife, it was evident, lifted up her heart in silent prayer for a blessing on the word.

I scarcely need add that the husband's anticipations of a "serenade" were not realized. His wife was too much respected, and the manly, decorous course pursued when the marriage was at last solemnized was a sufficient protection.

But what is a wedding without a "wedding tour"? Happy Mr. J——, desiring to please his bride by omitting none of the proprieties of the event, invited her to accompany him to the Mississippi. With an eye to business as well as enjoyment, he used for the journey the capacious wagon in which he came to be married, as it would enable him to bring back groceries for the neighbors, and also passengers, and thus pay the expense of the trip, and perchance earn a penny besides.

Twice sixty miles, over rolling, roadless prairies, broken at times by rough ravines; on seats of oaken boards laid across the wagon, — think of that for a bridal trip!

Returning, several couple occupied seats behind the owner of the team and his bride. Now, there being no springs under the seats, when the going was *very* uneven the jolting was violent and unsafe, obliging the lady passengers to cling to their lords or be shaken from the vehicle.

Mrs. J——, however, disapproving of such public freedom, and disdaining support, sat bolt upright and self-reliant.   Hold on by her husband
— not she !

But " dignity of character " is not an infallible
protection against accidents.   By and by came a
prodigious lurch.   There was a flutter of white
near the bridegroom, and stately Mrs. J—— was
sent flying through the air, and plumped down
among the prairie grass like a downy pillow.

Her husband did not turn to look at her, or
inquire if she was injured, nor dismount to assist
her in — he held her in too much awe.   Silently he reined in the horses, gazing meanwhile
straight ahead into vacancy, till she had with her
snowy kerchief smoothed her disordered apparel,
and composedly ascended to her place.   Then
he dutifully drove on.

Pain, however, will conquer both the mascu-
line and feminine will, and overcome even a mistaken sense of propriety.   The passengers were
scarcely well out of the perilous ravines, and on
the smooth prairie, when a groan issued from
the bride's unwilling lips.   The husband dutifully forbore to notice it.   Another, then another,
rising almost to a scream, broke forth.   She had
sprained an ankle, and the intense pain was too
great to be borne.   A mile at the left was a
cabin.   Driving there, the efficient settler's wife

was busy binding a soothing and healing lotion on the foot, when voices of men in altercation arose outside.

" 'Twas you that took it, you rascal; there was nobody else in our settlement mean enough to steal. Hand it over; quick, too!"

The passengers rushed to the door in time to see old Mr. J—— seize a man by the collar, and the latter, with a powerful blow of his fist, strike the gray-haired bridegroom to the ground, then, with astonishing agility, bound away towards the ravines.

It was Mr. Grey, *alias* Simmons, *alias* Grimes, on his way to the pirates' rendezvous.

"If I had my rifle here, and my sight was what it once was, I'd put an eend to his villanies quick 's I'd bullet a panther," exclaimed the fuming bridegroom, with an oath, as he reached the cabin door.

"Don't swear, husband," gently interposed his wife; and dropping his head for shame, he assisted her into the wagon, and resumed the journey home.

CHAPTER XIX.

THE WRONG CABIN. — THE COUPLE UNDER THE
UMBRELLA.

"LITTLE HUNCHY" tracked Simmons, otherwise Grimes, to the town of L——; saw him enter the village store; come out from thence; pass northward along the main street, and, just over the village plat, disappear in a better-class log house — the home, he afterwards learned, of Rev. Mr. Parsons, the missionary.

The dwarf then went into the shop. On the counter, his shapely legs pendent therefrom, sat the proprietor. A number of men were grouped near by, smoking and discussing local politics. At the Hunchback's entrance, conversation gradually fell off, the loafers, with curious stare and rough humor, greeting the advent of the misshapen young stranger.

"Well, squatty, what will *you* have?" asked the grocer.

"That is not my name," said the dwarf.

"Excuse me," replied the dealer; "I was not aware you owned any other."

"If that's not his *name*, it's his *natur*," said a bysitter, with a wink at the company.

"I'd thank you to speak when you're spoken to," retorted the Hunchback, losing his temper.

"Ah," ejaculated the other, offended in turn, "you're sassy as you're homely. If you wern't so small, now, I'd tweak your nose — if you had one — but you hain't!"

"Gentlemen," remarked the grocer, "we have no legal or moral right to insult the little fellow because he was spoilt in the making; and for my part I like his grit; if he don't look out for himself, everybody will tread on him."

"That's so," responded several.

"What'll you have?" he again interrogated.

"Nothing," answered the dwarf. "I came in to rest a moment."

"Well, you look as if it wouldn't hurt you, to be sure. John, bring a chair from the other room for this crooked mortal!"

The Hunchback seated himself, and gazed around. The color rushed to his sallow-pale cheeks. On the wall at the end of the apartment was a conspicuous poster, ornamented with the figures of a fiery charger and a man holding him by the bridle. And at the top of the handbill was printed, in bold type, —

FIFTY DOLLARS REWARD!

The circular commenced with, "Stolen from the subscriber," the description that followed of

the purloined horse corresponding precisely to
the one Mr. Simmons had left in the care of Ferdie and Georgie.

"Fifty dollars!" mentally echoed the dwarf;
"if I can only get that for mother to buy land
with!"

With his excessive weariness his confidence
had ebbed somewhat. But the offered reward
raised his spirits, and, embracing an opportunity,
he warily questioned Mr. Cowles concerning Mr.
Simmons; and finding that the shrewd trader
sympathized in his idea of Mr. Simmons's character, he related all he knew of him.

Mr. Cowles was interested and excited.

"*Mind* is the measure of the man," said he,
emphasizing the first word, "as Dr. Watts
expressed it; and you're a thundering illustration of the truth of the remark. How you
followed the serpent! And, my lad, don't
you fret; I'll see Edmonds about that hay,
and if anybody gets the money for it it shall
be you."

"You won't say anything so that it will get to
Simmons's ear?"

"When you catch a weasel asleep," replied the
grocer. "You'll pocket the fifty dollars for the
horse — that's my opinion. Can you be here
Thursday? Simmons has a case at court then,
and we are preparing to deal out to him, on that

occasion, his deserts. Bring along your mother or aunt, and the beast. Till then I'll keep mum. Simmons, as you call him, is living on the missionary. I'll see that the fellow don't visit your diggings till after the trial — then he won't care to." Then, pushing the dwarf with warm-hearted familiarity before him into the housekeeping part of the establishment, he called out, —

" Here, wife, give this big-soul-and-little-body a bite to eat, and a bed to-night for head and back — he won't need any for his legs."

The dwarf turned his face towards home next day, lightened of a load of apprehension, care, and solicitude. Victory over the wiles of a heartless villain was assured. Instead of danger and pecuniary loss, he had secured protection from the threatening peril, and there was a strong probability that a nice sum would be realized for the family. These considerations imparted a helpful impulse to his weak limbs as he walked; yet he was more conscious of the toilsomeness of the journey, now that he was alone, and the urgency of the extremity no longer existed. How much are the best of us creatures of circumstances!

Lamed from yesterday's exertions, the hours dragged wofully, and he seemed to have made exceedingly poor progress, he thought, as certain *markcd* spots did not appear. There, for example, was the creek crossing, where the two out-

laws met, — surely he ought to have reached it,
— yet it was not even discernible in the distance.
He had no misgivings as to his ability to retrace
the route. Had he not, coming, *studied* the face
of the prairies for this very purpose? Moreover, he could guide his course by the wind and
sun.

But, somehow, the monotonous meadows were
increasingly unfamiliar. And the creek, did it
mockingly retire as he advanced? By and by
he paused in suspense. Then he glanced to note
the position of the sun. But the heavens were
covered with clouds. How absent-minded he
had been! What about the wind? Ah, by that
he *must* be right in the main. Perhaps he had
veered a trifle,— enough to miss that jutting angle
of the creek, — and he would strike the stream
farther along.

This conclusion settled his doubts; yet he urged
his way with a nervous eagerness that betrayed
anxiety to behold the proof of the correctness of
his reasoning.

But the coveted creek did not cheer his strained
sight. Travel as confidently and energetically
as he might, the babbling brook broke not on
his longing vision.

Soon, however, there was abundance of water.
But it descended from above. Patter, patter,
came the pioneer drops. Then the air was a

liquid sea. How it poured — torrent joined to torrent! Had the upper ocean fallen through? Now heaven's artillery, discharged by electric fire, roared, and rumbled, and rolled, as if cannon balls of mountain weight were propelled around the aerial pavement. And how the chain-lightning flashes zigzagged!

Heroic dwarf, however, nursed a stubborn will. Panting, drenched, the water running in streams through his soaked cap over his face, into his bosom and back, — an animated mote of mortality on a watery waste, — he fought the elements, sure, soon, of shelter.

But the creek, where could it be? Perhaps he had waded some shallow ford unconsciously, the plains were so submerged. Ah, yes, it is even so. Joy! there's the cabin light! Thrice welcome, beaming taper, lighting the weary wanderer home! But how queerly the storm transfigures objects! Those trees do not resemble the straight growths of the Willard grove. And the dwelling, what is the matter with it?

"Ferdie! Georgie!" he piped, pressing towards the homely yet loved domicile. "Mother! Aunt Esther!"

No answer. But how could he hope his feeble tones would be heard in such a wild tumult?

"What a flash!" he exclaimed, stopping aghast; "and such a report?" He fairly reeled

with the shock.   Simultaneously with the mighty
crash, a giant tree burst into flame. The red
bolt had smitten it.   In the light of the lurid
glare, he looked to see if the dear cabin was unharmed.

He started as if a second bolt had smitten
him. A wretched loggery, unknown to him,
stood there. He had lost his way. The demonstration almost paralyzed him, so unexpected
and appalling.

" But," thought he, rallying, " how much better off I am than if I had found no dwelling,
and been obliged to spend the night on the bare
prairie !   Besides, no doubt the occupants of
the hovel will in the morning direct me how to
find the right course."

And with rekindled hope, he knocked at the
rude door. Hearing a reply within, the words
of which he did not distinguish, taking it for
granted to be an invitation to enter, he passed
within.

It was one of the wretchedest of structures —
low, half-roofed, every way uncomfortable and
unsightly. The one confined room was furnished with two "wildcat" bedsteads, on which
were ragged and dirty beds, a foreign-looking
trunk, a box, and two stout stools. The shanty
was inhabited by an old Norwegian couple, haggard, thriftless, and filthy — poor specimens of
their people.

The dwarf addressed them a question, but they did not understand his tongue. He tried to inform them by words and signs that he had lost his way, but did not succeed. This was another unanticipated dilemma. Cold, cross, tired, hungry, and baffled, he grew irritated because they could not speak English — ignorant, unaccommodating pair! He attempted conversation once more, and failed. How dull they were! He saw the mote in their eye, just as you and I do in our neighbors', forgetful that the same splinter was in his own — that he couldn't talk in Norwegian, their mother language. Had he been able, the chasm would have been bridged by a syllable.

The wrinkled housewife, however, pointed to the bed opposite the door, to indicate that he could remain till morning. This instantly disarmed the dwarf's foolish resentment, and he was in pantomime endeavoring to express his thanks for her hospitality, when stentorian shouting outside was heard.

The Hunchback opened the door, and there sat a smiling-faced man on a restless, wide-awake horse. From the rider's broad-brimmed hat streams were falling, but his manner was anything but " under the weather."

" O, yes, I am vherry vet," said he, jollily, as the dwarf invited him in, informing him that he would have to fasten his horse to the house, as there was no shed.

The German did as suggested, then, entering the room, drew off his boots, emptied the water from them, wrung out his hose, and hung them on the bedstead to dry.

"Did not know the road," he explained; " but I ride on, and I vas bother, but I tink to myself, my horse has fine instink, and I let him go. Phrarie beautiful — wide — flower — fine grass; phrarie hens fly — so many birds sing, sing, sing, feel as if I could stay dere. I get down to let my horse eat dat fine grass. Vell, it 'muse me vherry mootch, and I forget dat it cloud up, till I feel de rain; and den I say to my horse, ' Now ve hurry,' and I ride, ride. But it get quite dark, an it rain all de time; but de clouds vas so beautiful, vid de lightning, and de thunder roll so grand!

"Den I see de little house : ' Vhery nice people dere,' I say to my horse; but it 'muse me vherry mootch; so I go to sleep," nodding towards the bed, " till daylight, ven I shall have joy to see de sun rise. If de storm not come to make me vet, I vas not see de lightning ! "

So the dwarf and the tempest-admiring traveller went to bed together, and, unheeding the uproar without, and the neighing of the hapless horse, quickly fell asleep.

"Vat ish dat?" inquired the German, starting up.

The dwarf was already aroused.

Water was washing down upon them with a *consistent* copiousness that promised to convert their couch into a mud-hole, for the roof was *shingled* with *sods*.

By the tallow candle, which during their nap had been lighted and stuck in a potato, and placed on the box, the dwarf saw the aged Norwegians sitting side by side on the trunk, holding a huge umbrella over their heads.

Made wise by experience, they had in season forsaken their mud-and-water bed for their novel shelter — an expedient to which they were so accustomed, that their placid " of course " aspect set the Hunchback to laughing.

But the German lifted the door from its hinges, and tying it to the rafters lengthwise over the bed to keep off the rain, turned in again.

The repose of the travellers was, however, destined to another interruption. The waters collecting on the door began at last to drip from its sides, and as it was narrower than the couch beneath, a sudden splashing drove its occupants out, no more to return.

Next morning, as the German was departing, the dwarf begged the privilege of riding with him until they came to some cabin at which to inquire their course.

" It 'muse me vherry mootch, but that rascal horse jump up and kick up behind. No, you goes your vay, I goes mine; you valk. O, yes, phrarie looks better in fine weather!" and he was away.

The Hunchback was deserted, but through no unfriendliness ; and not once had the German, by look or hint, conveyed any allusion to the dwarf's physical appearance. The latter could forgive him almost anything because of that.

The Hunchback sat on the wooden step, endeavoring to decide what to do.

" I will," he finally resolved, "go back as nearly as possible the way I came. Perhaps I can find the village from which I started, and then I shall be all right."

But the ancient woman had boiled her kettle and steeped tea in the open air, several rods from the dwelling. She now brought in the tea-pot, placed three cups and saucers, a plate of corn-bread and of butter, on the box, and beckoned the dwarf to partake. As he concluded his meal, taking a large cake, he inquired by signs if he might have it, to which an affirmative answer was returned; and stowing it in his capacious pocket, he commenced to retrace his steps towards L——.

CHAPTER XX.

THE "CIRCLE" IN THE LODGE. — "WAKAN'."

In this wayward world it is easier to lose the right path than to recover it. Indeed, each subsequent step is apt to lead the wanderer more widely astray. This is true in creed and deed, intellectually, morally.

The dwarf found it true, also, geographically. Theoretically, it was a simple thing for him to preserve a sufficiently straight line from the Norwegian log shanty, and thus return on his own path. And the end would be the grocer's shop at L——. Such was the Hunchback's logic. But the logical conclusion and the practical result do not always tally. "The proof of the pudding is in the eating," and not in the formula. Nor even in the eating, permit us to add, but in the digesting. Please write that on the fly-leaf of your cook-book, madam, and your children, saved from many a cruel colic, shall "rise up and call you blessed."

All that weary day our hero breasted the billowy blossoms of the prairie solitudes. At the onset, his deep, large orbs, clear, penetrating, reflective, were undaunted, for his faith in his course was unwavering. Behind was the sod-thatched roof, in the blue canopy glowed the sun, and the wind steady : with these guide-posts, what cause to fear? The music of the birds resounded in his heart — he was not distrustful of them, — blithe and beautiful though they were, — as he was of his fellows. This toil, though wearing, was for his precious kindred in the home-cabin. To them, too, he was the courier of good news, which he longed to tell.

Alas, that our brightest anticipations are so often illusions! Sad was it for the limp-limbed dwarf to find at last the awful fear haunting him that he was again lost.

Behold how bravely he battles with the horrid misgiving, and with his fearful fate. Level with the waving grass of the upper land, his big head moves slowly forward, as you may see the spent swimmer striking for the dimly-discerned shore. Will he gain it? If not, too well he comprehends the fatal alternative. And the little Hunchback, should he not touch a familiar trail, or meet timely aid, would not the naked prairie, glorious as it was in its living verdure, be as fatal to him as ocean depths to the sinking mariner?

Till evening twilight he was alone on that wide sea of vegetation — walking, resting, hoping,

fearing, despairing, searching the remotest horizon for cabin or traveller. In vain. The west
grew golden. The stars came out. The moon
hung its silver crescent. The night-birds flitted.
The wolves barked. Chilled, faint, and at last
frightened, the dwarf tottered on, or, sitting on
the cold, damp earth, nodded and watched by
turns.

Lost and benighted on the uninhabited prairie,
what utter helplessness and desolateness are in
those words! The forest shuts your gaze in a
narrow circle. You hope that just through yonder vista is the old cart-path, or the well-known
pasture. But the prairie, swept by your sight
from sky to sky, gives ocular evidence that indeed you are lost.

Statisticians say that at about two or three
o'clock in the night more deaths occur than at any
other of the twenty-four hours, the sun has so long
been absent then, and the accumulated chills and
vapors are so powerful in their action on the en-
feebled system.

The blood circulated inadequately in the little
Hunchback's shrunken extremities. His respira-
tion was also weak, as his weak voice betrayed,
and the small vitality he possessed, drawn upon
too exhaustively by the over-mastering brain,
yielded readily to the cold night air. He shiv-
ered as with an ague. And later, neuralgic pains

tortured face, arms, and legs. Glad was he when the beams of day warmed his aching frame.

The Hunchback journeyed that day for the most part in irregular circles, having not the least conception of his whereabouts. Late, however, in the afternoon, he descried trees ahead. Any change was welcome to him after the discouraging sameness of the wild wastes, and with reviving hope he sought to mend his pace.

But a half dozen miles' view on level land, and in a transparent atmosphere, agreeably deceives the eye. The distance " holds out " " Quaker measure," come to walk it — especially if you are already overtired. And evening had far advanced when the wanderer neared the forest. Then, to his consternation, a line of light burst upon his gaze — he was in close proximity to an Indian encampment.

Here was an unforeseen difficulty. To retreat far enough from the place to escape the notice of the keen-eared, sharp-sighted, swift-footed savages, in his used-up condition, was impossible. He had terribly overtasked his powers of endurance, and positively *could* not journey farther. To go forward was capture, and he dared not contemplate what else. What could he do?

Lying in the grass, long he pondered the perplexing question. He had subsisted, since leaving the Norwegians, on the corn-cake his haggish hostess gave him at parting, and he was now half famished. There were a few figs in his pocket, that he had got at the grocer's, and had treasured for his much-loved mother. He ate those. The osiers at the wood's edge betokened the presence of water. Crawling there, he drank great draughts from the gurgling brooklet, and softly bathed his hot and fevered forehead.

Refreshed by the food, and drink, and bath, he could think more collectedly.

"Let me see," he soliloquized. "I can't find my way home, or to the village. That's settled. If I attempt it, I shall die on the prairies, for I should have nothing to eat, nor perhaps a drop of water to quench my thirst. So to go back is death. And the savages can only kill me. But it is better that it be me than Ferdie or Georgie. I'm so ugly-formed, and they are so handsome and strong!"

But the big, sad eyes swam in tears, and he pressed his hand to his jutting brow as if the thought-pain was there.

"Perhaps it will be best not to wait here and let them capture me; it might anger them worse. I will deliver myself into their hands, and appeal to their pity — if they have any," he added, shaking his head negatively. "But I can't do it yet. I'll delay as long as I can; after all, life is sweet even to me, deformed and despised as I am."

And he glanced shudderingly at the ruddy gleam, and the dusky figures moving to and fro.

"Wonder if every Indian is a demon?" he asked himself, weighing his chance of being murdered at a blow, or tortured. And the blood-congealing accounts he had heard and read of the barbarities perpetrated by redmen came trooping to his mind with heightened vividness.

"The Bible declares, however, that God made of one blood all the nations," he recalled. "'*One* blood;' that means, I suppose, that they are naturally alike in the main. If this is so, Indians differ in disposition, like other people." His face brightened at this idea.

But his countenance fell as he added, —

"Yet there are those who denounce the Bible as untrue. If these are correct, then I can't depend on the Indians resembling the whites. They may every one be perfectly fiendish. But whether the Bible is God's book or not," he continued, "I wish these savages went according to its rules. Some state the heathen better not be Christianized; but I guess if such folks were where I am," — and again he shrinkingly surveyed the flaming lights, — "they'd be very willing to have these savages converted.

"Suppose, now, they obeyed the Scriptures; how would I fare among them? There's the commandment, 'Thou shalt not kill.' I wish they'd mind that! 'Thou shalt love thy neighbor as thyself;' they wouldn't burn me if that was in their hearts.   The beatitude also, 'Blessed are the merciful;' wouldn't it be nice if that governed them?   And, too, Christ's words, 'Love your enemies.'   Well, I've no doubt but that they consider the whites their enemies, and no wonder, when their splendid hunting-grounds are taken from them."

How clearly and actively the intellect works in some dire crisis, when its owner crouches at the foot of impending doom!   Thus does reason assert its superiority over nature and brute terror.   The phenomenon is not unusual, and therefore the more instructive.   The soul cannot be trodden into inactivity by material agents.

And there lay the dwarf, despicable externally, puny, panting, physically powerless; but thinking, reasoning, remembering precepts, discussing, in the sanctuary of his own spirit, the mightiest questions, conscious all the while, O, so profoundly, that but a brief moment and his fate was fixed for weal or woe.

But the dwarf's cogitations were instantly arrested, as a mournful human howl floated out from the encampment on the calm evening air. With that sound also the light was suddenly extinguished.   How wild, weird, awful the wailing. Better the cry of the gray wolf than that!

What did it mean? He had read Indian history, and it occurred to him that a barbarous ceremony was being celebrated.

The din would favor his approach; so he cautiously crept along, a thorny thicket relieving him of his cap, which he did not try to recover; for what need had he of it, when so soon to be tomahawked?

The redskins were assembled in a large lodge, from which a smothered light issued through various crevices. In the centre was a smouldering fire, from which the dying smoke arose to find its way out at the cracks.

Should he move still nearer? He could hear his heart thump against his contorted ribs; would some quick-eared savage hear it too? He waited a moment, that the throbbing might lessen.

"Aunt Esther said she'd pray for me," came to memory just then. "Perhaps," he thought, "she's doing so now. God, who made these Indians, can hear prayer, and hold these Indians from harming me, if He sees best;" and strengthened by trust in the Infinite Defender, he crept close to the capacious wigwam.

Frankie, since that memorable first night on the prairie, when the *stars* enlightened him, had been under a controlling persuasion that on him depended important interests connected with the experiment of the family in immigrating.

The loss of his father, too, had thrown on him a sense of responsibility that otherwise he could not have experienced.

When he undertook any difficult duty, like that, for instance, concerning the outlaw Simmons, he uttered a presentiment in affirming as to his aunt, " It's put upon me to do it." This whisper within had sustained him while tracking the trackless prairies ; and now, in the shadow of the savage lodge, he had not entirely lost its inspiration, nor forgotten prayer.

The dwarf peeped through a crevice at the strange scene. The lodge was packed with savages of all ages and both sexes, sitting cross-legged in a variety of attitudes and postures, each with a blanket drawn over the head, singing in unison in a low key, the dirge-like notes rising and falling in guttural monotony.

" They are mourning for their dead," he concluded ; " now is my opportunity. Better discover myself to them when thus engaged than when their revengeful feelings are stirred. And after mentally preparing a short speech declarative of friendliness, and claiming their protection, he passed into the wigwam. His ingress was not at once perceived, such was the din, and so absorbed the performers. But when it was, the issue was as remarkable as unexpected. With a terrified yell the nearest copper-face scrambled from the lodge, his companions, men, women, and children, tumbling after.

If, as the dwarf had conjectured, he had stumbled upon an Indian powwow, and by the dismal ceremony the soul of a dead brave was being wafted across the dark waters into the Indian's Paradise, what the influence the dwarf's entrance must have been on said spirit, I can scarcely trust myself to contemplate. With what an inglorious flop the defunct warrior must have dropped earthward when the survivors dropped their vocal discordances! And as the powwow was not resumed, of course the tawny deceased did not go to hunt the brown deer, with silver bow and arrows like darts of summer lightning, in the blue forests of the happy hunting-ground.

But the dwarf was not wholly right in his conjecture concerning the nature of their convocation. They were not singing a dead brave into the Indian Paradise, but were invoking the spirits of the departed. The Dakotas are *spiritualists* — as we call those among us of the same faith and practice.

One of their sacred performances is the noted jugglery of rope-tying. A lodge is cleared of everything in it, and one of their copper-colored " mediums " produces ropes and thongs, requesting some of the stronger savages to tie him tightly. This is usually done by disinterested parties, who state that they have tied the arms, elbows, and feet so tightly as to break the skin, and then bound the feet and hands together, and wound up the whole body in knots and twists of the most formidable kind. The person thus secured is left in the empty lodge by himself, and the door secured from without. No one is allowed to touch or go near the lodge, and the Indian, thus bound, remains alone singing for a few minutes, when he cries out, the door is opened, and he walks forth free.

These Indians also believe that some possess the power to call up and converse with departed spirits. They often make feasts to the spirits, and seek from them information concerning deceased relatives and acquaintances. They assemble in the lodge, smoke, put out the fire, wrap their heads in their blankets, and sing, till the spirits make for them a picture ; and many queer tales are told by them of the occurrences at their " sittings."

The cause of the abrupt ending of the savage " circle " the dwarf partly divined. The painted barbarians were dealing, as they believed, with the dead, and his coming into such a ceremony had created a superstitious panic — something as if when you, imaginative reader, were consulting Planchette, a veritable ghost should glide into the parlor.

"They are afraid I'm a 'spiritual manifesta-
tion,'" thought the dwarf; and he resolved to
favor the error.

Altogether, their mistake was not so singular,
when the circumstances are considered.

"Ignorance" is *not* "the mother of devotion,"
but delusion. The sleight-of-hand tricks of dex-
terous impostors easily impose on the untaught
and the credulous, and natural phenomena are
readily construed to be the works of supernatural
agents.

Now, the great object of Dakota worship is the
TA'-KOO WAKAN', the *supernatural*, the *mysterious*. This *wakan'* includes all mystery, secret
power, divinity. And to the untutored savage
all around is to him *wakan'*. Without the illu-
minations of revelation and science, he under-
stands little. Forests, streams, lakes, springs,
prairies, hills, rain, thunder, lightning, sickness,
life, death, are to him, in all respects, awful mysteries. Sun, moon, and stars are gods and god-
desses. Multitudes of questions arise in his dark
mind, simple to us, to him unanswerable; and
with his hand on his mouth, he exclaims with
awe, "*Wakan'! A-tay, on'-she-ma-da!*" *Mystery! Father, have mercy upon me!*

To his apprehensions, heaven and earth are
peopled with invisible demons, monsters of hate
and evil, to propitiate whom he waves his pipe,

tortures his flesh, offers sacrifices, and by silly and horrid rites invokes. *Wakan'* — mystery, dead, slavish, whimsical, unearthly mystery, wraps him in fear from childhood to death.

Probably these Indians had never seen a hunchback till the dwarf disturbed their devotions. And — we will not disguise it — he was a *lusus naturæ*, though I doubt if the Dakotas understand what that means. His prodigious chest and back, baby legs, thin, dangling arms, large, long face, cadaverous, and — by reason of years of gloom, dejection, and ill temper affecting the liver — biliously yellow, a deeper shade being laid on by prairie exposures, his immense head out of all harmony with his height, surmounted by the wonderful *ridge* of coarse hair, which, when he was angered or deeply excited, seemed to stand more stiffly — picture such an apparition stealing in on a group of *wild* savages, in their own haunts, far from civilized neighbors, while engaged at their midnight orgies, connected with ghostly and demon consultations. And not the most alert of the assembled copper-faces had seen a trail or heard a footfall. Moreover, their unearthly-shaped visitor called voluntarily. He was not dragged there a protesting prisoner. He came unarmed. His expression grave, resolute, intelligent, his eyes large, spiritual, piercing — looking as if able to read their inmost thoughts.

How perfectly his advent, looks, bearing, time of his ingress, chimed in with their superstitions and the character of their ceremonies. Ah, he was *wakan'*!

The curiosity of the copper-faces, however, brought them back again -- peeping through the cracks, crawling cautiously a few paces into the lodge, grunting, calling out, yelling, drawing nearer and nearer.

In vain did the discreet dwarf preserve a majestic silence, and glance ineffable things. His power rapidly waned. He went heavenward as a rocket, in their estimation, and he came down like a stick. Morning found them wholly undeceived — he *was* flesh and blood, for they had pinched him. So do ghostly mysteries fade before a matter-of-fact handling.

His make-up, however, amused them exceedingly. And his voice contributed no little to the entertainment. To this mood, even when degenerating to ridicule, the dwarf was, for a wonder, submissive; for, he reasoned, while I make fun for them, they will not be likely to scalp me.

A savage might be seen "on all fours" squealing like a pig, to imitate his voice; another, rolling himself into a heap, would act the hedgehog, to caricature his bristles; a third squat like a tortoise, to take off his hunched back.

"Hands off!" the dwarf would pipe, when his hair was pulled.

"Look out, I tell you," as an Indian boy tried to trip him.

"Take care, there," as a squaw stuck a thorn in his arm.

His thin tones and puerile strength, contrasted with his ominous scowls and commanding head, excited roars of laughter.

But harmless mirth was fast changing to offensive and dangerous treatment. A tomahawk thrown at his head was narrowly dodged, and the Hunchback, beset by the clamorous crowd, saw that his risks were fearfully increasing, when from a fine large tent there looked forth a beautiful Indian girl; and instantly after an aged chief came to him, and dispersing the savages, led him to his wigwam.

The dwarf, overcome by the unexpected interposition, would have fallen at the feet of the chief's daughter, and poured forth his gratitude, and begged her to complete the kindness by sending him to the white settlements; but she appeared now scarcely aware of his presence, and her silence compelled his.

CHAPTER XXI.

AUNT ESTHER'S TROUBLE. — THE LAMP IN THE WINDOW.

AUNT ESTHER was troubled. Evening was falling, and the dwarf had not returned. A score of times had she peered anxiously from the cabin window, a score of times donned sun-bonnet with assumed carelessness, and repaired to the gentle eminence beyond the stable, and shading her eyes with her neat hand, scanned the landscape.

She had hoped he would not have so far to go but that he would be back by dark, at the farthest. She blamed herself bitterly for consenting to so ventursome a project. What if Simmons should chance to detect the pursuit, or the dwarf fall sick, or be torn by prowling beasts, or get lost! The last thought sent a deathly pallor to her cheeks.

And now the family were wondering at his absence. How would they regard her when it transpired that she was secretly a party to it?

A clandestine enterprise, even when entirely

defensible, indeed praiseworthy, if it lacks success, is apt to react against those concerned in it. That aunt Esther's motives were every way what they should be, in fitting off the dwarf, is entirely apparent; but would Mrs. Willard appreciate them? — especially if the dwarf met with misfortune in his singular and hazardous undertaking? And a woman will rarely excuse it if not counted in, in a secret where her husband or children are involved.

True, it was necessary — or appeared so — that the confiding Mrs. Willard should remain ignorant of the proceedings against Mr. Simmons; for, if she were informed, she would most certainly inform him — and what then? A knave would have them at his fingers' ends. Nevertheless, Mrs. Willard could not see this, for she trusted Mr. Simmons. What defence, then, could poor aunt Esther offer, should the lad miscarry in his schemes?

"Where can Frankie be!" the mother repeated.

The exclamation set aunt Esther trembling.

Supper was eaten, the dishes washed, — save the absent one's unsoiled plate and cup, — the candle lighted, and no Frankie.

Aunt Esther, unable to bear the tumult in her own breast, walked about on the moon-lit grass, longing, O, so much, that the distorted, though ever dear form of the Hunchback would appear, and she be spared the pain of telling his mother the cause of his tarrying.

But there was no alternative, and ever resolute in duty, she went in, and laying her hand in her sister's, she said, —

"I must tell you all. Frankie, I fear, will not be here to-night — he mentioned that he *might* not when he went away."

"Went away!" repeated Mrs. Willard, dropping the sock she was darning. "Went away! Where?"

She related all the circumstances.

"You and Frankie are both crazy!" exclaimed the mother, deeply agitated. "That poor, weak, wee thing following a person of Mr. Simmons's strength across the pathless prairies! You've lost your wits, Esther! And keeping it hidden from his mother, too! It's wicked for a child not to confide in its mother. He had no right to leave, and not let me know it. You have encouraged him to deceive the best friend and the safest counsellor he has in the world; and what will come of it God alone can foresee. How could you be so foolish and cruel, Esther?"

Esther sobbed as the mother wept.

What could she say? She intended it nobly, heroically, at serious cost to her own affections. She deemed it a resistless necessity. But now that Frankie did not return, and while witnessing

the parent's grief, and listening to her arguments
and accusations, so sharp-edged, touching, and
vehement, she forgot the real reasons for her part-
nership in the affair, and came to view herself as
heartless, weak, and sinful in the extreme.

Besides, she was instinctively aware that this
new sorrow had unsealed anew that other; and
that the bereaved wife and mother now mourned
a double loss.

Mrs. Willard arose, lighted a second candle,
and placed it in the window; and that night aunt
Esther saw her frequently rise and trim it, that
the blaze might be steady and strong. And
each succeeding night the flame of that friendly
lamp, kept bright by the vigilant watcher, shone
out on the velvet grass, and gleamed far over the
unbeaten waste.

"He may come home, belated," said she.

When Frankie had been gone four days, there
was, one evening, a welcome arrival at the Willard cabin. A clerical-looking gentleman rode
up, and introduced himself as Mr. Parsons, the
missionary at L——. He apologized for calling
at that hour, by mentioning that young Jones had
informed him about the family, and desired that
their whereabouts might be ascertained; but he
had had some difficulty in finding them. Besides,
he said, he had a little errand to do for Mr.
Cowles, on behalf of a Mr. Swallow.

"It appears," explained the missionary, "that the latter had a horse stolen from him, and our storekeeper, having reasons to suspect that the missing animal is about your premises, has commissioned me, if I find the beast, to take him along with me."

Then drawing Mr. Swallow's advertisement from his pocket, he read it aloud.

"Why," cried Georgie, in amazement, "Mr. Simmons's horse is exactly like that!"

Ferdie ran to the stable, and with marvellous quickness rode the horse to the door, and the Willards, with their reverend caller, carefully compared the animal with the printed description. The clergyman was satisfied that it was the stolen horse.

"What is your opinion, ladies? and yours, my lads?"

"It must be the one," gasped astonished Mrs. Willard.

"It is, and no mistake," echoed the brothers.

"Mr. Swallow has authorized Mr. Cowles to pay the person recovering the animal," observed the minister, "the amount offered as reward. The money is in my charge. Where is the lad who brought the information to Mr. Cowles?"

"Do you mean Frankie?" eagerly asked aunt Esther.

"He was somewhat deformed, the grocer said, but he did'nt learn his name."

"It is — it is Frankie; can you tell me, sir, where he is?" cried the mother.

"Is he not here?" counting the bills into Mrs. Willard's hand. "He left our village next day, promising to bring the horse on Thursday. And as he did not come, and Mr. Swallow was in a hurry to reclaim the animal, I hunted you up, as you perceive."

"Then Frankie has perished on the prairies," exclaimed the mother, sinking into a seat, faint and trembling.

"My good woman," gently exhorted the minister, "do not too hastily abandon hope. Persons frequently go astray on the prairies, and long afterwards return alive and well. Some out-of-the-way cabin may have given shelter to your boy. I will rouse the settlers, and diligent search shall be instituted.

"And now, if you can stow me away in a corner — no matter where — till morning, I will not try to go home in the darkness."

Mr. Parsons's visit was timely and comforting.

"I cannot infer," said he to Mrs. Willard, "that your Frankie is hopelessly lost. It was an eminently worthy and courageous deed that he left you to accomplish, and I have lived long enough to know that a kind Providence is intimately concerned in the interests of such heroic and self-denying persons. And his bodily infirmity would serve to attract to him the special care of God. How is it with yourself, madam? Is your *afflicted* son less dear than the two well-formed boys before me? Do not the weakness and deformity of the other elicit from you a peculiar tenderness? And is Frankie's heavenly Parent less loving and considerate than you?"

"Frankie was very brave and disinterested in undertaking such an enterprise," observed aunt Esther.

"Nobly so," answered the minister, "and that fact gives me a pleasing assurance of his ultimate success. When the young engage in such services, they usually come out splendidly."

"Did you do such things when you were a boy?" asked Georgie.

"I did not live on the prairie then," he smilingly replied, "and therefore had no occasion, like your brother, to chase a scoundrel across one. I dwelt in a crowded city, and had no call to such a peculiar mission."

At this point, Mrs. Willard handed a Bible to her visitor, and reading a cheerful Psalm of trust, he knelt down, and fervently prayed for the little household, not forgetting the two mysteriously missing members. His words were like "apples of gold in pictures of silver" to the afflicted household, and as Mrs. Willard bade him good night, her radiant face reflected her inward peace.

CHAPTER XXII.

AN INDIAN LOVER. — THE MAGIC MOCCASONS.

IF the dwarf wondered, at first, why the Indian maiden persuaded her father to deliver him from the savage rabble, a week's tarrying in the chief's wigwam did not solve the problem. The tawny miss was far from being as amiable as her interposition might lead him to expect. She certainly did not interfere to save him because of his personal beauty, for now that he was sheltered by the same tent, from her invincible stolidity of countenance he would suppose she was totally unaware of his presence, except when she ordered him to some menial service. Then her broken English was short, harsh, and domineering.

" White boy, bring water ! "

" Pale-face, get wood ! "

It grated on the Hunchback's self-respect to be thus addressed by the feminine Sioux, but " hard words break no bones " he remembered, while tomahawks crushed the skull ; and how speedily that blood-shedding hatchet would cleave his cranium, should he rebel, he could easily calculate. Over-sensitiveness to the remarks of others, leading to a morbid irritability of temper, was the dwarf's "besetting sin." He was taking lessons in self-control, now, with a Dakotah girl for his teacher. But we all have to submit to the pruning-knife sooner or later.

"She wanted me for her slave," the meditative prisoner concluded; "that's why she didn't let the savages kill me."

It puzzled him, however, that while she ordered him about insultingly, his tasks were not more burdensome.

But one thing amused him. One afternoon a young brave stalked into the chief's tent, and casting down a freshly-shot deer, went grave-faced away. His coming was so frequent and peculiar, that the observant captive saw that an Indian courtship was in progress. The tawny maiden, however, deigned not to notice her suitor; evidently he was not in favor with her; but her unrelenting coldness only added fuel to his ardor, and for hours he would lie on the grass chanting, in minor key, his love-song, promising her abundance of game to eat — the highest good of the hunter's life.

> "Cling fast to me, and you'll ever have a plenty,
> Cling fast to me, and you'll ever have a plenty,
> Cling fast to me."

Heartless heathen! how often she heard this ditty, droned over and over again, as if she heard not; even though accompanied by the *cho'-tan-ka*, or flute, made of sumac, in the best style of savage art, decorated with ribbon streamers, yellow and red paint, the carved likeness of a horse, and a brass thimble for a mouth-piece.

Some evenings after the dwarf's discovery of this affair, as the undiscouraged red-skin was pouring forth his unrequited passion, the Hunchback was ordered to the spring. It struck him that the maiden had a double purpose in despatching him among the bushes. So, concealed by the shrubbery, he stopped to look back, and he saw the tawny beauty glide from out the door, and chant a brief response to the pleading lover, who instantly stood at her side.

"Had she changed her mind, and was now confessing it!" thought the dwarf.

A moment more and fear superseded curiosity. She had been unusually tyrannical through the day, and now her conversation seemed to be concerning him, for she pointed in his direction. Was she devoting him to the knife of the warrior? But the latter disappeared in the darkness, and the thankful dwarf returned to the wigwam.

Next day the dwarf endured much from the tongue of the Indian girl. All the epithets ex-

pressive of the hatred of her race towards the
pale-faces descended on his head. What a prospect, should his captor's dislike continue to in-
crease! Worn with sad forebodings, that night
he fell into a dreamful slumber, from which he
was awakened by a gentle touch. The chief's
daughter, bending over him, made signs for him
to be silent, and led him to the forest. Then
handing him a pair of moccasons for his feet, she
said, —

"Indian girl send pale-face home. Pale-face
no lose moccasons — *understand?* When he get
to his people, pale-face look in moccason; no
forget?" She spoke low and impressively, and
before he could utter a syllable, glided towards
the chief's tent.

The round yellow moon hung above the trees.
By its shimmering beams he saw a dusky form.
It was the Indian beau, who silently started off,
followed by the astonished dwarf. Travelling
slowly, they came to a small stream. Pushing a
canoe from the bushes that lined the bank, the
savage motioned him to lie down in it, and then
paddled swiftly away. The succeeding forenoon, after threading the woods on the opposite
shore, they struck an Indian trail. Pointing to
it, his guide said, —

"Go in that; don't leave; find white cabin,"
and left him.

Freedom, how sweet to all! Home, however homely, how dear!

Did you ever trace an Indian trail, worn by the feet of the Indian pony? The narrow path, clear cut, goes straight to its destination — you cannot well miss it. Observed you what choice spots it led to, just where a tent should be pitched, or a cabin stand? And thus it comes about that the white man, pluming himself on his superior judgment in selecting so eligible a site for his wilderness home, finds, after all, that he has chosen second-hand; the uncultivated child of nature kindled his wigwam fire just there.

No danger that on this journey the little Hunchback would go astray, for he trod a well-defined path, conducting him by the sweetest springs to the lands of the settlers. That night he slept in the rude shanty of a pioneer, and by twelve the day succeeding, — still retaining the trail, — reached a cultivated field in the alluvial river-bottom. Climbing the rail-fence, and crossing the enclosed lot, he struck the trail again.

It ran parallel with a lessening creek tributary to a river, near which he saw a log house, and, higher up on the bank, a neat cottage in process of erection. The cabin door was open. At the opposite extremity of the room stood a woman before a small looking-glass, arranging her toilet, her wealth of glossy-black hair hanging to her waist.

"Madam," said he, entering, in his eagerness, without knocking, "can you tell me —"

Not waiting to hear his question, she dashed past him, screaming, —

"Husband! husband! the Hunchback's here!"

At which an athletic, pleasant-faced man rushed in, and seeing the dwarf, vociferated, —

"Why, where did you rain from? Where've you been? The whole country has been scoured to find you. There's a gathering to-day at the missionary's, to decide what else to do about it. I must carry you right there."

And putting his head out· of the door, he shouted, —

"William! the Hunchback's come. Clap the horse into the buggy quick as you can. I'll help you;" and hurrying out, the two hustled the horse into harness, and the dwarf was whirling towards the minister's.

"How far is it?" inquired the Hunchback.

"Only a short piece — you must have crossed the parson's ten-acre lot in getting to my cabin."

"What are they doing at the missionary's?"

"Why, Tom Jones — we call him Tom, 'cause he was brought up about here, as you may say — is there. The settlers had about given over the hunt for you; but Tom has brought with him an Indian, — a great friend to the Joneses, — and they set this afternoon to state where each one had searched, and then the Indian — he's a hound on a scent — is to try. But here's the house."

And hitching his horse among the trees, out of sight of the cabin, saying, with a humorous twinkle in his honest dark eye, "We must be careful not to scare the folks — you just wait outside a minute," he entered the dwelling without ceremony, and in an unnecessarily loud voice said, —

"Tom, there's a gentleman at the door that wants to speak to you."

The surprise of Tom when he saw who was there, and the joy of the company, cannot be described. They made the air resound with their lusty cheers, and the firing of their guns gave notice to the settlers around of the gladsome event, bringing even the women and children to see and hear for themselves. And the dwarf, overwhelmed with gratulations, learned that even a dwarf need not be despised.

The Indian, however, retained, amid the universal rejoicing, the immobility of feature characteristic of his race. But for his bright, gleaming eye, you would pronounce him immovably indifferent. When the excitement had measurably died away, pointing to the Hunchback's feet, he said to Tom, in low, earnest tones, —

"What for white boy wear moccason?"

Tom saw that Long Hair detected something

significant in his discovery, and he quietly beckoned the dwarf and the Indian into the missionary's attic study.

"Long Hair thinks it strange that you wear moccasons," remarked Tom, when they were by themselves; "how does it happen?"

"The Indian girl gave them to me!"

"No; Indian pappoose no give pale-face moccason," contradicted Long Hair.

"He means," interpreted Tom, "that it would be unlike an Indian to do so."

"But she did," warmly asserted the Hunchback.

"Long Hair want see moccason," said the Indian.

"He wishes you to take them off, that he may examine them," explained Tom.

The dwarf complied, passing each in turn to the Indian.

"What dat?" he asked, secretly calling Tom's attention to an object smoothly secured within one of them.

The inspection sent the blood with magical suddenness into Tom's face, and moved him so deeply that the dwarf was alarmed.

"What is the matter?" he inquired, anxiously.

Tom did not reply, but after whispering aside to Long Hair, asked, —

"How long were you in the canoe?"

"All night," answered the Hunchback.

" Did you go up or down stream? "

"Down."

"And kept the trail all the way? "

"Yes."

"Good," grunted the Indian. " Long Hair know ! "

CHAPTER XXIII.

FOREBODINGS. — SHINGLING THE CABIN.

"MOTHER, you'll have to see to those boys," said the dwarf, querulously. "They wouldn't accomplish anything if I didn't drive them to it."

"He's fine at bossing," retorted Ferdie, "and that's about all he is good for. Georgie and I work from morning till night. We don't sit round directing other folks — do we, Georgie?"

"But Frankie likes that. Wonder if he intends to follow it for a business," chimed in Georgie.

"Now, there's the roof needs shingling; and the stove must be moved into the house. The weather is growing cool, and winter'll be here before we are half ready for it," continued the Hunchback, unheeding their taunts.

"There isn't much winter in this climate," affirmed Ferdie, "and we have plenty of time to prepare for it."

"Where'd you get your information?" sharply questioned the Hunchback.

"All the settlers say so."

"But they are new comers, like ourselves. Mother, look here;" and the dwarf took down a school atlas, and pointing with his immature finger, said, "You see we are in the same latitude as Burlington, Vermont, where the winter is very severe."

"It's warmer west than east," urged Ferdie.

"Well," replied the Hunchback, "you can risk it if you wish, but you'll be sorry for it when everything freezes up. Mother, hadn't these youngsters better get ready in season?"

"Youngsters! Wonder what you nickname yourself — *oldster*? ' returned Ferdie. "One would think, to hear you talk, that you were Methuselah, and I your youngest great-great-great-grandson, and that Georgie and I were too lazy to pick our teeth after dinner, while you was a miracle of industry, by whom the whole labor of the country is performed."

"Hush, Ferdinand," gently interposed the mother. "Frankie is worrying lest we shall not be comfortable. He is not fitted for hard work. And I agree with him that it is wiser to be early ready for winter than to trust to having a mild season; and as there's only you two to depend upon, it is the more necessary to take time by the forelock, as the old saying is."

"I'd like to see the shingles, before I'm required to nail them on," said Georgie.

"We shall have to buy them," answered the dwarf.

"How far is it to the lumber-dealer's?" asked Georgie, donning his cap with a comical grimace, and starting for the door.

"A Mr. Gregory, near L——, has them. He makes them by hand, and, as it is a slow process, it will be necessary to go over and engage them ahead. If you and Ferdie will put the horses in the wagon, I'll ride there with you."

In front of a wretched loggery, open to wind and rain, sat the settler, a stump of a black pipe in his mouth, leisurely manufacturing shingles. An oak tree, straight-grained as can be had, is selected, cut down, and with "cross-cut" sawed into segments shingle length. The huge blocks are then split into smaller ones, and these in turn into thin parts, with a heavy steel instrument cleaver-shaped. This last operation is termed "riving out."

The dwarf inquired the price of the rough oaken shingles, and when he could have some.

"When mought you be wantin' on 'em?" inquired the man.

"Soon as possible," answered the dwarf.

"Isn't your ruff kivered?" asked the manufacturer.

"Only boarded," said the Hunchback.

"No pertick'ler hurry, then, youngster, if it's boarded, as you say."

"We want them in two weeks, without fail," returned the dwarf.

"Well, jist ride over. Perhaps I ken 'comadate you to enough to begin on."

"Why don't you tighten and shingle your own house?" asked Georgie, gazing at the leaky structure.

"No need on't sich weather as this."

"But how do you manage when it storms?"

"Couldn't 'tend to it when it rains, no way you ken fix it."

So the easy frontiersman did not repair his shanty in pleasant weather, because then it was not necessary, and in foul he preferred not to work in the wet.

"What do you use in your cabin — fireplace or stove?" he asked.

"Stove," promptly answered Georgie.

"Mebbe you don't want to trade for some funnel? Got some to spare."

"Old woman!" he bawled, entering the loggery and climbing into the partly-floored attic; "here, take this as I pass it."

The wife extended her arms as directed, and a shower of ashes and soot saluted her head.

"Wall, if that wan't a miss-go!" exclaimed the husband. "Brush it off, Roxanna!"

Georgie giggled outright as she rubbed her blackened face with her wet, greasy apron.

"My wife don't look like a beauty just now," remarked her lord, "but I've seen the time when she'd dance the cow-tillion with the best on 'em."

"What are these four lengths worth?" inquired the dwarf.

"They might be wuth more, and they might be wuth less. Give us fifty cents, and we'll consider it a bargain."

"Put them in the wagon, Georgie," said the Hunchback, handing the man the money.

"An' now, youngster, seein' you're flush, 'spose you take a turn round the cabin, an' see if there's anything there wuth dickerin' for."

The dwarf smiled; for piled against the building were a number of bundles of shingles.

"Them's engaged, but the man hasn't come for 'em accordin' to agreement. Told him he'd have to be on hand to the minute. They are yours if you've got the cash; if not, the next person that has gits 'em, whomsomedever he be."

"I'll take them," replied the Hunchback; and the seller, tossing them on his brawny shoulders, piled them in the wagon, and the lads left.

"But what is the matter?" suddenly asked Georgie; "you look dreadful sick."

"Not much," answered the dwarf, his contracted brow, pallid cheeks, and feeble utterance refuting his words.

"Yes, there is, too!"

"Please stop the team, and let me rest a moment," said the Hunchback; "the motion hurts so."

Georgie checked the horses, and, alarmed, watched Frankie, who, moaning, curled himself down on the leathern cushion.

"Georgie," said he at last, fixing his deep, sad gaze on his brother's frightened face, and articulating with difficulty, "promise me you won't tell mother of this."

"Why, she ought to know if you're sick, so that she may get you well."

"No, Georgie; it would worry her; and you know how she grieves now. It isn't anything she can help."

"But where do you feel badly?"

"You will not mention it to her?"

"No," was the hesitating answer.

"Nor to Ferdie or aunt Esther?"

"No."

"It's all up and down my back. It seems, sometimes, as if I should screech right out, every bone in my spine is so hot and raw. And here," placing his brother's hand against the "false" or "short" ribs, "it hurts me there when I breathe. My stomach, too, is awful weak."

"You ought not to come over here, to-day," said Georgie, his eyes blinded by tears.

"Yes, I had, Georgie. Perhaps I shan't live

long, and the house must be made comfortable
for mother — she isn't used to roughing it.   And
now you and Ferdie will shingle it right away —
won't you?   I'd help, but I can't.   I'm only trying to keep along till father comes."

"Father," cried Georgie; "do you expect to see
him again?"

"Yes," returned the dwarf, "I *feel* that I shall
some time — perhaps, though, it will be when I
die," he softly added.

"Frankie," cried Georgie, dropping the rein
and clasping him around the neck, "*don't* talk
so!   I can't have you die, you're so good, and I
love you so dearly!" and the impulsive boy
sobbed aloud.

"I am better now," said the dwarf; and a sadly-
satisfied light played over his features.   "But
look, the lines are dragging under the horses'
heels.   Pick them up very carefully, Georgie, so
as not to set the span running.

"Wait! I'll get them," he added, as he saw that
Georgie's impetuosity was disturbing the animals;
and, leaning cautiously over the whippletrees
with the whipstock, he gently raised the rein
and deposited it in Georgie's hand, the latter saying, enthusiastically, —

"You can do anything, Frankie!"

"It's because I stop to think," answered the
dwarf.

The day following being fair, Ferdie and Georgie commenced work on the roof.

Georgie, under the stimulus of his recent conversation with Frankie, was foremost in the enterprise, and had a half row of shingles nailed next to the ridge-pole, when Ferdie shouted, —

"What you doing there, chick? You've got the cart before the horse. In shingling, they always lay the lower tier first, and lap the next upon it, and so on till the top is reached."

"That's too bad!" ejaculated the disappointed young house-carpenter, scrambling to the ground.

Ferdie, producing a ball of cord and a piece of chalk, telling Georgie to hold an end of the twine, rubbed the chalk back and forth upon it. Then, tacking a nail to one end of the roof, near the edge, he tied the twine to the nail, and stationing Georgie at the opposite side with his end of the line, the same number of inches from the edge, with his finger and thumb he quickly pulled upon the line and let it go again; and Georgie saw that it left a perfectly straight white mark all the way across.

"We must lay the shingles by this mark," explained Ferdie, "that we may put them on evenly."

"How fast our carpenters get along!" remarked the mother, stepping out to view their progress. "Don't fall, Georgie."

"No danger of that," he proudly replied; and the hammers of the lads vied with each other, sinking the nails into the tough wood.

Meanwhile the dwarf had managed to cut a circular hole in a square piece of sheet iron, and directing Ferdie where to make a similar aperture in the roof-board, the iron collar was fastened over it, to be subsequently covered by the shingles.

"That will prevent the stove-pipe from getting in contact with the wood, and setting the cabin on fire," said the dwarf.

A fireboard also having been constructed, with which to close the fireplace, and thus prevent the air from drawing down the wide-mouthed chimney into the room, Ferdie and Georgie, with the assistance of the women, moved the Great Western stove into the dwelling, and the funnel Frankie bought was fitted together, and run up through the roof.

"Now," said the dwarf, "the fire will also warm the attic next winter."

But the Hunchback, Georgie saw, constantly suffered; and the latter often checked his boyish mirth, or ceased his blithe whistling, to marvel at and grieve over his drooping, deformed uncomplaining brother.

CHAPTER XXIV.

THE SILENT BOATMEN.

"YEES'LL niver find him there. My Dennis isn't drowned at all, at all. I wouldn't belave it if ye saw him fall into the strame wid yer own eyes. Sure an' he'll turn up safe an' sound, an' put yees all to shame for misdoubting me."

And the young wife turned away from the silent boatmen, as they continued dragging the river for the body.

They were common Irish laborers. Who would have thought that those coarse, brawny men would be so tender of her feelings as to make no reply to her assertions of her husband's safety. And yet so certain were they of his fate, that, leaving their work, they had searched the waters far and near for long, weary hours, and intended to continue at their sad task till the corpse was found.

The missing young Irishman had formerly been a workman in an establishment near by. Driven by poverty from the old country, he had come to these favored shores to find work. He had made his way to the hospitable west. Dun-leith, rising so beautifully from the Mississippi, caught his eye.

He had a good share of natural shrewdness, and he foresaw that the place would grow, and he decided to seek work in the rising town. Two years of regular employment passed, enabling him to take a trip into Minnesota, and buy a quarter section of fertile land on the line of im-migration, fencing it, and building a neat cabin, by the avails of his earnings as stage-driver from —— Landing, on the Mississippi, inland. Then he sent to "ould Ireland" for "the wife and the babe." With what an anxious, longing heart he looked for their arrival! and when at last he clasped them in his arms, his cup of happiness seemed to overflow. He was an intelligent, warm-hearted man, and had been taught that it was "no harm to take jist a drop now and thin." The family reunion could not, of course, pass uncelebrated, and what with joy and excitement of the event, and a growing love of the fiery liquid, he was led to drink more than his wont.

"It is all the wakeness Dennis has, sure," said his wife, as with heavy heart and many tears she begged the one who sold him his drams not to let him have any more, at least "till he's him-self again." But how could the rum-seller continue his traffic if he heeded the sorrows of the heart-broken?

That very night the young husband, walking with pale face and unsteady step along the river brink, staggered in, and was swept away by the current.

Have you ever been at Dunleith? Then you know how romantically it stretches along under the limestone bluffs, and how luxuriantly in summer the grape vines clamber over the warm, bare face of the rocks. Two weeks after the disappearance of Dennis O'Brien, mine host of —— Hotel was conducting Mr. Parsons, the missionary, over the place, plucking the luscious natural plums from the garden, loading him with rich, ripe clusters from the graperies, introducing him to various objects of interest, embarrassing his retiring modesty with blandest attentions, from respect, I fear, not so much to the clergyman as to the column he chanced to fill in a Boston weekly — another illustration of the power of the press, you see.

But no genuine tavern-keeper is a fool. He knows men. He talks with all sorts of folks, and hears from year's end to year's end discussions on every known topic. And there is no subject from tea to theology on which he may not say something apt.

"The Catholics are very strong here," said he

to Mr. Parsons, " and there is a church of theirs that you would like to visit. You will find in it some quaint old pictures from the masters."

" Will the edifice be open this week-day?." asked the minister.

" Certainly : a Catholic church is rarely closed. And I tell you there are some things about the Catholic system that you Protestants, if you were wise, would imitate. Let me see," he added, giving him a careless but penetrating scrutiny, " you are a clergyman — are you not? "

" You have guessed correctly," said his guest, smiling.

" So I supposed. Now, isn't it said in Scripture, ' My house shall be called a house of *prayer?* ' and he emphasized the last word; " but do not the sects use the meeting-house more for preaching than devotion? Why, I have often heard ministers and church members style the invocation, singing, Bible-reading, and prayers, ' the *preliminary exercises.*' Even public prayers — how like orations! so that the people say, ' Wasn't that a fine prayer?' ' What an *able* prayer!' ' How eloquently Rev. Dr. Blank *addressed* the throne of grace!'

" But the Romanists go to church to *worship ;* and the cathedral doors stand open all the week for devotional purposes; while with us, once in seven days the church-going bell invites us to the sanctuary, where the attendants are treated to great sermons, learned essays, sensational subjects, elocution, rhetoric, eloquence.

"Besides," he continued, "the poor and the rich are on an equality in the Papal church. The ill clad and the well clad sit and kneel side by side. But Protestantism is shutting out the masses by high-priced pews and fashions, making religious show mock the woes of the lowly. But I must leave you now. Good by."

And the missionary entered the Romanist church alone.

The "dim religious light," the silence that might be felt, the kneeling men and women scattered among the pews, the pictures of saints and representatives of the passion of Jesus, the gliding in and out of ecclesiastics, and in a niche the "confessional box," spoke voicelessly of things unseen and ghostly.

Returning to the open air, as the clergyman was going musingly through a street inhabited mostly by foreigners, a crowd, gathered before a door, led him to ask what had happened.

"Dennis O'Brien is found, sir," said an Irish woman, with eyes red from weeping. "His body's jist brought in from the river, sir, swollen an' soaked so yees would hardly know it."

The deceased had temporarily occupied rooms in the second story, and through the open win-

dow came a wild wailing.   It was the voice ₵ f
his widow, who "refused to be comforted."   And
alas ! what a sorrow was hers, so soon and suddenly after her lonely, stormy ocean voyage, and
the long-wished-for meeting with the companion
of her youth, to be torn from him in so awful a
manner !

The priest's carriage, with its elegant span and
equipage, stood by ; so the clergyman knew that
he was there to administer the last rites of his
church.

"But what comfort," thought the Protestant,
" has the priest to offer the stricken woman? or,
indeed, any of the bereaved among his trusting
followers, when, according to his teachings, the
flames of purgatory wait to seize the saintliest of
his flock at death."   As he pondered this perver-
sion of the " glad tidings of great joy," and there
came thronging to mind the sweet words of con-
solation for the afflicted with which the Bible is
freighted, how he longed to break the darkness
that brooded over the benighted minds before
him !

"And O," he exclaimed, " the cruel horrors
and tragedies of the rum-traffic !   When will its
days be numbered?   When will the deluded immigrant cease to pay the rum-seller for robbing
him of property, reason, and life, and murdering
his dear ones? "

Of the men and women who rode in the long funeral procession at the burial of Dennis O'Brien, few were wholly sober. Over his dishonored remains they drank the deadly draught that had hurried him into eternity. And the dead man did not rise to rebuke them!

How like a kaleidoscope is real life! Forty-eight hours had not completed their rounds, when the gathering suspicion that whiskey was not the only agent directly concerned in the fate of the interesting young immigrant, culminated in the arrest of a man for his murder. As the officers —one on each side of him—hurried the suspected criminal along, Mr. Parsons elbowed his way through the excited throng to get a glimpse of the prisoner. It was his ex-workman, Mr. Grey *alias* Simmons, *alias* Grimes.

Mr. Parsons obtained a private interview with him. He affected entire ignorance of the clergyman, pretending, with craftily affected surprise, that he was not Mr. Grey, that he had not before seen Mr. Parsons, and that the latter had assuredly mistaken him for some other person.

" Grey," said the missionary, indignantly, " you are in the hands of justice, charged with a capital crime, and it becomes you to remember that if I volunteer to testify in the case, I can tell a hard story."

The convict was as cowardly as cunning, and,

with blanched cheeks, he asked, in abject terror, —

"Do you think, Mr. Parsons, that I shall be hung?"

"The prospect is dark for you," replied the missionary; "for if you are tried, and not convicted, the people are so enraged that they may take the law into their own hands. If you wish me to show you the least favor, answer me in a straightforward manner. Where is Scroggs, the scoundrel you met on the prairie as you went from Mrs. Willard's to L——?"

Had a bolt from a cloudless sky fallen at his feet he could not have been more amazed.

"He doesn't stay in any particular place; he keeps moving round."

"He's afraid he shall run across Mr. Willard — isn't he?"

"Yes."

"And where is Mr. Willard?"

"None of us know, for certain. Scroggs says he was picked up, and is in one of the river towns; but Merrow, who helped him do the job, don't really believe it. *I* think he's alive somewhere."

This was all the information concerning Mr. Willard that Mr. Parsons then elicited.

As to the ill-fated Hibernian, it appeared that Grimes was with him at the groggery on the

evening of the tragedy ; that he was seen again
in his company after leaving the rum-shop;
that O'Brien had on his person considerable
money, with which to buy housekeeping articles
to take with his family to his Minnesota farm :
and that when the body was recovered, his
pocket-book was gone, while a five-dollar bill
paid O'Brien the evening of his death was in
Grey's possession.   It was identified by the ini-
tials of a fellow-workman of O'Brien's, written,
with the date, on the back of the note, the afternoon of the fatal day.

CHAPTER XXV.

THE CAPTIVE MAIDEN.

But what of Alice McElroy?

Let us go back in our narrative to her mysterious disappearance, the resulting search for her, and her flight from the wigwam of her captor.

Her father's soldiers were within call. A moment more, and, environed by those brave-hearted men, she would have been secure against a hundred Indians. But by one of those unaccountable coincidences with which human affairs are replete, just as she espied on the opposite bank the uniform of Captain Manly, the hand of the pursuing savage was placed upon her mouth, and flinging the struggling girl over his shoulder, he bore her to his waiting canoe.

What a terrible revulsion! So near escape, and so frightfully to fail!

The malignant-featured savage uttered not a word till he carried her the second time into his wigwam; then, throwing her to the ground, he said, with a fiendish look, —

"White squaw fool; Injun killee her!"

What motive impelled her captor to spare her life at first, and then to be so anxious to hold her as to pursue and bring her once more to his hut, Alice tried fruitlessly to determine. That it was not hope of reward for ultimately restoring her to her parents, the rage he exhibited when she held out that bribe fully disproved. It was plain, however, that he held a deadly grudge against the general; for when Alice mentioned her father's name, the face of the savage glowed with hate, and he fiercely muttered, —

"White chief kill Injun — many! Injun killee him!"

It was evident, too, that the savage held a spite against her. As she pondered she suddenly recalled where and under what circumstances she originally met her implacable foe. The recapitulation of certain incidents, and a brief historical statement, will show why the discovery filled her with the worst apprehensions.

One day Mrs. McElroy and her charming Alice, on their way home from a visit to friends in Northern Iowa, were detained at the hotel at L—— for several days, while a party of Indians graced the village with their presence. And Alice, flitting hither and thither, bird-like, often tripped across the street to brighten Mrs. Mather's sitting-room with her coming, and fill the house with music as she swept the piano and sang her favorite songs.

Now, it chanced one morning, entering the back door of that lady's dwelling, she came suddenly upon an Indian helping himself from the good housewife's newly-packed "meat barrel." Startled, she cried out, —

"Mr. Mather! here's a horrid savage stealing!"

The announcement brought quite a group of spectators to the spot, before whom, the town-owner, who was a quick-tempered, stern man when aroused, lifted the blanket of the copper-colored thief, disclosing to view, hugged under a dirty arm, a number of pieces of salted pork, which, with angry threats, he compelled the reluctant red-man to return to their places in the barrel.

That Indian was the chief. That chief was Alice McElroy's captor. The threatening expression of that evil face terrified her at the time, and it was the same evil expression, reproduced with increased intensity, that now enabled her shudderingly to identify the swarthy demon into whose power she had so strangely fallen.

Now that she was hopelessly in his power, her mind intensely revolved the awful question of her fate. Between the hut and stream was a solitary oak. Around this the Indian began to heap brushwood.

"Is he intending to burn me to death?" she queried. The preparations indicated it. The expression of his hideous face and glare of his diabolical eye confirmed the appalling inference. Unable to cope with the white soldiery, his breast rankling with traditional animosity and personal revenge, he would gloat over the slow agonies of the helpless member of the hated race he had captured.

With ghastly, white face the maiden noted the ominous preparations. The pile was completed. Repairing to a swamp at hand, he brought from thence fibrous grape-wood to bind her fast, and was trimming it with his scalping-knife, when, as if he heard a sound, he dropped the vines to listen. An instant after there was a report, and a bullet pierced his chest. The wounded savage pitched forward, and commenced his death-song.

"It is the soldiers!" cried Alice, joyfully.

But to her surprise a party of Indians rushed from out the bushes, the foremost of whom struck his tomahawk into the skull of the dying savage.

Alice fell to her knees, as, after slaying her captor, the Indian entered the wigwam. Instead of the dreaded stroke, he beckoned her to follow him, and, returning to the Indian village, took her into his own tent, and delivered her to his squaw.

Alice knew that her condition in that barbarous home depended largely on what sort of a being the woman was, for the chief would necessarily be absent much of the time, while his wife would dwell ever in the tent. The trembling captive therefore rapidly scrutinized the feminine form before her, to determine, if possible, her disposition and character.

But it is difficult to read the Indian countenance, young or old, male or female. This specimen was short and thick, untidy in person and apparel, with a broad, wrinkled, haggish face. Whether she was as old as she looked, Alice could not judge, as the Indian women, from exposure, want, and toil, become prematurely decrepit. Her face wore a gloomy, sullen expression, which Alice supposed was evidence of hatred to her.

From the squaw Alice's eyes passed to the survey of the little habitation she was destined to occupy, how long and under what circumstances she knew not.

Like the Arabs of the desert, the Dakotas live in tents — in their language, *tecpccs*. Like the army-tent, they are usually of a conical shape, covered with buffalo-skins, or, when these are scarce, of cotton cloth, or bark, the latter being more pleasant and cool for the summer.

This of the chief's was composed of not less than a dozen buffalo-skins, dressed and sewed

together by his squaw, and supported by a number of poles fastened together at the top, and
spreading out at the bottom so as to suit the skin-
covering, which was drawn around the poles
and fastened in front with a row of pins, leaving
a hole at the bottom for entrance, and one at the
top for the smoke to pass out. The lower edge
of the covering was confined by pins driven into
the ground, while at the smoke-hole was a flap
arranged so as to be accommodated to the wind.
The "draught," however, was not perfect, Alice
concluded, as she wiped the tears from her eyes
caused by the smoke in the tent.

On the ground inside, dried grass had been
spread by the squaw, on which were placed skin-
mats and robes — the carpet by day and bed by
night. In the centre was a space for the fire,
the fuel for which the squaw always provided.

When the chief brought Alice there, he said
something concerning her to the squaw ; but as
he used the Indian tongue, Alice was not able to
understand the purport of it. That it was not
ominously harsh, however, she gathered from
the forbearance of the Indian woman to ill-treat
her at the outset, as their way is towards captives.

The sharp pangs of hunger reminded Alice
that she had "lived on excitement" already too
long, and by signs she sought to signify to the

squaw that she was hungry; and bringing her some hominy and a boiled egg on a wooden plate. with a horn spoon, Alice ate the food with avidity.

It was evident from what the chief's wife proffered Alice that provisions were not any too abundant in the *tecpee;* and that was the reason the husband had left so soon. He did not return that night, nor the next; but each morning the squaw, with haggard looks and dishevelled hair, wearing a ragged skirt and leggins, with an old piece of buffalo-skin thrown over her shoulders, walked round the wigwam, wailing, "*Me-choonk-she! me-choonk-she!*"

She was mourning for her only daughter, slain by the Ojibwas. Bitter was the lament of the Indian mother, which, if rendered in English, would be somewhat like that given by Mrs. Riggs — "*Me-choonk-she! me-choonk-she!*" (*My daughter! my daughter!*) "Alas, alas! My hope, my comfort has departed, and my heart is very sad. My joy is turned into sorrow, and my song into wailing. Shall I never more behold thy sunny smile? Shall I never more hear the music of thy voice? The Great Spirit has entered my *tecpee* in anger, and taken thee from me — my first-born, my only child! I am comfortless, and must wail out my grief. The pale-faces repress their sorrow; but we, children of nature, must give vent to ours, or die. *Me-choonk-she! me-choonk-she!*

" I have cast from me all comfortable clothing, and robed myself in skins·; for no clothing, no fire, can warm thee, my daughter. Unwashed and uncombed I will mourn for thee, whose long locks I can never more braid, and whose cheeks I can never again tinge with vermilion. I will cut off my dishevelled hair, for my grief is great. Me-choonk-she! me-choonk-she!"

The return of the Indians from the hunting expedition was announced, while they were yet far off, by their rejoicing song. This showed, too, that they had been successful ; and when they appeared they brought quite a little supply of game, which, however, they staid at home to eat up, before getting more.

While the chief was at home day by day, Alice pleadingly inquired when he was to take her to the fort, his vague guttural reply uniformly being, "Take pappoose dere bimeby!"

What motives led her present captors to show her special consideration we cannot say. Certain it is, however, that Alice McElroy was not subjected to the sufferings that befell her less fortunate captive sisters. Who can paint her thankfulness at their forbearance towards her!

She resolved to show her appreciation of it. And as her grateful looks and winsome ways evoked additional kindness from her captors, she trusted that ere long their softening natures would yield, and they would grant her one consuming desire and oft-uttered prayer, and restore her to those she knew were mourning her loss, — a quenchless grief.

Conceive her dismay, then, when, one day, the childless couple gave her to understand that they had concluded to adopt her!

"O, no; carry me to my *true* father and mother!" she cried, convulsed with agony.

But the brow of the chief grew portentous, and his squaw changed into a fury, and seemed about to pounce upon and tear her in pieces. In anguish and terror she lay and pondered that night, and by morning had wisely resolved to submit to their whim, — making a virtue of necessity, — and patiently wait the issue. For were not her condition and prospects enviable, compared with other captives? Would it not be suicidal folly to offend those who held her prisoner? Moreover, as a chief's daughter, if she used discreetly the advantages of such a position, she could win the respect and confidence of the tribe, and when her plans were ripe and the opportunity opened, farewell, Indian captivity; welcome, liberty and home!

Alice's acquiescence in their wishes gave great satisfaction to the swarthy pair; particularly as, with girl-tact, she became an Indian of the Indians, as Paul was "a Pharisee of the Pharisees," conforming to their habits, customs, and prejudices as far as she possibly could — outwardly at least.

The use of paints, the Dakotas aver, was taught them by their gods. I think their gods must have been poor artists — do you not? *Oonktay'-he* showed the first "medicine-men" how to paint themselves when they worshipped him, and what colors to use. *Ta'-koo-shkan-shkan'* whispers to his favorites what colors are most acceptable to him. *Ha-yo'-ka* hovers over them in dreams, and communicates how many streaks to make upon their bodies, and what tinge they must have. And no rite in worship was considered acceptable if destitute of the *wakan'*, or sacred application of colors.

So Alice, from those skilled in plants that dye, obtained liquids to change her auburn locks to raven black, and her skin to a tawny hue — of course the gods directed in the transformation, and in the added hues and daubs.

Her manner became grave, composed, and dignified, as became the child of the chief. Here her birth and training helped her. Accustomed all her life to the sight of military discipline, and to her father's commanding carriage, she easily bore herself with a quiet authority eminently adapted to impress the savage mind.

One thing I liked to have forgotten. Alice could turn to black her eyebrows and lids, but her *eyes* were "*true* blue," and neither of the god painters, nor the trio combined, could undo what "the true God" had done for her as to color in those couspicuous parts of her visage. So, after all, I guess our God is God, and "the gods of the heathen are vanity."

In becoming an Indian, Alice was honored with a new name. The Dakotas, however, have no family names; so she was not named for her Indian parents, as would be the case among us. They employ proper names only, and these all have a significance. Generally they are formed of two nouns, or a noun and an adjective, as *Good-House*, *Scarlet-End*, *Good-Road*, *Long-Buffalo*, *Iron-Cutter*. Sometimes they consist of a verb or participle, as *Walking-Spirit*. And often the name is affixed to the individual because of some peculiarity or defect, as *Crooked-Feet*, *Burnt-Legs*, *Sleepy-Eyes*, *Bit-Nose* (how would you like that?), *Big-Eyes*. It was perfectly natural, therefore, that they should designate Alice, the chief's daughter, *Blue-Eyes*. However, black eyelids cause the peepers beneath them to seem darker than they really are, and even in some lights to appear black; so Alice was not afflicted with a serious defect.

Many phases of life among the Sioux must

have been terribly repugnant to the petted child
of the general. But she had will and wisdom,
and was working for a precious object; and one
can do, and dare, and endure when inspired by a
high purpose.

Blue-Eyes became the idol of the old chief and
his squaw, while her queenly air and personal
grace and beauty made her the admiration of the
younger warriors, to win whose notice they
wrestled, and ran, and exhibited feats of physical
prowess, and sang their impassional love-songs.

I should insult the intelligence of my reader
to explain, at this point, that the charming "child
of nature," who broke so unexpectedly on Tom's
wondering vision, the beautiful chief's daughter,
she of the "coffin cough" and grave demeanor,
was Alice McElroy, otherwise Blue-Eyes; and
also that it was to her interposition the dwarf
owed his escape.

Ah, had Tom known into whose yellow palm
he poured the healing globules; had he been
conscious of the concealed tremblings of those
girlish limbs that walked so unswerving a gait,
or noted the latent glances of the eyes that gazed
straight ahead, as if unaware of his presence;
if to the ear of the soul there had been conveyed
the unwhispered word of recognition aching to
burst from the voiceless lips, — then might he have
comprehended, in part, what self-mastery and

self-abnegation it cost her to preserve her composure, that he might not be put in jeopardy.

O, how she longed to send a message by him to her parents, letting them know that she still lived, and thought of them! Must she keep her secret, and remain a captive? Could she see him depart, not once dreaming who she was? Ah, how hateful then the Indian ornaments celebrated in the songs of admiring braves! Ah, how odious her disguise, if she might cast it off sufficiently to show that she was not Blue-Eyes, the chief's daughter, but only Alice McElroy!

But keen eyes and ears were in ambush. She must act her part for Tom's sake, and to secure a future chance. How magnificently she triumphed over the trying ordeal, the chief's personal application to Tom for "more medicine for pappoose," and Tom's unharmed dismissal, demonstrated.

From that test-hour the confidence of the Indians in Alice's fidelity to them was almost unlimited.

She readily divined, however, that Tom was on his way to visit his mother at the fort. From that interview she was on the alert for an opportunity to send a message to him. The coveted occasion came when the little Hunchback strayed into the chief's encampment, after the Indians had returned there.

CHAPTER XXVI.

A BIRD-SONG IN THE NIGHT.

Tom and Charley lay in the shadow of the wood, intently listening. Save the liquid lullaby of the gently-flowing stream, and the whisper of the trees stirred by breath of zephyr, silence reigned.

Wary watchers they. Only those trained where the stealthy step and keen senses of the death-dealing savage must be watched by a foot as noiseless, and a vigilance as acute, could preserve such motionless quietude and alert wakefulness.

Past their covert slunk a large, black wolf, unsuspicious of their proximity. Over their heads perched a monstrous owl, his staring eyes stretched to see the first creature to his taste that moved; then on downy wing he swooped to their very side upon a plump field-mouse, and supped at his leisure on raw rat steak. An antlered deer proudly guided his mate to the stream to slake her thirst. Tempting game; but the

bullet sleeps in the pioneer boys' rifles. The
deer drink deeply, and browse the pendent
boughs, and wander away unharmed.

What a scene for the stars to look down upon
through the rifted clouds and glimmering tree-
tops — that solitary pair of youthful faces, patient,
resolute, unwearied, keeping brave vigil far from
the haunts of civilization, the gloom of the forest
at night enshrouding them, and rolling off im-
measurably from the woods the uninhabited
prairie.

Hush ! A faint sound from out the far-off darkness. Was it the dip of an oar, or the feathered
plunge of a night-bird? None, save an ear
educated to it, sharpened and rendered preternaturally quick, would have caught the muffled
indistinctness. The eyes of the venturesome
young scouts shine, and they scarcely breathe.
A lengthy interval of unbroken quiet succeeds.
Were they deceived ?

Suddenly, up-stream, a robin carols. How hard
for birds that can sing not to sing ! Perchance
tuneful red-breast, in dreaming of his true-hearted
mate, uttered his love-lay unawares. None the
less sincere, however, for that.

What now ! From the bushes where Tom and
Charley wait is wafted a responsive warble. Did
bird-wife wander in the swift-descending twilight

from her husband's side, and the darkness com-
pel her to alight on the first object her tiny foot
might press, and wait there in loneliness for the
dawn of a new day? And did she fold her wing
on Tom's lips? for the answering notes seemed
to rise therefrom.

If, however, you will notice, as well as you can
for the darkness, the countenances of the frontier
brothers, you will perceive an aroused expec-
tancy that was not apparent before. Did the bird-
note telegraph important news that the young
men now peer with strained vision through the
gloom? That's a secret, confided only to the
prudent few. "Won't you tell?" Then let me
whisper that no bird was concerned in the song
you admired so, and the tuneful reply. It was
the signal agreed upon between Long Hair, the
friendly Indian, and Tom.

And observe. Down the narrow river, through
the black vista of overarching trees, shoots a
canoe. It pauses opposite the brothers' place of
concealment. A savage, with cat-like agility,
springs ashore, and swiftly drags the light craft
into a sheltered baylet, hidden by tangled thickets. The bird-call is sounded cautiously again.
Tom and Charley hurry noiselessly to the Indian's side. It is Long Hair.

"Quick; got pappoose dere!" said the latter,
pointing to the canoe, from her prone condition

in the bottom of which an Indian girl arose, and, aided by Long Hair, stepped upon the bank. It was Blue-Eyes.

"O, Alice!" whispered Tom, trembling with excitement, as he extended his hand.

"O, Tom!" she answered; and, overcome with the tumult of her feelings, in a very un-Indianish way, flung her arms around the squatter son's neck, sobbing wildly for joy, while Tom, giving the reins to his long-pent-up emotions, in an exceedingly unmasculine manner, fell to laughing and crying together : and Charley , forgetting military property and fear of pursuing savages, turned an old- fashioned somersaults crashing the bushes with his descending heels.

"Pappoose fool; Tom fool; Charley fool," rapidly whispered angry Long Hair. "What for make noise? Want Injun come?"

"Nature will have its way." It did, in this instance, with white and copper-face. Fortunate for the escaping captive that Indian nature was there as an ally. Clapping his ear to the ground, Long Hair said, —

"Injun come bimeby — *quick!*"

The trio understood by this that the pursuing Indians were close upon them. You should have seen the change this startling intelligence caused in Tom and Charley. Active, adroit, sagacious, their faces like marble, yet expressive of fearless determination — from weak weeping to heroes in deportment. Thus do great emergencies bring out and invest with the sceptre the nobler elements of the soul.

Alice understood her three friends not to be panic-stricken. She had intrusted her safety to their hands, and felt assured that they would not undertake the dangerous and difficult enterprise of her rescue from captivity and restoration to her home without adequate preparation; and she hopefully accompanied them, as they glided rapidly through the forest towards the open land.

Alice's heart beat with a joyous, grateful throb, as Tom, taking her hand, guided her to a sheltered spot, where stood her own dear pony. Hidden also near by were spirited steeds for himself, Charley, and Long Hair. Dashing out upon the prairie, the whiz of an Indian's arrow gave notice that their foes were pressing them hard.

"Let them come on," said Tom; "we are safely out of their ugly claws."

"Safe!" ejaculated Alice, as a spent bullet smote Charley's horse.

"Look! Injun over dere," said Long Hair, pointing ahead, slightly to their right.

He was correct; dusky forms were hurrying to intercept them.

"No matter," coolly replied Tom; "we'll turn

a little to the left. They'll soon go back faster than they came."

The assertion was not mere bravado; for suddenly there was a bright flash in the prairie grass, followed by a simultaneous discharge of fire-arms, and, with an astonished yell, the savages recoiled to the woods. At the same instant, on the extreme left, there was similar firing on the advancing Indians at that point, with like result.

"Good," grunted Long Hair. "White soldier fire from de ground."

But their defenders remained flat on their faces, and the prairie seemed as destitute of military force as before.

"The Indians won't molest us any more," said Tom, exultingly. "They'll think the prairie is sown with soldiers. Captain Manly is a splendid tactician. He can fight the Indians better with a score of picked men than some officers could with a regiment at command."

And the three rode courageously on.

CHAPTER XXVII.

BLACK NANCY SHOUTS. — A DREAM. — THE TWO
SAVAGES.

THE lad that goes from the old homestead to seek his fortune, but of whom nothing is ever heard afterwards; the dear ones who set-sail in the ship that makes no port, and concerning whose fate the ocean is dumb; the child, missed from your side in the dense city or flowery field, who answers no more to your call, — these "lost" ones are mourned for with an unceasing and peculiar sorrow. The mystery of their destiny fills the mind with a yearning disquiet. Years drag by, and we think we have seasoned ourselves into the immovable conviction that they have entered, "where the wicked cease from troubling, and the weary are at rest;" but we start at a familiar voice or step, and find ourselves, with aching hearts, waiting for the wanderers.

Over long-lost Alice her parents ceaselessly wept. They conversed less of their strange bereavement, but their grief gnawed as remorselessly. General McElroy's tall, erect form be-

came bowed, and his locks white.   His elegant
wife wasted as if in a slow consumption, and her
brilliant smile was the wan semblance of its
former radiance.

The fond parents had left no measures untried
to solve the painful problem of her disappearance;
but no news of the absent daughter was borne to
them from prairie, grove, or river, cabin of the
pioneer, or wigwam of the red-man.   Grasses
waved, birds carolled, trees waved their brawny
branches, waters ran, but spoke not a syllable
concerning the fair form for whom they witnessed
such pains-taking and heart-breaking search.

Nor did her family grieve alone.   Before the
sad event gayety and mirth often held carnival in
the many-roomed dwellings of the frontier fort,
for the long, four-storied, brick buildings, enclos-
ing the spacious square, contained not a few
choice spirits — ladies and gentlemen of culture;
and the fortress itself, what was it, but an armed,
compact town?   An advanced outpost, remote
from the large settlements, it was dependent on
its own resources for improvement and diversion,
and each person contributed something to the
social stock.

But the loss of the commander's child caused
a marked change in the little community.   The
sympathy for him and his wife was sincere and
profound.   Soldiers spoke low and stepped softly

as in the chamber of death; for the beautiful girl was a universal favorite.

Prosperity affects children very differently. It is the ruin of some, a blessing to others. Alice McElroy was "born with a silver spoon in her mouth," as the quaint old phrase has it. Wealth and position commanded attention and petting, and the winsome child of the general would inevitably have been spoiled had she naturally lacked the ballast of sound common sense. Just as sweet, unaffected, and unselfish was she, despite fine clothes, personal charms, and unstinted praise.

Ah, that shut piano, which used to gush with music beneath her fairy fingers, the varied tones of which all the fort rejoiced to hear, — sacred instrument, closed now, for no hand since hers had vanished might woo the ivory keys, — how its eloquent voicelessness depressed the fort people! And the dumb woe of the dispirited pony, listening in vain for the loving call and the tripping step, increased the prevailing gloom.

A Scripture fragrant with wisdom and love exhorts us to console the sorrowing, "with the comfort wherewith we ourselves are comforted." Mrs. Jones, Tom and Charley's mother, was first brought to the fort by the soldiers who had rescued her from the scenes of tragic horror in which her husband was mortally shot and her daughter tomahawked. The fate also at that juncture of Charley and little Bub was involved in doubt, as no trace of them was found.

Mrs. McElroy welcomed the weeping woman with large-hearted and sympathizing hospitality, and did all in her power to calm her grief and cheer her spirit; with tender consideration she caused the widow to become governess in the McElroy household, that congenial employment might at once divert her thoughts and give her the independence of self-support. Little did the general's wife then imagine that the hour was coming when, instead of ministering comfort, she would lean on Mrs. Jones for sympathy, as that lady had on her. So do good deeds return to bless the doer.

A union of the best qualities of head and heart fitted Mrs. McElroy to counsel and plan for Mrs. Jones in the time of the latter's troubles. She could suggest a silver lining to the stormiest cloud, and argue aptly and cogently against despair. Nor did she omit to point the sufferer to faith in an all-wise and gracious Providence. Nevertheless, this, to a large extent, was *theory* to Mrs. McElroy. Her life had been scarred by no notable misfortune — on the contrary, it had been happy beyond that of most.

But the unexplained disappearance of Alice smote down the stately woman as by a murderous blow. Wild with anguish, day and night she moaned and wept. Such a sunbeam as Alice had been, and so swift the quenching of that light! The mother's vigorous mind, stored with philosophic maxims and Bible texts, was in a whirl of fear, anxiety, sorrow, foreboding, and not one of the well-turned truisms she was wont with soothing smile to offer Mrs. Jones availed for her own soul.

Her extremity was Mrs. Jones's opportunity. What could she have done in that hour, had it not been for one who had tasted the same cup of bitterness? When the cry was wrung from her, " Never was sorrow like my sorrow," the gentle governess reminded her of the terrible days when brave, romantic Charley was, none knew where ; yet both he and Bub were restored to her embrace.

" Best of comforters ! truest of friends ! What should I do without you? " often would Mrs. McElroy exclaim.

One morning, after a sleepless night, Mrs. McElroy, adjusting a shawl to her shoulders, feebly descended to the door, to breathe the prairie air a moment before eating, she said, then took her seat at the breakfast table. The ashen lips, sunken cheeks, languid eye, fickle appetite, bespoke the chronic invalid. Yet it was not bodily disease that had wrought the sad change, but a mother's mourning love.

Black Nancy, with hair in short, crisp pig-tails, adorned with fluttering bits of bright ribbon, bustled about, recommending "missus jest to taste of dish sher berry nice fricassee prairie chicken, an' dat ar light biscuit and new butter." But neither odorous coffee from the silver urn, though seasoned with rich, thick cream, skimmed "preticklerlally for missus," nor the neatly laid cloth artistically covered with tempting dishes, could provoke the sorrowing woman to eat.

"It's mos' *des*couragin'; de little bird ud die eatin' no more'n missus do," ejaculated the sable waitress, as Mrs. McElroy arose. "I'se a great min' neber to set dish sher agin;" and she clattered off the plates indignantly. "Anybody'll tink de food wasn't fit for de pigs — dat dey would. An missus growin' dat poor, — specs she'll blow away some ob dese fine mornings, when dere's no wind. An' massa, too, follerin' on jest de same way. So poor now de crows wouldn't pick dere bones, ef 'twas ter keep dere selves from breakin' de commandment, and stealin' de farmer's corn! But, laws, *Miss* Jones," she exclaimed, suddenly confronting that lady, "what am de matter wid you? Eber sense Tom was here de las' time, you fly about, fly about, jest as if de wings were sproutin' on yer shoulders, an' you was spectin' to be a sure enough angel, an' fly out ob de winder up to de sky. You do conduc berry singlar!"

"Nancy," said Mrs. Jones, striving to look very grave, at which the quick-eyed image cut in ebony rolled up her eyes most comically, " it is quite desirable that you do not call attention to my manner in the hearing of Mrs. McElroy. I do not wish her to notice it."

"Can't help it, no ways, Miss Jones; you do behave so quar," shrewdly replied the African. " Ef, now, I understood jes' what am de matter wid you, 'twould be diffrunt — dat's de fac, truf."

"Won't you let a soul know, if I tell you the secret?"

"You wont ketch dis chile in no sich imprudency — won't tell myself — dat's so!"

Mrs. Jones began to whisper in her ear, her dark-skinned listener's fat, shining face glowing with the consciousness of the honor conferred on her by being made the confidant of the governess. Better than a show was it to watch the varying expression of the colored woman's mobile countenance. The large, round eyes grew larger and rounder, the generous mouth slowly opened, revealing by degrees double rows of comely white teeth, breaking meanwhile into a widening grin, that threatened to involve her ears; and the fleshy arms and hands were gradually upraised in ineffable astonishment.

"O, bless de Lord! Praise de *good* Lord! Jes' what I'se bin prayin' for," she bellowed, " an' long ago He gub me de witness dat de honey sweet — "

"Stop," interrupted Mrs. Jones; "you promised not to tell, and you are proclaiming it to the whole fort."

"Can't help it, Miss Jones; " and sitting flat on the floor, and swaying back and forth, her ample body exercised in every bone and muscle with her happy excitement, she shouted, "I *shall* praise de Lord, if all de worl' say I mus'n't. Bless de Lord! Praise de *good* Lord!"

"Nancy," asked Mrs. McElroy, drawn to the dining-room by the uproar, "what does this mean?"

"Dish chile can't possibly splain, missus; but she mus' praise de Lord, or she'll bust; dat's de Bible truf."

"What has come over you? Get up, and be yourself again," commanded her mistress.

"Now," said Mrs. McElroy, as the servant arose, "state to me calmly what agitated you so?"

"Dat are ain't possible, missus. But I'se terr'ble happy. 'Fraid if I keep still de berry stones ob de court ud cry out. Praise de blessed Jesus! he's jest bin de *besterest* friend dat eber any poor sinner eber had — been monstrous good to all in dish sher fort!"

"I wish I could realize it," said Mrs. McElroy.

"Bress de Lord, you'se gwine to right away, missus. You'll shout bigger'n I did, when —"

"Nancy!" sternly interposed the governess.

"Laws," ejaculated the forgetful waitress, clapping her great paw over her widely distended lips, "I jest gwine ter break my promise — but I didn't, thank de good Lord for dat!"

"An unusual scene," observed Mrs. McElroy, as they ascended to that lady's apartment. "You can, however, interpret it to me, if I mistake not;" and she laid her thin hand in that of the governess.

"It appears," replied the latter, "that Nancy has made your great loss a subject of prayer, — you know what a simple, child-like faith many of the blacks have, — and she is confident that the evidence is given her that her petitions are heard; in other words, that Alice is alive, and will be restored to you."

The mother sighed, then asked, with a penetrating look, —

"What do you think in regard to this matter?"

"Stranger things have happened," she answered.

"Mrs. Jones," cried the general's wife, gazing into the governess's truth-telling face, "has anything been heard of Alice?"

"There has been a new search instituted by my Tom, aided by his Indian friend, Long Hair, and

Tom is sanguine that all will end well. But of course the young are hopeful. Do you think the joy will be too much for your debilitated frame, should his efforts result as we all so much desire?"

"No. I can bear anything better than this awful suspense. But I have not mentioned that I also have a presentiment that Alice is not dead, and that I shall once more clasp her in my arms. Lately, when I am most desponding, a secret voice seems to whisper, 'She's coming; she's coming!' And therefore, if she should return, she would not find me wholly off my guard. But what is this?" she inquired, as, hearing the clattering of hoofs, she went to the window. "Two mounted Indians! How queer!"

"Why, so there are," Mrs. Jones responded. "One of them looks like a squaw. It is the Dakota chief's daughter, Blue-Eyes, so famed for her beauty, intelligence, and fine character, I'll wager. Tom told me about her; he saw her on one of his adventurous expeditions. Yes, it must be she, for there's Tom just alighting, and my wide-awake Charley. Suppose we return to the dining-room, and make the acquaintance of the tawny miss."

"A remarkable beauty, surely," murmured Mrs. McElroy, raising the window, and gazing spell-bound after the Indian girl. "What a

graceful, queenly carriage — a perfect figure!
But I feel faint," she suddenly added, and staggering to a sofa, reclined a while, Mrs. Jones anxiously fanning her. "What do you suppose,"
said she, recovering her equanimity, "affected
me so? You don't know how my heart jumped.
What is the matter with me? My load of sorrow
is gone. I begin to be happy again. How
singular! One night I had such a sweet dream!
I thought Alice came. I didn't recognize the
dear child at once; but it proved to be really she;
and O, how happy I was! But why should that
same peace fill my heart now, when, alas! she is
still away? Strange — isn't it? If I did not *know*
to the contrary, I should believe that the dear
girl had now come. But perhaps it is because
I am not strong, and my mind is overtaxed."

"Perhaps it will interest you," said Mrs. Jones,
wiping the tears from her own cheeks, "to go
down and see the chief's daughter."

Tom's eager, yet respectful greeting of Mrs.
McElroy, as she entered the room, was cordially
reciprocated.

"This is Long Hair," said he, pointing to the
Indian sitting nearest.

"I am pleased to see you once more," she remarked, shaking his hand. "You were a good
friend to the Joneses, and I am grateful for it.
And who is this?" she inquired, advancing towards the beautiful Indian girl.

"Blue-Eyes," answered Tom, with choked utterance.

"I have heard of you," politely said Mrs. McElroy, addressing the dusky maiden; and she was about to take her hand also, when, sinking into a chair, she said, "O, how strangely I feel! Just as in that blissful dream. I am not deceived — Alice is coming! Nancy, open the door, she must be in the court. I *know* she's near. Throw the door wide open. Nancy, do you hear? Alice, my own darling Alice, is coming, I say!"

"Mother, mother! dear, dear mother! don't you know me!" cried the Indian girl, starting up, and casting herself on Mrs. McElroy's bosom. "I was captured by the Indians, and adopted by a chief!"

"Happy, happy! just as I dreamed," murmured the mother, folding her closely.

It is said that evil tidings travel fast, and that "a lie will go ten leagues while truth is putting on its boots." It is delightful to mention one instance in favor of the reverse.

The news that the fairy of the fort, gentle. lovely Alice McElroy, was in the fortress, went like a flash of light through the buildings. "Beautiful upon" the prairie "the feet of them" that hasted to spread the joyful intelligence. Officers and privates shook hands over the event, and war-begrimed comrades embraced each other with brimming eyes.

That evening, when the grand old star-spangled banner, waving from the lofty flag-staff, was, as usual, lowered, jubilee was kept. How the big cannon roared, and the musketry rattled, and the band played! Flash followed flash, report succeeded report, one tune rose after another, till the air was ablaze, and the prairie vocal. Meanwhile the ladies, — did anybody ever " get ahead of their time" ? — while the lords of creation supposed them to be dutifully applauding their performances, were getting up a little celebration on their own hook. To each window-pane of the entire fort they affixed rows of candles, and at a signal the tapers were lighted, and the spacious buildings illuminated as if by enchantment.

The result was striking. The drummers stopped drumming, the musicians forgot to blow, the gunners neglected to load; then splitting their throats in their enthusiasm, cheer on cheer greeted the brilliant spectacle.

I do not know what the prairie wolves thought of the military thunder and lightning, the radiance and deafening voices; they did not tarry to express their feelings at any great length, but with their tails between their legs they scampered off, snarling and howling. As for prowling savages, they slunk away with the wolves.

CHAPTER XXVIII.

THE MYSTERY OF THE MOCCASONS. — THE MAN WITH THE LANTERN.

IT is related of an artist, who, secluded from observation, was working on a masterpiece, which it was for his interest not then to make public, that his bosom friend begged permission to invite " only two " of his acquaintances to view it.

The painter smilingly answered, —

" You do not reckon right ! "

" How so ? " inquired the other.

Taking his pencil, the artist replied, —

"*You* have seen the painting ; that's *one ;* " and he indicated it by the appropriate numeral. " Mr. E—— would also be one, and Mr. G. one ; that makes," said he, significantly marking a numeral, III — one hundred and eleven."

The successful escape of Alice McElroy was due largely to the fact that she had sufficient discretion to confide the enterprise to so few persons, and those able to keep their own counsel. Tom and Long Hair were every way fitted to prosecute the undertaking, for they were well acquainted with the Indian character and habits, and could devise and execute her rescue with little risk of alarming her captors and imperilling her safety. Had a squad of soldiers been despatched to deliver her, the Indians, discovering their approach, would have spirited her away, or, failing in that, sacrificed her life.

What a cute thought, placing those moccasons on the dwarf's feet! For if the Hunchback had worn away his shoes, some straggling savage might have struck his trail, and the temptation to take his scalp be too strong to resist. But wearing moccasons, a score of bloodthirsty Indians, seeing his footmarks, would suppose them those of a native Sioux. But there were in them, in Indian symbol, for Long Hair, her name and that of the old chief, and where their encampment was; also, in English, a message to Tom, suggesting that Long Hair be employed to come alone first, and arrange the time of her flight.

Words cannot convey the anxiety with which she waited the issue of her experiment. When she slept, her heart was awake to catch the coveted signal. And one kind night the full round harvest moon " took the black veil," and the prairies went into mourning for her absence. At midnight, when the swarthy occupants of the wigwams snored in their blankets, the faintly audible carol of the robin threw up her eyelids with spasmodic suddenness. She understood well what bird of hope sung that song, — so well that her strength for the moment utterly forsook her, and, unable to rise, she lay pressing her little hand over her heart to suppress its loud palpitations.

Long Hair, however, was too sagacious immediately to repeat the signal; and stealing softly out into the thicket, from whence came the call, in the heavy dew-damp and chilly night air, was the patient red-man. In terse language he appointed the time when he would convey her to the fort, and when the hour rolled round he was there.

The lives of some persons have little incident to vary their hackneyed monotony; others are crowded with great and solemn events. Tom Jones's was stirring and eventful. Even his vacation, which he anticipated as a peaceful visit to his frontier friends, had been filled with adventure.

How remarkable the occurrences that had drawn Alice McElroy and himself into such close connection! What did these experiences foreshadow? He dared not trust himself to ponder this question. His honor would not permit him to presume on the strength of the service he had rendered her. On the contrary, he was sensitive lest she might fancy he expected to be specially noticed on this ground. " For," he reasoned, " I am only assisting to pay the debt of gratitude due her parents for their kindness to my mother. And who am I — Tom Jones, the squatter's son — that she should think of me?"

But, when the day arrived for him to set his face eastward, and, at parting, Alice leaned from a window, just as he once dreamed, and with evident agitation said, "You won't forget me while you're gone — will you, Tom?" his heart was so moved he could not answer.

On his way to the river, Tom called at the cabin of the Willards. The very logs seemed to brighten, so glad were the inmates to see him. And the dwarf's eyes swam as the loved visitor handed him an appreciative letter from Mrs. McElroy, complimenting him on his heroic deeds for his family, and thanking him for the part he bore in the recovery of her daughter. The fifty-dollar bank-bill, enclosed, was to buy, she said, if he would oblige her by parting with them, the moccasons Blue-Eyes furnished him.

The proud-spirited Hunchback had no opportunity to decline the money, for, as he commenced speaking, there was a thundering knock at the door, which, as he was sitting nearest, he hastened to open. A short, stout man, with a cross face, which misrepresented its owner, stood before him, the butt of his formidable whipstock uplifted for a second rap.

"My name is Edmands," said he. "I've come to see about that hay I bought of Simmons!"

"'Twasn't his to sell," piped the dwarf, bristling with combativeness.

"Wal, wal," replied the settler, surveying him with a comical squint, "you're a buster — ain't ye, now? Going to swallow me? I suppose you've no objection to showing me where the stacks are."

"Mr. Edmands," said Tom, starting towards him.

"Ah, Tom, how are you? I drove round here on *business ;* didn't expect to have the pleasure of seeing you."

"Nor I you," responded Tom. "But about that hay —"

"That's none of *your* concern," he brusquely iuterrupted, slyly winking at him. "I bargained for hay that's on this claim, and if this youngster, or oldster, whichever he is, ain't afraid to do the square and honest thing, he'll show it to me."

"I will do that," answered the Hunchback; "but you can't cart off a wisp on that Simmons's account."

"Can't, eh? Wal, that can be tested, I reckon."

Ferdie and Georgie, with lengthened visages, accompanied the two.

"You'll want to reserve enough to winter your span," remarked the farmer.

"We shall reserve it all," retorted the dwarf.

"Don't get riled, my little friend," the man observed. "I expect to control the major part of that dried grass, anyhow. You can spare ten tons, and leave plenty for your horses. I contracted with Simmons for it at two dollars and fifty cents. There's been more grass cut this season than anybody expected. It won't be over five dollars a ton till next mowing. I'll give you that, my lad, if you are willing to spare the hay, and I'll pay you this minute, to clinch the bargain;" and he tendered the dwarf fifty dollars.

"It's too much," replied the Hunchback, his tones husky with emotion.

"That's *my* bread and butter," said the settler; and as if offended he tossed the bills upon the grass, and began to walk away.

"Don't be angry, Mr. Edmands," cried Georgie, running after him; "we all thank you."

"How wonderfully the hand of Providence has marked our history since we left the steamboat!" exclaimed Mrs. Willard, as the boys reëntered the dwelling, and related Mr. Edmands's kindness.

"I trust you have had no reason to regret settling on a prairie claim. I would not advise every family as I did yours, but was impressed that it would be best for you."

"There is one lesson we ought to learn from

this affair about that Simmons," remarked aunt Esther, " and that is, that opposite qualities balance one another. Mrs. Willard and the boys were too confiding. Frankie and I are apt to be suspicious. Yet, if there had been no over-confidence, the haying, breaking, and fencing would not have been done, nor the stolen horse left here. But if, also, there was no distrust, Simmons might not have been foiled, and no profit have accrued to us. Shall we not appreciate each other better after this?"

"Learn, too," added Tom, " that the sickly and feeble may be eminently useful and honored of Providence, as was our Frankie."

"O," sighed Mrs. Willard, "if I knew how we should pass through the winter! and if the other lost one could be restored to us."

"It is good to hope and quietly wait for the salvation of God," tenderly quoted Tom. "Trust your husband in God's care, madam. And, as to lesser troubles, do not be unbelieving; when you need help, it will come — just as it has. How often I have seen this illustrated here at the west!

"A clergyman was once called from home on a mission of mercy. The case was urgent. A dangerous marsh must be crossed, which it was impossible to reach before nightfall, and he could scarcely expect to pass over in the darkness unharmed. But he recognized the call as imperative; 'love constrained' him; and, casting all care on the heavenly Friend, he pushed on through the gloom. Urging his horse along the dangerous pathway, he at length reached a frightful point in his perilous journey. The darkness was profound. A single misstep might be fatal; and for an instant he paused.

"At that moment a light appeared. Nearer and nearer it came. What could it betoken in that lonely, uninhabited spot? Directly a stranger came in sight, bearing a lantern, and courteously guided the benighted minister to a place of safety.

"'And thus,' said the man of God, 'have I ever found it through life. When all has been enveloped in gloom, and in no way could I extricate myself, "a man with a lantern" has come to my aid. God has said, "Let there be light."'

"A missionary, when pressed by poverty and want, was in the habit of specifying in prayer his most important needs. One day potatoes, meal, and salt were lacking. Nothing could be hoped from the 'subscription.' A great financial crash had fallen on the whole country, and distress was upon all the settlers. What could he do? Prayer was his only refuge.

"Next morning a rough, swearing man, living

miles away, came driving his team through the bushes. Presently stopping, he tossed some bags into the grass, saying, in a frank, off-hand way, —

"'There's a trifle for your babies; that's a bag of potatoes, the other is meal, and at the end of the sack you'll find a few pounds of salt; perhaps you'll smile when I tell you that I had a queer notion that I must put that salt in; but if you don't need it, it won't do any harm.'

"Who would have thought this messenger would have come 'with the lantern'? How happened it that he, and not one of the members of the missionary's church, should be the almoner of God's goodness to His servant? Answers to prayer often reach us through unexpected instrumentalities. And God may be nearer those accounted not his people than we think.

"Sickness on the frontier! Ah, the terror of that thought — an entire family prostrated, and none to help! Thus it was one fearful autumn with the Fosters. First the parents, then the children; the former, rallying, bent over the wasted forms of their little ones, in great weakness watching them through long nights and sultry days, until, exhausted, they could watch no more, and sinking upon the floor, besought the Lord to send them a friend.

"Morning broke, and with it came an answer to their petitions, in the person of one least expected or desired, and who, under happier circumstances, would have been greeted coldly. Little did they know till then that under that repulsive manner throbbed a tender heart.

"'I could not sleep last night,' said the comer, 'I was so troubled about you; and now, if you can put up with my rough ways, I should like to help you.'

"Such words from her, while those who ought to have been there, afraid to trust themselves before the dreaded contagion, keep safely at a distance!

"And what a help that strong-armed woman was, as she tenderly arranged the sick ones upon freshly-made beds, and laid their aching heads upon smooth, sweet pillows.

"Ah, she was a messenger with a lantern, and verily the place grew beautifully 'light about her.'"

Dear reader, let us not only pray that in our hours of darkness a messenger with a lantern may come to us, but that we, in our turn, may bear to the benighted and tempest-tossed its cheering rays. Farewell, till we meet again.

If you are interested in continuing in the
Family Classic Collection,
or desire a catalog of other
Mantle Ministries' books, videos, and cassettes,
send a self-stamped addressed envelope to:
MANTLE MINISTRIES
228 Still Ridge
Bulverde, TEXAS 78163
or call:
OFFICE: 830-438-3777
FAX: 830-438-3370
E-MAIL: mantle3377@aol.com
HOME PAGE: http://www.jcmac.com/mantle